SIDETRACKS

Where one wrong decision leads to disaster
and life itself depends on finding the strength to triumph over destiny.

∽≈∼

Valerie Connelly

∽≈∼

Nightengale Press
A Nighengale Media LLC Company
First Edition ©2004 All Rights Reserved
Second Edition ©2009 All Rights Reserved

SIDETRACKS

For information about Nightengale Press please
visit our website at www.nightengalepress.com
Email: publisher@nightengalepress.com
or send a letter to:
Nightengale Press
10936 N. Port Washington Road #206
Mequon, WI 53092

Library of Congress Cataloging-in-Publication Data
Connelly, Valerie, 1947 –
Sidetracks / Valerie Connelly
ISBN: 0-9743348-2-0
ISN 13: 978-0-9743348-20
Fiction, Mystery, Magic Realism
Copyright First Registered in 2004: TX5-945-961
First Published by Nightengale Press in the USA

Second Edition
January 2009

9 8 7 6 5 4 3 2 1

Printed in the USA at
Lightning Source, Inc.
LaVergne, TN

Dedication

To my husband, Michael A. Connelly, who was waiting for me on a sidetrack in my life to change everything for the better by providing me a new path of friendship and love.

Acknowledgements

Thanks to my editor, Brandi Reissenweber, who turned my draft inside out and encouraged me to restructure the whole story, all for the better. And, I want to mention how much I valure the support and encouragement of my personal friends and my colleagues in the book industry, who have reviewed, printed, read, and talked about my books to so many others.

TITLES BY VALERIE CONNELLY

SACRED NIGHT

Once I started reading "Sacred Night," I could not put the book down. Valerie Connelly did an excellent job with writing this debut novel. I look forward to reading other books that she has written since this one. I highly recommend this book to people that enjoy a good mystery with touches of the paranormal thrown in. You will not be disappointed!

—Paige Lovitt, Reviewer

SIDETRACKS

We have all made decisions in our lives that we often wonder about later. What if I had said "Yes" instead of "No"? What if I had turned left instead of right? We drive ourselves crazy wondering about how our lives might have turned out had we taken a different route. "Sidetracks" will interest anyone who has ever asked "what if". Ms. Connelly presents the subject in such a unique way, allowing us to completely follow along with Hannah and Peyton in their "alternate" lives. While I hopefully will never be placed in such a precarious position as they were, reading the book has forced me to consciously look for the sidetracks in my own life and carefully consider all possible choices and consequences before making a decision. I guarantee it will start you thinking as well.

—Cyndy Zoch, Reviewer

ARTHUR, THE CHRISTMAS ELF

In the tale of Arthur, the Christmas Elf by Valerie Connelly, two misguided children are reminded of the joy that Christmas can bring to those with open hearts. Connelly's story is meant to be shared as a family. Part of Arthur's strategy for convincing the children is to provide them with ideas of gifts they can make with their own hands for their loved ones. The tale, along with the craft instructions, contains colorful illustrations to engage the reader. The crafts emphasize the meaning of the story: that one does not have to lack money and possessions to be poor, and Christmas is not about cherishing gifts, but the people behind the gifts.

— Barb Radmore, Editor, Front Street Reviews

CALLING ALL AUTHORS –
How to Publish with Your Eyes Wide Open

This may be the best information that's come out in years for aspiring new authors. It will definitely guide them through the many land mines that exist in today's complex publishing scene.
—Patrika Vaughn,President, A Cappela Publishing

I think the book provides outstanding guidance to authors and should give them helpful information about issues that publishers, editors, etc face and how an author can help simplify those issues. An excellent work! Congratulations!
—Bob Gussin, Oceanview Publishing

Valerie Connelly has written a down-to-earth book that will be of benefit to all authors in their mission to write and sell their books. It will be of value not only to the first-time author but also to the established writer as a constant reminder of the necessity to not only write a book but the requirement to help the publisher market and sell the book. Both the neophyte and the experienced author should keep this book at their fingertips and refer to it frequently.
—John A Henderson MD, Author of: **God.com: A Deity for the New Millennium** and **FEAR FAITH FACT FANTASY** and **Judging God**

Regardless of your publishing method, Ms. Connelly's **CALLING ALL AUTHORS**—***How To Publish With Your Eyes Wide Open*** *is a must-read for anyone attempting to publish a book. Vital "how-to" information to make the publishing journey easier and more successful!*
—Yvonne Perry, Author, Founder and Owner of Writers in the Sky Creative Writing Services

"Calling All Authors is a well-organized – and much-needed guide."
—Maryglenn McCombs, founder of Maryglenn McCombs Book Publicity

SIDETRACKS

PROLOGUE

As the humidifier shut off, the tumbling of her bras in the three-year-old Whirlpool dryer warmed the chill Hannah Sebastian forced onto the night by keeping the furnace turned low. The trembling of the machines kept silence away, even though quiet settled around her any way it could, between shudders of the furnace as it awakened to blow comfort up from the cellar of the house and the subtle ringing in her ears that became intense as silence engulfed her day, swallowing it, and grinning as might a Cheshire cat having eaten the canary. The whir of the blades ran faster to consume the last splashes of water in the reservoir. The humidifier didn't know it had run dry. It only whirred faster, trying to produce the mist that kept the plants from dropping their leaves all winter long. But in her mind, the disappearance of her family, dispersed in different directions seemed unnaturally comfortable. That she endured the noise of young people, that she no longer suffered the moodiness of her husband, that she wondered how she can feel closer to a friend from her ancient youth who lived in the capital of some desert-confined country half a world away than she did to her neighbors next door, all this came up from her psyche at the end of the weekend, at the end of the day she noticed would soon be at the end of the hour.

Who could even be moved by this reflection, so un-necessary, so insignificant against the death throes she would never see in others who lay dying? If Hannah knew someone, had met someone who was dying, trying not to, in the suburbs and inner cities of the world, she put it aside.

Life is to be lived. Dying ends the struggle. One ought not to die. Her thought provoked her. The provocation pulled her back to the sounds in the silence populating her awareness like friends standing in a circle, tossing a ball about in fun, mocking her inability to catch the ball or even swat it in a new direction.

Life is accidental. Death is unfathomable. Why spend time fearing it? Inevitably, it will come. Life will go on. Remaining unchanged for those who are not yet initiated, who have not lost love and loved ones to death, the day to day is forever altered for those who have.

Between these dark ideas forming in her mind, Han-nah noticed the minor triad of the train whistle—or was it a horn?—piercing the distance between the hot breath of the furnace and the humming purr of the humidifier. The dryer had stopped. The duet was quickly again a trio as a new voice added a counterpoint of melody to their static baseline. The ceramic wind chime hanging from the curtain rod above the floor vent in the upstairs office played its cheerful—if atonal—melody against the symphonic rhythm of a squeaky tap of the gas meter and the tympanic belching of the cooling furnace pipes, the simmering humidifier and the whining train.

But it was the train that permeated her thought, seep-ing into Hannah's drifting consciousness the way cold seeps into the bone to chill and cause the body to tremble, uncon-trolled, in waves of convulsive resistance. The train seemed to draw closer though the tracks were blocks away—or was it miles away—just distant enough to pull her mind back to the nights of her childhood when she could discern the first vibrations of a train's approach, determine whether it were a commuter or a freight by the sound of the wheels' clacking—slowly meant freight, fast meant commuter—and fall asleep in the space of the time the train took to pass. What might have her life been had she taken the sidetracks, always apparent, offered to her in various disguises so that to choose one direction or another made her life turn toward and away from the alternate story she might have lived?

Trains travel icy rails, laid to conduct the impassioned pulse of human endeavor from beginning to end; yet, occa-sionally trains do take the sidetrack, perhaps to refuel, to let another train pass on its right of way, to wait for a tunnel to clear the oncoming locomotive, or the maintenance wagon or the cross-country zephyr. So much like the wind, trains billow the anchored vegetation whose misfortune it has been to germinate beside the tracks. So much like dreams, mysterious, ephemeral, impossible to capture and hold, trains flash by, powered by infinite energies of combustion and wheels, hard-edged to grip the imagination from the unseen point of departure to the inestimable destination. Trains are so much like life, seemingly designed to flow along a predictable web of cities and towns joined by switches and levers, to send serpentine sinew and muscle of the economic body into regulated contractions and releases of humanity, never to vary or wander from the chosen route—except for the sidetracks. When unavoidable circumstances, unforeseen or previewed, force the train to sidetrack or derail, so rarely does it derail. The sidetrack is a safe haven from imminent disaster, or so it seems.

1

Good girl, Sandy, that was a good one."

My dog yipped, calling me back from my remembrance of the evening just past. We both were still winded from the customary pre-dawn walk and jog along the lake front, my heart still pounding and her sides still heaving between her playful yelps. Then looking over the recently re-painted black wrought iron fence into my small front yard, my eyes wandered over the vegetation, some dead branches hung low and limp from the trees in the parkway, still indistinct in the half light.

"The pines need trimming." Sandy wagged her tail in agreement, shifting her weight to show me her eagerness to go inside.

Overgrown, the burning bushes lining the borders of the small patch of grass city folks call a lawn would soon be turning vibrant colors, as Fall stretched long and warm from a temperate summer, uncommon in the central Midwest. Begonias and hostas that rimmed the curving walkway leading to the front steps yellowed and drooping from the effects of the first light frost, the fountain that ran clear all summer now algae coated and silent, clarified how the yard and I could have been so alike, decayed, dilapidated, fading and in need of serious attention, if I hadn't been financially successful in life. I gave in to Sandy's urging and went inside, escaping the temptation to prolong this comparison and hoping that the act of paying attention to my dog would alleviate the pressure building in my temples from the pressures of responsibility the day would bring.

"Come on, you deserve some cheese." Sandy wriggled with happiness. When I opened the iron gate and then the heavy oak door flanked by my favorite bevelled and stained glass windows that caught the first rays of the morning sun and refracted them into rainbows on the foyer wall, the dog knew it was also time for cheese. Simple pleasure. Simple reward. We crossed the few feet into the gourmet-chef designed, untidy kitchen. What a stye. Who lives here? A crazy person with no hygiene? The cleaning lady had yet to arrive. Her efforts every other day couldn't keep up with my inattention to housework, a curse I probably suffered because of my mother's fanaticism over dust and clutter during my childhood.

I flicked on the solitary light above the sink, avoiding the garish overhead fluorescent that so often triggered migraines. Sandy's eyes followed my every move, as if cataloging the rhythm of my actions to arrive at her moment of reward. I left the fridge door ajar as I chipped a few chunks from the block of sharp cheddar. They fell on the counter the way the events of the last few months had chipped away large chunks of my self-confidence, which had fallen on the future with nowhere to go. I was glad my boss hadn't yet noticed how few of my big accounts were still ordering as they once had. It was only a matter of time, and a review of the system before I'd be found out. I squeezed the yellow wax into the crevices of the rawhide bone, which, when at last licked clean, Sandy alternately hid in corners and under the chairs. Taking the dog's face in my hands and peering deep into her eyes, into the wells of wisdom I sought there, looking for the answers

I knew could not be found in the myopic glance she returned to me, I continued to question her, knowing she could not respond. A perfect sounding board.

"Sandy? How the hell did we get here, anyway?" Her tail swished the air lazily, slowing to the rhythm of my words, hoping I would soon give up the gab and give her the bone. I nudged the door closed with my hip.

Always an attractive enough woman, I didn't let anyone know that my hair, turning gray under the salon auburn coloring, and that the mirror, shouting that I had gained more pounds than I wanted to admit, upset me rudely and were intimately connected to my routine inspection of wrinkles deepening around my eyes and age spots appearing on my hands. The high-priced lotions and pommades to bleach the spots and fill in the wrinkles were not nearly as effective as advertised. I knew, but couldn't admit that living had become harder for me over time, not easier, in spite of material success. I petted Sandy's head, again looking into her eyes.

"What should I do?"

Sandy's tail sagged to the floor as she sat down. Her gaze jumped from my face to the bone and back. No human could speak more clearly. Cheese bone.

"Nice, take it nice." I slowly placed the bone horizontally in front of her nose.

Sandy's drooling mouth very gently took the bone from my hand. At the moment she owned it, she bounded off to her sleeping quarters at the top of the basement stairs to lick away every bit of cheese. I poured the last bitter cup of day old coffee from the pot, set up the baby gate to keep Sandy contained on the tile flooring of the kitchen and off the silk, hand-woven carpets, and then headed upstairs to my home-away-from-the-office office. Sculpted into the guest bedroom were mahogany filing cabinets and an antique French armoire from Normandy, whose re-configured interior served as a computer desk that engorged the overly decorated space into a cavern-like cubbyhole of solitude and isolation. This is where I kept my memories, family photos and treasures handmade by my children, reminding me of happier times as I frantically tried to survive the downturn in the economy and my self-esteem. Maybe I'd find some answers here.

The phone rang as I settled into the compact lumps my sculptured derrière had moulded into the cushion of my husband's aging office chair, the one I had given to him for Christmas ten years ago, the only real relic remaining from my marriage. I picked up the receiver and automatically punched the speakerphone button, giving no thought to the fact that someone was calling. Very few people other than my attorney ever called me at this number anymore. I preferred the silence and its implied distance, resenting to have to speak on command.

"Hello?"

Only a soft whisper of breathing answered me.

"Hello? Who is this?" Annoyance camouflaged the hint of fear I heard in my own voice.

"Hello?" I hung up. "Wrong number—damned kids playing a prank."

The caller ID, I had diligently embraced the frantic acquisition of every kind of frivolous techno toy in this world of high speed DSL lines and Internet viruses, gave a 'private caller' reading as I turned on the odd assortment of overly expensive decorator lamps and booted up the computer. Unpaid bills leered at me from the desk in-box where I relegated them to enforced stagnation. Perhaps they would evaporate if I left them there long enough.

"Damn the bills! Why can't you ever earn enough money?" The words pummeled me with guilt, a habit ingrained since childhood when my math grades could not satisfy my over expectant parents. I clicked on the computer program where I dutifully logged in Bills to Pay on the financial spreadsheet pretending they would get paid if they were logged in, just as I dutifully opened math books pretending to finish homework I would never understand. The amount of my commission checks had dwindled to barely cover the mortgage, electricity, and water bill. The small amount I received from my late husband's social security paid the phone bill, in-town transportation and food. After that, I couldn't keep up; juggling money had become like an incurable disease that sapped my strength and denied me any comfort.

"Lawyers! Why do you listen to them?"

Talking to myself had become my only means to vent the accumulated anger of the past few years, the unconscious act of isolated souls needing to hear a human voice. I shuddered with blame as the rant came on. Taking responsibility for my own shortcomings had become my new means to emotional liberation, unsatisfying and useless though it was, a scrim curtain to cover the guilt of my perceived tragedies and failings as a human being.

"You had the biggest orders in three years. You had loyalty from your customers. You had contacts and business friends. You had chronic migraines."

My voice grew in decibels as the litany of sins rose from my often repeated, self-inflicted, verbal battering. "You risked your health. You drove yourself to achieve ever higher profits. On that gloomy afternoon in the last snow storm of early spring, you couldn't resist temptation. You guzzled the last glass of whiskey with the men, without considering the consequences." Memories ran headlong into the abyss of my loneliness like water over a cliff.

"You never play it safe!" I slammed my hand on the desk. "You have to play it safe!"

I knew I wouldn't. Who I had become tormented me. I closed out of the spreadsheet and waited for Google to load. Every day I secretly searched online for a job. I scanned the job boards, filled out the resume wizards, looked for responses that rarely appeared. Why should the charade be different on any one day?

"Earn $6000 a day at home—Put your computer to work for you—Hot jobs—Scams, phantom jobs!"

Some days I thought I could simplify my life, maybe teach again—yet I was over qualified, they told me. Just routine excuses. I was too old and with twenty years of real-life, business experience and a Master's degree, too expensive. Fresh young graduates got the teaching jobs. Professional silence infuriated me.

The phone shut off my thoughts. Second ring.

"Hello?" No response. "Hello? Who is this? Stop calling this number, whoever you are!" I slammed down the phone. "Get hold of yourself. Breathe deep drags of the stuffy air. Open the window."

It rang again. Fifth ring this time.

"Hello?"

Lynn Hargrove's voice chirped at me. Kindness flowed from her like honey from the hive. Her gentle manner calmed my terror when she handled my divorce from my first husband fifteen years ago. In one crisis after another her sweet confidence reduced to non-existance a couple of traffic violations, one job related suit trying to preserve both the job and my reputation. Lynn, my guide in many ways, in the purest sense of goodness attempted to keep me in contact with my four children out of some altruistic concern for me. She saw my deserted personal island as a liability to my health and well-being. I saw it as a refuge from the disasters of my life. Distance removed me from my children, like personal oblivion removed me from reality. Death had forced me into my own prison where so called family issues locked the cell door. I stayed sequestered and shut in as much as possible. Lynn remembered the outgoing, vivacious personality. She wanted to rekindle that spirit. I was tired. I was enraged. I wanted to be left alone.

"Hannah? Good news. The DUI charges have been dropped. You're a free woman."

"That's that? Oh. Okay, that's good. I'll be gone for a while. Taking a little trip to sort things out. Thanks for your help. Take care of yourself. Bye." I heard the apathy in my voice. Did she?

Lynn couldn't respond before I hung up the phone. Computer on, I went down stairs. Sandy's eyeballs rotated up at me, but she never stopped licking the bone.

"I'm losing it, Sandy." Sandy wagged her tail as if she knew I was right as I sat on the Victorian chaise longue and stroked the maroon satin upholstery.

"I need a drink." Looking through the open blinds, the familiar wave of sadness washed over me like a tide washing up on a beach. Tears flowed hot, again, blurring my vision with the steam of impossibilities. Wrapping my arms around my own shoulders, hugging myself as I rocked slowly forward and back, I sobbed. Grief dropped over me like a net some astral being had thrown to capture me.

"I need you. Come back to me." I moaned at a framed photo of my second husband. Sandy left the bone. She came over to lick my tears, wagging her tail slowly to comfort me. My memories of his laughter mingled with my own gasps for air.

What was it like to die instantly at seventy miles an hour? I hugged Sandy. "You're my best friend, Sandy. I'm glad you're here." Hiding my face in Sandy's fur then looking out the windows again, a man at the bus stop in front of my house, like so many others, flicked a cigarette butt into my yard. I hated these arrogant strangers who thought my property was their personal ashtray. He pulled a cell phone from inside his coat. I approached the small English armoire, opened the door and stared at the array of liquor bottles, begging me to break their seals and taste of their spirits.

"I'll pour these into the sink later." I closed the door. One demon restrained.

Shivering from the sweat that had cooled since my return and heading back upstairs to the luxurious bathroom/spa I had installed right after buying the brownstone, I turned on the spigots, polished brass and antique French design, to banish the passing spell I had managed to break with the simplest act—drawing a bath. The bubbles frothed cheerily from the stream of soap I was pouring generously, releasing the fragrance of lavender into the steam that filled the room. I zipped off the designer Gortex jogging suit, tossed my shoes into the corner, and flipped the socks toward the hamper as I climbed into the churning, hot bath water of the whirlpool tub intent on letting the water rise around my body and wash away my cares.

As I turned to sit, something caught my eye. I straightened up and glanced into the street through the oval window above the tub that allowed me to view out, but no one from below to see in. A delivery van pulled in front of my building, and a uniformed man climbed out. I recognized him as he circled the vehicle and then opened the side door towards the sidewalk. His name was Peyton, unusual and sexy. He reached into the opening and lifted a large bouquet of red roses, wrapped in cellophane and tied with an enormous crimson bow, from the van and placed it on the curb. I recalled his soft-spoken demeanor and how each time he delivered flowers to my door, his muscles rippling under his brown shirt had made me feel nervous, like a schoolgirl at her first dance. He looked up at my windows as he secured the truck.

Sandy began to growl, her rumbling floating upwards from below as it always did when she heard someone in the street. Peyton turned as if to approach my door. Her growls erupted into warning barks, low and menacing. It was a good thing I had set up the gate to her space so she couldn't actually have the run of the house.

I strained to watch him take the bouquet to my door, at the same time as I reached toward the matches on far end of the shelf ledge, so I could light the fragrant candles perched like so many birds on a wire along the shelf above the tub. The gesture caused me to over reach my balance point. I slipped, trying to catch myself on the shelf, but it tore away from the supports as my hand missed its grip. The board flung the candles at the ceiling, as I fell back. It was all slow motion. I saw the board slam between the tub and the wall. I heard the candles thud like fallen apples onto the ceramic tiles. I smelled the lavender as my head hit the faucet full force, all my weight and the speed of the fall catching the nape of my neck on the brass curve of the pour spout. It didn't hurt, I was just surprised. I felt the water rising against me. I couldn't move. A distant train whistle sounded in my ears and I was gone.

I hate looking for the street numbers again and again, wandering for fifteen minutes, finding myself turning the wrong way on one way streets. But as I remembered the frustration I had faced every day in the IS department of Dayton-Holland Industries, the simplicity of delivering flowers seemed like heaven. I was not one to cheat, lie or steal another guy's glory, or ideas or wife. I believed that playing fair was the only way to success, lasting success. I believed, apparently wrongly, that saving a guy's reputation instead of destroying it was the way to the top. I had been down the ladder of success so often that I had given in to the unemployment line in favor of selling my soul to the lowest bidder. I could not eat the shit they served up on my plate. So, I quit. Walked away. What is big money anyway, but a trapdoor into the prison of yes men.

SIDETRACKS

My thoughts ran free as I watched for details in the houses, the gardens, the light. It's just how I pass the time when I'm on my route. Keeps the boredom at bay. The sunlight cast hotspots between the shadows of the trees, though the chill was definitely on the breeze. Finally, there it was, the address of familiarity on a street I knew. It felt good to arrive at her brownstone. I could smell the autumn as I threw the van door open and jumped into the street. I looked up at her second floor windows. The oval one peers out at the world like a cyclops, not evil, just odd. I missed my step.

"Ouch! Damn that knee!" I kept forgetting the weakness in my right knee, the effects of early onset arthritis. I broke my leg playing football on the empty lot with a bunch of other guys, showing our kids how it's done. I took a tackle that snapped my shin, weakened from the five mile runs I had been making everyday to train for a marathon. They couldn't set it right, too many fragments, so they left it out of alignment. The wear and tear of walking brought on the arthritis. A guy my age shouldn't feel the way that thing made me feel in cool weather, like I had a wooden stump for a leg, a stiffened log hinged by rusted irons, a hobbled appendage that kept me off balance. But, the weirdo standing at the bus stop distracted me from the ache. Scraggly hair, dirty coat, cigarette hanging from his lip, cell phone to his ear, unmoving, not quite alive. Why he nodded at me as I slid the cargo door open, I couldn't figure.

Flipping the addresses on the receipts until I found the right one, "1411 State Parkway—whew! Rich digs!" The huge bouquet, all wrapped in cellophane and ribbon, fanning out from the Lalique crystal vase, filled with water and moss grass, the whole thing heavier than my grandmother's Thanksgiving turkey stuffed and filling her enormous porcelain platter, was from some guy whose name I hadn't seen before.

"Ungghh!" God, I couldn't believe I had grunted like my eighty-year-old grandfather when I picked it up. Balancing it so I could see the ground as I walked, I felt my way up the steps to the brownstone's oak door. The bell chime played a phrase from a Mozart sonata or something like that.

"What ever happened to a simple ding-dong?" No answer, except the barking of her dog from deep inside the apartment. "Shit!"

Disappointed by Ms. Hannah Sebastian's absence, I had to try the neighbors, company policy, like anyone would know if I skipped the routine this once. The vase was getting heavier as I worked my way next door on the left. No one home. Across the street—no one home—next door on the right—silence. "Damn! Well, at least I tried." I hate talking to myself like this. I noticed that the greasy statue-guy didn't get on the bus that stopped at the bus stop. Made a mental note of it—you never know when you'll need to remember things. I decided I'd try the door at 1411 again, just for luck. Sometimes people wake up when the doorbell rings, and it takes them time to answer. It was early yet.

I rang the bell again, but, nothing. So, rather than take this gargantuan greenhouse with me, I set the roses down to give my back a rest, a little too close to the door. They started to tip over, and I over reacted, shoving them against the oak door, which swung open like an invitation to enter.

"Hello? Anybody home?" My voice echoed from the ceramic hallway and across the hardwood floors that shone like polished amber in the light from the front. My shadow darkened my silhouette onto the wall. I heard water running upstairs, kind of sloshing like in a deep vessel, a bathtub maybe. I also heard her dog growling, deep, rumbling, throaty growls, like a big dog would make. There she was, standing in the hallway, head lowered, menacing from the other side of the gate Ms. Hannah Sebastian had put in the door to keep her dog confined.

"Hey, Sandy, a baby gate for a German Shepherd? Hey there baby, aren't you part husky too?" I loved dogs, had a bunch of my own. "What are you doing all cooped up?" Sandy actually settled down and sat quietly as I spoke to her. She allowed me inside, whimpering for me to come play with her. I put the roses on the foyer table, one of those god-awful antique polished mahogany monstrosities that rich people think are so cool. I glanced toward the stairs just as water poured down the bare wood steps.

"Maybe you can help me out here," I said to the dog as I released her, patting her head, setting the baby gate aside. She bounded up the stairs, leading the way to the bathroom, her big paws sloshing through the water like galoshes on a child's feet. I followed her up the flash flood steps to the half opened hallway door of the bathroom. As I shoved the door open wider, I pulled my cell phone from my pocket. The dog stood front paws on the tub, barking at the naked woman whose auburn hair floated on the surface of the water. I grabbed her hand, pulling her up and out of the water, dropping my cell phone on the floor. I knew I was in trouble now, my hands grappling with her naked body, limp, heavy, still warm, still breathing, but not conscious. My heart pounded, my knees buckled as I put her down face up on the wet floor, and turned off the spigot. Then I saw the blood spreading like oil on the water that pooled in the cervaces of the designer slate tiling.

Sandy, whimpering, crying, whining, licked Ms. Sebastian's face as I salvaged my cell phone from under the tub.

"9-1-1. What's your emergency?"

"A woman tried to drown herself in the tub, or she fell, I don't know, but at 1411 State Parkway, we need help here."

"What is her name?"

"I just delivered her flowers, and—"

"What is her name?"

"Uhh—Hannah Sebastian is the name on the delivery ticket." I knew her name all right, but I didn't want to seem too familiar with her. Who could tell what had happened here, and if I knew too much, I might be in trouble.

Sandy turned, baring her teeth, exploding in fury and hatred at the man who stood in the bathroom doorway. The bus stop statue had come to life. Her spring from the floor, airborne in a second, stretched her full length, roaring like a starved lioness attacking her prey, took her to the upraised arm of the intruder, who accepted the crushing jaws without remorse, and who curled his free arm around Sandy's neck, and raising his trapped arm upward violently, snapped the dog's neck. Ninety pounds of canine loyalty fell to the floor like a sodden sack of wet towels, heavy and lifeless.

His fist flattened the left cheekbone of my face. My cell phone flew against the wall, and landed somewhere behind the commode. I countered with a jab and a power punch to the guy's rib cage and solar plexus. He doubled over in pain. Go figure, a dog bites him, he's unmoved. I hit him, and he's a noodle. The guy rose up and smashed the back of his head into my jaw, simple but effective head butt technique. I fell backward into the shower door, shattering it. I think my head cracked the tiling in the shower stall just before I slumped to the floor. I watched as the bus stop guy staggered from the room. I dragged myself to my hands and knees and crawled after him, stopping at the doorway into the hall. He staggered into the office, raging through it like a campground bear in search of food in a camper. He was looking for something and he apparently knew vaguely where to find the lock box he grabbed from inside the filing cabinet. As he came out of the office, he saw me watching him. Just as the realization he meant harm pierced my consciousness, the guy panicked. He reached into his pocket for his handgun, raising it towards Hannah and me. I heard the clicks and the two reports. He ran down the stairs like he was escaping a flash point fire, two risers at a time, staggering like a drunk, slipping on the wet floor, falling out the front door, taking no time to stop for the cell phone that had dumped out of his pocket. Maybe he didn't know he'd dropped it. A train whistle, urgent and harsh, broke the sudden silence and shattered my mind as I fell to the floor, my chest burning, my sight fading, my thoughts evaporating into the dark.

2

*M*arjorie? Be good to me and call the garage and have them bring my car around," Lynn said to her secretary as she hung up the phone. "I'll be back in a couple of hours. Long lunch date."

"Sure, Ms. Hargrove—lunch with Hannah, Ms. Hargrove?" Marjorie said to the office door as it slammed shut.

Lynn pulled her Lexus up in front of Hannah's brownstone where a delivery van had parked in front. She couldn't remember driving here, responding to Hannah's odd comments on the phone. She had to maneuver around the van, into the short space before the fire hydrant. Shivering, she looked at the front door through the misty windshield. It stood open, beckoning to her. Hannah always kept that door shut. The porch light was off. She always kept the light on. But most worrisome was the silence. Sandy always barked when anyone's car drove up and stopped in front of the building. She grabbed her day-timer and her cell phone and got out of the car, all in reflex mode, not thinking. She felt the biting cold air slap arctic rouge onto her cheeks as she walked cautiously up the stairs to the porch. Peering into the entrance hall through the open door, she saw water soaking into the Persian rug from a wide puddle on the ceramic tile floor.

"Oh God!" She pulled out the antenna on her cell. Her numbing fingers dialed 9-1-1.

"Police Emergency. State your name and why you are calling." Lynn could hear the woman's overly calm voice, but she couldn't get her throat to utter a sound. She coughed to shake it loose.

"My name is Lynn Hargrove. I'm an attorney. I'm standing on my friend's front porch at 1411 State Parkway. I'm sure a crime has been committed here. I can see a flood of water in the front hall, but the dog isn't barking, and the door is standing open. Send an ambulance and the police to 1411 State Parkway. Hurry!"

"Yes ma'am, right away. Don't go in. I repeat don't go into the house."

Lynn was trembling so hard that she had trouble putting her phone back into her pocket. Sitting on the ornate wrought-iron chair set diagonally in the corner of the porch near the door, she had to grip the arms to fight the tremors. To keep her brain from freezing in terror, she took in the details of the house. The drooping begonias, the silent fountain, and the clouds blocking the sun contributed to the mood of doom sweeping over the scene. Leaves swirled across the sidewalk. The paint was peeling from the window frames in some places, flaking in others. Cobwebs draped the corners near the ceiling of the porch where resident spiders feasted on a smorgasbord of trapped cocooned delicacies. Garden dirt encrusted the edge of the bottom step, where Hannah's gardener probably had scraped it from a shoe. But the dust gathered in the corners and along the base of the stonework, indicated that only the wind had swept the porch for some time.

Her gaze settled on red spots spattered on the stoop. Her eyes followed the trail leading away from the house and down the sidewalk. Lynn shuddered.

"Blood. Oh Hannah! What's taking them so long?"

Unwilling to wait any longer, she stood at the front door, hesitating as she stepped inside. She was unsure of her next move, but her brain snapped mental pictures as she headed up the stairs. The water had pooled on the treads where a century of foot-traffic had worn down the wood. Lying halfway into the hallway was a man, shot and bleeding. Bending over, she felt his jugular for a pulse. Very faint, but palpable. She left him to go into the bathroom.

"Oh, my God! Oh, my God!"

The sight was gruesome. There on the floor were Sandy's twisted carcass and Hannah's pale, naked body. Shock rubberized her knees, and Lynn crumpled to the floor beside her friend. The moisture from the pool of water and blood seeped into her skirt and soaked into her undergarments. She felt for a pulse as a sobbing sound gushed from her throat. She put her free hand down to balance herself as a dizzying sensation struck her. Lynn caught the dog's muzzle in her line of vision, and saw there was blood on the lips that were curled back from what must have been her last moment's emotion. She thought there was a slight throb in Hannah's neck under her fingers, but the police and ambulance sirens wailed into her consciousness. Lynn wanted to stand and run from the house, but instead she heard herself screaming, "Oh, please come help me. My friend is dying in there. She's barely alive. Please, help her, please!" until a female officer took her arm.

"Let's wait over here. I am Officer Parker." She helped Lynn to her feet, supporting her shaking form as she led her past the man lying in the hall, down the stairs and toward her squad car, where another female officer was in touch with the station by radio. There were four or five other squad cars in the street, and one ambulance.

"They're going in now, Sir," the officer said into the microphone.

Again, the cold autumn air slapped Lynn's face, kick-ing her autopilot professionalism into gear like the derailleur on a ten-speed racing bike. Her mind cleared enough to allow her to speak with an attempt at authority.

"We have to protect this crime scene. There are blood drops on the sidewalk. It's still fresh. The attacker can't be far away. Order a forensic team to secure the premises. We have to preserve the evidence. Alert the hospitals to watch for someone with dog bite coming in for treatment. Sandy must have gotten her teeth on the attacker, judging from the blood on her snout."

"Ms. Hargrove?" the male crime scene officer called out to her. "Could you come here? My name is Detective O'Riley."

As in a dream, she walked back into the house. The paramedics had placed Hannah on one gurney and the man on another. They were bringing the gurneys down the stairs to the front hall and to the waiting ambulance.

"The dog got her attacker. There is blood and skin on her snout and canine teeth," Detective O'Riley said.

"Can you preserve it? Can you put it in something to preserve it?" Lynn babbled the questions like a rookie, the façade of composure flaking away like moisture laden plaster.

"Routine, ma'am, we've already done that. But from the looks of things, it appears Ms. Sebastian fell in the tub and was shot in the thigh after the guy in the hallway pulled her from the tub. He is most likely the delivery man who belongs to that florist's van out front."

"And the bouquet on the entrance hall table," Lynn responded, trying to fill in details for her own sanity.

"He's been shot in the chest. The bullets may provide some help in identifying the attacker."

"Anything else?" She was losing my focus.

"Well, yes. The office upstairs was ransacked. We're dusting it for prints right now." Detective O'Riley was way ahead of her.

"Thank you. I'll need every bit of evidence I can get to prosecute the guy who did this." What was she thinking? She's not a criminal attorney, just divorce, bankruptcy and family matters.

"Ms. Hargrove? Officer Brown. We've finished taking photos and secured the scene," he informed me. "We found this under the table in the front hall."

Officer Brown handed Lynn a plastic bag containing a cell phone. Turning the bag like a kaleidoscope to better see the contents, she read the identity tag aloud, "Property of Dayton-Holland Industries—if found, return to PO Box 135928, Chicago, IL. 60601," and then she copied the information on the tag into her day-timer and returned the phone to the officer.

"Thank you, for all your help, officer. I'm going to take some of her personal things for her: her husband's picture, her nightgown, her toothbrush, that sort of thing. All right?"

"All right. We've got what we came for. Officer Parker here will lock up."

"I can do that. I have a key to the house. I'd like to be alone for a moment before I go."

"No ma'am. We'll wait out front for a few minutes, but we can't close the scene until you're gone." Again, Detective O'Riley took her power with him as he headed toward his car.

The other officers left the yellow-crime-scene-tape draped porch, and the silence returned. Lynn stared after them for a few moments until her eyes burned, and then she re-entered the house. She took her time searching Hannah's bedroom and then her office in that spellbound mental state, which grief and concern impose to keep the bereaved lucid enough to function. Lynn gathered the items she had men-tioned to the detective, but she also liberated Hannah's personal phonebook, her daily journal, and her identification thinking ahead to what she might want to have with her when she came to.

Lynn couldn't say exactly how she managed to leave the house, drive to the hospital and not remember doing so, but when she became aware of herself, she was standing in the lounge of the emergency room at County General looking out the window, sipping from a bottle of spring water. Is this how the elderly feel when they begin to lose their minds?

"Ms. Hargrove?" The young doctor tapped her on the shoulder.

Lynn could see in the doctor's face that he was going to have trouble telling her the facts.

"Just give it to me straight, doctor."

He cleared his throat several times as he led her into the emergency room consultation office. "Hannah's been gravely injured. The blow to her head has crushed part of the skull. The injuries are critical, but we think the team of surgeons will be able to save her. The pressure that has been building in the cranium may possibly have stopped the blood flow to her brain long enough to compromise her mentally. The loss of blood from the gunshot wound increases that possibility. We won't know for sure what this will mean until she wakes up . . . if she wakes up at all. That she is alive is a miracle. She should be dead. We're hoping for the best, but need to caution you, the road back for her may be very long. Does she have any family?"

"No. Her husband died just under a year ago. She's estranged from her brother and sister. Parents are dead. Her children are grown and have nothing to do with her." Lynn's eyes fill with tears. "She's so alone."

"Then she's going to need you. Victims of attacks like this one need to have a reason to live. Without that, there's not much hope."

Running her fingers through her hair, as if returning a straggling wisp to its proper place would set everything in order, Lynn said, "That's up to me, right?"

"It's not for me to say. But if you think you can help her—then

I hope you will," the doctor said. "Could you come take care of the paperwork for her?"

"Of course. What about the delivery man?" Lynn asked, not really wanting to know, as she took the clip-board from the doctor. Such fine hands, trim, perfect nails. No guy has hands like that unless he's a doctor. Lynn's thoughts strayed from her immediate concerns.

"Well, the most information we can get for now is from his driver's licence. Peyton Staley is his name. He's from Michigan. The police are checking the address, the delivery company and his I.D. numbers now—should have more to go on in an hour or so."

Lynn looked away from him, thinking. I know Hannah's brother controls her family's estate; he controls her portion of the inheritance and keeps it from her. Over the years, Hannah simply rejected her family's attempts to manipulate her choices. It angered everyone, especially her mother. I know her brother manipulated the funds to get back at her. And, I know I have go after that money from the legal side of things. Her insurance won't cover all this, not even the best insurance does.

"Certainly, I'll sign whatever papers you have. She deserves a break. And besides, as her attorney, I can find the means to help in more ways than this," she said.

"All right, then. Come this way." The young doctor opened the door for her.

"Do you have the bullet?" Lynn asked him, walking through the doorway knowing she was walking into a long, difficult, solitary battle for Hannah's life.

≈≈

3

≈≈

A rocking train compartment came into focus as I became aware that a recliner chair was supporting every muscle of my head and neck, back and legs, a welcome comfort. The memory of the bathroom, falling, slipping under the water, softened and faded from my mind the way the sunset fades into a night sky at the end of a film. In the emptiness of forgetting, I felt the rumbling of the train and curiosity shook loose from where my brain had gone blank. The night countryside flashed by too fast to see where the train was passing. The lights in the distance gave no indication of place, not farms, not towns, just lights outside the windows. The darkness itself was a blur. Curious, I stood and moved toward the door, thinking I would find my way to the dining car and a glass of water, or Coke, or wine. A soft series of tones crackled through a speaker.

"All passengers are to remain seated." The voice was baritone, like James Earl Jones floating over the intercom, as rich and velvety as caramel over flan. "The call to dinner will come in a few minutes. Please remain seated."

With the obedience of a well-trained canine, I re-turned to my seat and relaxed into the recliner.

"Ms. Sebastian, you are here to determine your fate."

"Excuse me?"

"Your soul is in shock. Your body has shut down enough to seem dead to others—something like playing possum. You have no control over the reflex. You could survive, or you could die."

I laughed. "What a ridiculous thing to hear on a train."

"Life is like a journey on a train. Each journey has a beginning and an end. The tracks intersect many others. When a sidetrack is offered, a person can to choose to stay on the original track or take the sidetrack. It is a simple matter of choice. Each individual finds many sidetracks leading to a life of purpose. However, every track is littered with obstacles to overcome and sidetracks that can lead to derailment. You have come to a moment where your life has been threat-ened."

"I slipped in the tub," I said to the voice, unable to resist defending myself against this invisible presence.

"And hit your head, a particularly nasty fall. And you took a bullet in the thigh, near the main artery. Bloody mess. You could die. The sidetrack is before you. You will have to take it this time. No options."

I was wearing clothes meant for traveling, jeans, walking shoes of the comfortable sort, a pullover sweater and a windbreaker. I still felt no pain.

"I am unclear on your meaning. I have done well. I have been successful. Made all the right choices, or so they tell me every year at the Powerhouse Banquet honoring the best sales people."

"Understand, I'm going to say this as clearly as I can." The Voice sounded closer, although not louder, more conspiratorial in tone, nearly a whisper. "You are going to have to prove why you should live. This is not easy. The criteria are rigid and clear."

"Criteria?" I was beginning to listen to the Voice as if it were another person using a microphone hidden behind a screen, like the Wizard talking to Dorothy in the castle in Emerald City.

"Yes, you will be given very little help in this area. It makes no difference whether you know all the regulations ahead of time or not. You cannot change the facts of your life to fit them. The Processor knows all the facts. If you lie about them for any reason, you return and must live with the results. Some die. Some live out their days in a vegetative state. Others go on without the use of limbs. Others suffer the rejection of their families and friends. Still others just get on with things as they had been before. The possibilities are limitless. But," the pause was melodramatic, like an exaggeration of time to create suspense in an otherwise boring tale, "no one goes back to the previous life unchanged."

"I get it. This the moment when a person's life passes before his eyes right before he dies."

"No."

I scoured the walls for evidence of some sort of speaker.

"Coming here became part of your life's design a long time ago. But, the only way you will leave here is according to the decisions of the Processor."

Rubbish. "Do I have to stay in this depressing little compartment?" I was checking behind the moveable panels and curtains for the connection to the voice. I tried the door. Locked.

"No. You will travel to other Environments, as we call them. You will relive certain events in your life. You will meet our agents in a short while. After concluding your first level inquiry before a tribunal, others will direct you, each to a new Environment, where you will engage certain important decisions of your life. Any other questions?"

"Will I meet this Processor of yours?" I was still thinking of the Wizard even though I could not find any evidence of such a person.

"If you do meet the Processor, it will happen at the Final Decision Symposium, the FDS as we call it. You now will have a few moments to reflect before the first agent appears. I suggest you begin to think about the value of your life."

I saw my reflection in the mirror above the small sink across the compartment from my recliner. I was tired and rubbed my fingers over my sallow face trying to ignore the gray circles under my eyes and to rub some color into my ashen cheeks. "I haven't looked this bad since I had dysentery on safari in Africa."

"No, you haven't," said a woman's lucious voice. "But then, you haven't been mortally wounded before either."

Appearing in the mirror, standing just behind me, a young woman with long blond hair, bare feet, and dressed in a multicolored flowing robe, held a large book, resembling an album commonly used for photographs, tied with a red ribbon.

"It's time to start your evaluation. Come with me. I am Agent One, but you may call me Annica."

Annica touched the door to the corridor and it opened into a barren white corridor with dark purple plush carpeting and illuminated from above by a gentle flow of light that highlighted the arch of the ceiling. The softness of the floor was so palpable through the soles of my shoes, I felt the urge to kick them off and walk barefoot. This was no ordinary train. The rocking and swaying of the train car lessened with every step.

"Here we are," Annica said, stopping. Again, she touched a door which disappeared into the wall. "We call this the FORMATION ENVIRONMENT. The first level inquiry will take place in here."

Annica and I descended from the train outside and behind a modest sized house that seemed at once strange and familiar. At first I heard only the slow chugging of the train, as if it were pulling away from a nearby station, but as the sound diminished into nothing, the chirping of birds and the buzzing of insects intensified and replaced the silence with the sounds of summer.

I wondered if Annica could be privately making a fool of me. But Annica knew what was happening next, so I followed her into the back yard of the house in spite of questions swirling in my mind like cottonwood caught in a summer breeze.

Three other beings appeared, walking toward Annica and me, shining in the sunlight, watching me like sentinels taking stock of the enemy. They moved like robots, the skin colors were wrong, like a child's toys that had been painted with flesh tones that were too intense. None of these beings had facial hair of any kind, neither eyebrows nor eyelashes, giving them an air of authority and making them seem more powerful simply because their faces were untroubled by details.

Annica explained the next sequence of coming events. "The Processor provides three events from your childhood for you to relive. After each one, you must tell us how the experience influenced your life. The Processor may require us to ask direct questions, if you are not complete enough in your answers. Do you understand?"

"Seems simple enough. Yes." But why did she and the others seem so mechanical, so matter-of-fact? The question escaped my mind as the sunny warm day disappeared. Without moving I was suddenly a little girl kneeling on a cushion, gazing into the snowy backyard from the back porch addition my father had built so the family could use the space in the winter. I was about four years old.

My mother, the homemaker of the year, middle class, nothing was ever wrong with her Margaret Miller, was baking cookies in the kitchen.

"Oh God, I remember this."

"Lenny, where are you going with that bee-bee gun?" Mother's voice called out from the kitchen.

"Just into the back yard. I want to try it out. I saw a rabbit I want to add to my collection," Lenny shouted. "I'll be right back."

"Lenny—you really should go to the forest preserve for that," Mother said, with no force in her words.

She always was as limp as a dishrag around Lenny.

"I'll be right back!" Lenny shouted again. He got his way with Mother by taking his way and not obeying her. No one else in the family, not even my father, could get away with that. Only Lenny, my eleven-year-old brother got away with anything he pleased. The stretched and drying skins of a hundred small animals: mink, musk-rat, rabbit and squirrel hung as neatly categorized testaments on the basement walls. Lenny trapped the animals and sold their pelts for cash. Always the entrepreneur, he supplied the local taxidermist with quality skins taken from the dwindling wildlife popula-tion soon to be extinguished by urban sprawl, his traps and now his new Christ-mas gift bee-bee gun. The stink of death and tanning of the skins per-meated the whole house.

Pulling on his coat with his gun in hand, Lenny headed for the door to the back yard. A small rabbit, loping with difficulty across the deep snow seemed unaware of danger and out of place trying to hop through the drifts inches deeper than its body. It was clearly trying to reach the woodpile for shelter from the cold and snow. I looked back toward my brother as he opened the door, moving very slowly a short distance into the yard, stalking the rabbit, not wanting to startle his prey.

"No!"

Lenny raised the gun to his shoulder and sighted the rabbit in the aiming notch on the barrel. He squeezed the trigger. The rabbit leaped into the air.

"No!" I was screaming and running the length of the porch and into the yard. Lenny stood still, stunned that he had hit the rabbit with the first shot. Blood spattered in the snow as the rabbit writhed in pain, squeaking, trembling and digging a hole with his squirming body. The snow lining the hole was pink like the satin of a miniature coffin.

Mother came running. I was stomping in circles around the rabbit, crying hysterically, shouting at my brother. The air was still as I felt the snow burning my ankles. No shoes, just thin socks offered no protection for my tiny feet. I didn't care.

"You shot my bunny! You shot my bunny! No! No! You killed my bunny! I hate you! I hate you! I hate you!" The hot blood melted the snow where it fell. Reaching as high as I could, I pummeled Lenny's arm with my tiny fists. Mother looked at the rabbit.

"It's not dead, Lenny. You have to kill it. You can't let it suffer." Cold blooded murderer.

"I can't shoot it again." He was crying. "I can't shoot it again."

"Then you'll have to find another way to kill it. You can't leave it like this," Mother's tone was hard-edged and stern. Lenny ran over to the wood pile. He loosened one of the smaller frozen logs and ran back to the rabbit. I was screaming and sobbing at the same time. Mother grabbed me to carry me back into the house.

"You'll have to take care of that rabbit before you come back in." She tossed her words, carelessly over her shoulder.

"I hate you! I hate you!" I screamed inconsolably as Lenny raised the log and brought it down as hard as he could on the rabbit's head. The rabbit stopped moving. Mother sat down on the couch trying to keep me from running outside again.

"Now Hannah, it'll be all right. People hunt rabbits for food all the time. It's a natural thing to do."

We never ate rabbit.

"No! Lenny shot my bunny!" I was sobbing on Mother's shoulder.

"There, there. You'll be okay. Stop your crying now. That's

enough." Mother was losing her patience. "You'll have to go to your room till you calm down if you don't stop now."

"No! We never eat rabbit! Lenny shot my bunny!" Involuntary gasps for air from sobbing broke the cadence of my words. "Lenny—shot—my bunny!"

Mother carried me up the stairs to my bedroom. She put me down on the bed with no comfort intended.

"Then, just stay here, young lady, until you can stop crying. If you can't do that, then you'll have to miss dinner." The door shut just short of slamming.

Lying on my stomach, I cried into my pillow. Images of the bloody rabbit, leaping into the air, squealing in the snow and dying before my eyes tormented me. I cried for a long time. The frost, sparkling on the window as the sun shone through it, caught my attention. I scratched the frost with my fingernail, watching it fall like feathered diamonds in soft shavings that melted intantly on the window sill. My sobs stopped. Among the stuffed animals scattered on the floor was a little blue bunny. I picked it up, snuggling it against my neck.

"I'll protect you. I'll keep you safe. . . my sweet little bunny. He won't shoot you."

The scene faded. I was sitting on the ground next to the sand box, sobbing, all emotion. The tall, young man, dressed in a simple dark blue body suit, handsome, clean shaven and completely bald, stared at me without feeling yet in a way that made me want to explain his silent question.

"I was helpless that day, so unable to stop my brother from killing the rabbit. What were they trying to do to me? I was helpless in my family. I couldn't stop him from killing an innocent animal. Later on, in many areas of my family life, I would choose a path of resistance."

"But your brother was crying—unable to shoot the rabbit again."

"He beat it to death! With his own hands, he beat it. Jesus! With no remorse, like a serial killer in the making. That made the whole thing personal for me. I knew right then and there he could do the same to me, if I ever crossed him. He got used shooting animals, too. So, I grew up keeping him happy, so he wouldn't have a reason to turn on me. Until later on."

"What time later on do you mean?" the young man asked, too logically, too coldly, too dispassionately for my taste. Sitting cross-legged, I made myself more comfortable, thinking I'd have to make a long explanation and taking time to consider the question.

"I want someone to remind me why I have to answer these questions. How can I explain a point of my life I haven't thought about for decades?"

"For the Processor," the young man said again without inflection. I then recalled what I was supposed to do, to reveal the results of this experience in my life.

"It wasn't a particular moment. Over time I began to see that Lenny, like so many arrogant and calculating people, became outwardly successful—money, big house, world travel—and inwardly corrupt. Self-indulgent to a fault."

I was describing myself, too, an idea that bothered me and silenced me.

"Other reasons, please," the young man said like a toy robot.

"Well, I always felt like he was spying on me whenever he came to visit. He showed up at odd times, often uninvited. He made my private life his business. But his intent became clear when he convinced Mother that I didn't care about her as she grew older. And after she died, he took control of my portion of her estate. But that is a long, complicated story."

"We know all about it," the young man agreed. "We'll come back to that if necessary. Did the rabbit die in vain?"

"Hell if I know. I was so little when it happened."

"You must respond. We are waiting. Time is fleeting. Your answer is required. Now." The young man's face became completely passive, not a muscle twitched, but his eyes held mine. I felt compelled to speak, but my words flowed slowly.

"I never learned to read character. I had trouble standing up for myself. I couldn't tell who to trust and who not to trust. I became the queen of denial and over-achiever of the year, every year of my life. I trusted others with my life when they were uninterested in protecting me."

I wiped the fragile anguish from my face with my trembling hands, hoping to relax my cramping facial muscles and to assess the responses of those otherworldly automatons listening to her. No valid reaction.

4

I was suddenly standing in the front yard of my childhood home, bigger and older—about ten years old.

In the blistering heat and humidity of summer 1957, the sun burned the shadows into the ground. I had just arrived home from playing with friends on a mission to get the old bedspreads from my basement, so we could make a small tent village by stringing ropes between the trees and securing the cloth to the ground with bricks and rocks.

I caught a glimpse of a pink Ford sedan pulling into my driveway, and without much concern I opened the front door. Shouting from the second floor of the house stopped me at the top of the basement stairs. Mother was enraged over something. I hurried down into the musty underground to grab the bedspreads. On my way up the stairs, the lights went out and the door slammed, shutting out my view of the hallway, but not dampening the sounds of anger raging above me. A creepy chill shivered up my spine as I stumbled on the bedspreads, landing hands and knees hard on the wooden risers. This time it was not a panic induced by the fear of an imagined monster lurking below that frightened me. It was my initiation to adult rage, unrestrained and vicious, pouring through the cracks in the door. Could this only be a nightmare? Make it be a nightmare.

My mother's voice was tinged with blood-curling ugliness, "I'm going to kill him! I'm going to kill him! She can't go with him!" My young ears had no reference for the sounds, and so I recorded them as hatred exploding from her hysterical ranting, like pulses from an engine with no muffler. "Leave me alone! Let go of me! Let go of me!"

Oh, God, I remember this. Oh, God. I slipped into the picture as if drawn into a cartoon by the hand of a gargantuan artist who placed me at the basement door, trying to escape the darkness.

As the door cracked open, my father, at home in the middle of the day, was holding my mother's hand up and away, trying to disarm her as they struggled in the small front hall. The sight of an enormous kitchen butcher knife froze me in my tracks. My heart was crashing against my lungs, pounding like it was going to burst from my chest. Too real. Too painful. My father saw me. His face showed a kind of desperation my ten year old mind could not comprehend. He shoved Mother aside and wrenched the knife from her hand. Until that moment, my docile father, the unflappable Jack Miller, had never in my life yelled at me. The heat in his voice was trembling with his attempt to soften his tone. Poor man. He was so unprepared.

"Hannah, get outside! Go to Verna's! Stay there till someone calls for you!" His eyes pleading with me to obey left me no choice. I ran, dropping the green spread on the threshold of the door, the yellow one slathered onto the front steps like mustard, and the blue one poured into the driveway like a puddle of terror. I ran past the pink car and into the sunlight. When I reached the neighbor's house about two blocks distance down the street, Verna was waiting at the front door, arms outstretched. Her hug was warm and safe.

"Why is Mommy screaming like that? What's going on?" I gasped, still panting from the run down the block.

"You'll understand—someday—when you're older," Verna said softly.

How could she know? I felt my face flushing as I took the peanut butter and jelly sandwich Verna handed to me from the kitchen counter. Everything fell into place in my ten-year-old mind. My father was home at the wrong time of day; Mother was screaming in the wrong voice, it was the wrong car, the wrong knife. Every detail was wrong.

"Donna's my sister! I have to know now!"

The sandwich plopped onto the floor as I ran outside and back home to the front yard just as Donna escaped from the house lugging her suitcase. My father, glancing nervously back toward the door, helped her put it in the car. I saw them in slow motion. The sun was too bright. I couldn't see who was driving. I heard nothing. I just observed how the car was getting smaller as it drove away. I watched my father, stoop-shouldered and defeated, go back into the house. He hadn't noticed me standing there. In just a few moments, Mother came out of the house looking for something as if she'd lost it and would find it out here. She stopped a few paces away from me. I stood silent as a statue, attempting conversion to invisibility. I failed to disappear and was disbelieving of the pain in my arms as she grabbed them roughly. She pulled me face to face with her.

"Let me go! Leave me alone! Don't touch me!" My mother's hands in some unspoken way violated my privacy, another intimate sensation I was meeting for the first time. That was the way I would feel her touch for the rest of my life, as if she would pollute my whole being when she touched me.

"No one is ever going to know what happened here today. No one. It's secret." Mother's voice was nasty, snarling like a rabid dog. "You can't tell this secret to anyone. Not to your friends, not to your teacher, not to anyone. Just forget what you saw and what you heard."

She grabbed my shoulders. "Don't you ever do anything like what your sister did to me today, hear? Never!" I remained silent, unsuccessfully willing myself into another dimension.

"Do you hear?!" She shook me hard, as if to rid me of demons. Her rage precluded any resistance to her demands.

"Okay," I murmured softly, my eyes staring at the tips of my shoes as the tears stung behind my eyeballs, tears I have never let fall. The artist erased the vision, and in my very distorted new reality, I was back with the agents. Damn, this was getting to me.

The young man spoke after a moment or two. "Tell me what your mother's insistence on secrecy meant to you in your life."

"In a word? Destruction." Then I laughed to soften the intensity of my realization.

All three tribunal members frowned. Apparently, laughter was not a generally acceptable response to their questions.

"My mother stole my honesty. The most important choice any person ever has is the choice to be honest. She meant to steal it, too. She lied so many times, and to so many different people, in as many different ways, that the lies became the truth. Lies can do that. I felt utterly alone, a feeling I knew I would never completely shake the rest of my life."

Suddenly, I was choking on sobs. I was losing my sense of detachment.

"Did you ever take back your honesty?" the middle-aged woman tribunal member asked casually, the way one asks for a drink of water. Her gray hair was swept back in a tight bun, her clothes equally gray, severe and unflattering.

"Not from them. I struggled with deceit in most areas of my life as I grew older. You know, cheating boyfriends, fickle back-stabbing girlfriends in school. A time came when I was no longer willing to lie to myself. By the time I was twenty I wanted to begin my life over again."

"Did your return to honesty put an end your problems?" The third tribunal member finally spoke. He was quite old, feeble in movement and manner. His back was curved and he looked downward toward the ground, involuntarily forced to twist his head to the side to look into anyone's face.

"No, it was just an act of desperation. I tormented my mother with rejection. I wouldn't let her hug me. I berated her constantly."

"Rather cruel, don't you think?" the young man asked, pumping me for more rhetoric.

"No, I don't."

5

The old man took my hand. Instantly, I was fourteen years old and standing alone on the windy, wintry hilltop of my father's house in the country, my second and last home with my parents where I lived as an only child, since both my older siblings had left home by then.

"Here King! Come here boy! Here King!" I called into the darkness. I punctuated my shouts with the loudest whistles I could make. I relived the fear and panic of the young girl I had been that night. My father came out of the house and walked up the hill toward me.

"Come in now, Hannah. He's not coming home tonight. We'll go look for him in the daylight." My father knew the loneliness I was feeling and tried to lessen it with gentleness. He and Mother had been living separate lives in the same house for years by the time this took place, just another great lesson in avoidance for my survival handbook.

"No, Daddy, he's out there. I want him to hear me calling. Maybe he'll find his way back if he can just keep hearing me call him." Tears streamed down my face.

"I'm sorry, honey. You've been out here for an hour. He's not heard you. We'll look for him in the morning. Now, come inside and eat dinner." The cold bit into my skin like an airborne piranha, whose teeth made no marks but caused a stinging pain only hours of warmth could cure.

"But, how could he be gone? His chain is still on his doghouse. He didn't run away without someone letting him off the chain. Who would do that?"

"Come on. Let's go in and warm up." He walked back to the house and I followed him.

By the end of this third vision, the others were silent, listening with a strange interest cloaked in detachment. How did they do that?

"Daddy took me into the house. They told me there had been a lot of dogs stolen in the neighboring countryside. It was just before Christmas, and an unusually large number of pedigreed animals were reported missing from the exclusive homes in our part of the village. They both told me King had probably been stolen along with all the other dogs."

"That's what they told you. But that's not what happened."

It was early afternoon of the same day. The garbage truck was coming up the road. It turned into the long driveway leading up the hill. My mother stood in the parking area at the top, waving at the truck to stop on the incline rather than coming all the way up into the parking area. The driver leaned out the window of the truck's cab.

"What's the matter, Mrs. Miller?"

"Stop right there! I need your help!" She was shouting hysterically.

"Help with what?" The driver was curious. Her behavior was odd for no apparent reason. The excitement in her voice seemed forced, planned, just like all the manipulating women he had known.

"Our dog. Come here and take a look." She walked toward the white and blue frame doghouse my father had built years earlier in the corner of the parking lot. The driver got out of the truck and followed her. "Look inside the house. I don't know what to make of it." She said this last with the same lilt in her voice she would use to ask someone to look at a photo album.

The driver looked into the dim interior of the dog house. The collie lay on his side, his body contorted, eyes open with a look of terror frozen in the dog's stare.

"Looks like he's dead," the driver said with no emotion. "Do you want us to take him off your hands?"

"Oh—could you?" Her tone settled into a sweetness that sounded more like a coquettish ploy than an honest wish. "It would make things so much easier."

"Sure, but, you know, it looks like your dog was poisoned. I had a dog die once that looked like that when he got hold of some rat poison."

"Oh, I'm sure no one would give our dog poison." She shook her head in disbelief. He looked at her sidelong and responded in a forced courtesy, her child-like demeanor seeming odd to the driver, as it would have to any normal human being.

"Well, we'll just put him in the back of the truck and take him with us. You go ahead inside. We'll take care of it for you."

"Thank you. Thank you so much." Laughing the shakey little laugh that accented nearly all her sentences, Mother retreated inside, watching from the bedroom window until the garbage men had taken everything and gone on their way. Turning away from the window, smiling, she picked up the phone on the dressing table and dialed Daddy at work.

"Hello, Jack? The garbage men came today. I gave them all the extra stuff we've kept around here too long, okay?"

"What are you talking about? And why are you calling me at work?"

Mother was not supposed to call Daddy at work. But, what ever kept her from doing any damned thing she pleased?

"The dog is gone, too. Got rid of all the stuff. Aren't you glad?"

"Stay home, dear. I'll be there as quickly as I can ."

"Hey, Daddy! Mother is out of control again," the child's voice in my head spoke aloud.

"Don't let Hannah know about the dog."

"Oh, she's still at school. She won't ever know anything about this. Don't you worry about that!" Mother's laugh caught like a broken record between her sentences.

The scene disappeared and the tribunal along with it. Annica reappeared, back in the yard behind the house.

"What do you think?"

"I'm not surprised. So many personal losses grew from these three events. How could I not know? Was I just a stupid, trusting kid?

"You had incomplete information to go on. Do you remember that shortly after the dog disappeared, your mother went to the hospital?" the young man asked.

"Yes, she had trouble with the veins in her legs." I looked at the group. Jesus! Even these creatures knew what really happened. They all shook their heads.

"Okay, I'm game. Where did she go, then?"

"Your father had her committed to a mental health facility for evaluation and treatment," Annica said, "for manic depression and delusions, as they called it in those days. Basically, she was bi-polar. With time, treatment and drugs, she was able to return home and lead a fairly normal existence after that," the middle aged woman said.

"Information a little late for the jury, huh?" I asked. No one responded.

"But she took care of my father in his old age the same way she took care of the dog. When he grew weak from strokes, she didn't poison him. She just put him in the worst elderly care facility she could find to let him waste away. The result was the same, it just took longer."

I couldn't fight the emotions with sarcasm any longer. The break is jagged when it happens, and from the fissure flows all the grief I had kept bottled inside.

"Oh, my God! Oh my God! I never knew—I never knew." The tears pulled all my anger from inside me. "I needed this."

"We know."

Annica and I returned to the compartment of the train.

"My whole life was based on lies."

"No, the road you travel was mined with lies during the first years of your life. But your life is not marred by lies of your own. You are searching for the truth, and with difficulty, you are finding it."

"But I'm dead!" I screamed at Annica.

"Are you?"

I heard the call of the train whistle, once again tearing me from the moment, gathering speed; I felt only the rock and sway of the train taking me away.

6

As my memory of Hannah's bathroom faded, I heard a woman's voice.

"Are you Agent Two?"

I couldn't respond. Someone nudged me on the shoulder.

"Are you Agent Two? I was told there would be an Agent Two."

"Well, this is something! Wake up! Wake up!"

Someone pushed me several times, trying to get a response.

"Hey! What are you doing!" Sitting bolt upright, I pushed my face close to the woman's face. "I was having a wonderful dream."

"Did you have an accident, too?" She looked at me with interest.

"What 'too'?"

"An accident. Are you here because you had an accident? I fell in my bathtub."

"Where am I? The motion is making me sick." I caught myself from falling off the chair as I craned my neck to see the full three-hundred sixty degree panorama.

"Well, I can't explain it very well, but we're in this compartment on this train because the Processor wants us here."

"The Processor?"

"Well, he's—uh—sort of like—uh—God, I guess." A dawn of recognition lit up her face. "What's your name?"

"My name?" *I wonder if I should tell her.* "Peyton Staley."

"I thought I recognized you. You deliver my flowers every week. My name is Hannah Sebastian. Don't you remember me?" She smiled her glamour girl smile, and I shook my head and pretended I didn't know her.

"What am I doing here?" I said, dodging her question with my own.

"That was my question. The Processor knows the answer to that. I'm waiting for Agent Two to come and take me to the next environment."

"The next environment? This is insane. Let me out of here!" I searched the compartment for a lever or a button to push. Finding none, I searched the walls, tried the door; locked. No way out. I returned to my recliner and sat on the foot end.

"I think we'd better just wait. I already went through the first inquiry and returned here. I suppose we're to wait. What else can we do?"

"First inquiry? Do you want to explain that?"

"Oh, I don't think I'm qualified to do that, but I'll try. The way I understand it, everyone is born with a track to travel—like on a train." Her voice was serious. Her face was sad, her hair, disheveled.

"You get many chances to make something of your life by taking or not taking sidetracks. If you have an accident or something violent happens to you, then you get sent here to find out if you will live or die. You have to prove you should be allowed to live. Some people do and some people don't. If you do, you go back to the life you had before, and you have to live it in whatever condition your accident left you in. They told me some people are vegetables, or paralyzed, or hated by their friends and families. Others go back and just pick up where they left off, but with a whole new outlook. You are on a sidetrack even if you weren't looking for one. I guess that means you get a chance to start all over. See?"

"No, I don't see." This has got to be just a bad dream. "I'm supposed to finish my deliveries and get to an important interview with new corporate owners. I have to be there or I'll lose my chance at a good new job. I am now going to wake up." I slapped my own face. "Wake up!" I shouted at myself. "It's as simple as that. I want you to show me the way out of here. Wake up!"

"She can't do that." The baritone voice booms.

"Holy shit!" I jerked involuntarily.

"You're here and you can't go back. The Processor has indicated you need to wait for Anthony, your Agent One. You may wait here or be placed in another compartment—alone. Which do you choose?"

"I'll stay here." At least Hannah was a known commodity in this unrecognizable place.

Somehow I was wearing the same kind jeans, pullover and jacket as Hannah. A barefoot young man appeared from nowhere. He was wearing multi-colored clothing and carrying a large book tied with red ribbon. "Gay pride day, is it?" I said.

"Peyton Staley? I am your Agent One, Anthony. You will come with me now. We will begin your inquiry in your FORMATION ENVIRONMENT. Please follow me."

"Sure, to the ends of the earth." I raised my eyebrows at Hannah in surprise. She smiled to reassure me. "See you later, maybe."

I followed Anthony through the door, hoping Hannah would be there when I returned, if I returned. The hallway was dark and barren. One door glowed at the far end of the corridor. Walking behind Anthony, my heart began pounding, my stomach churned. I felt my movements becoming more and more agitated. Anxiety attack. Anthony waited a moment before touching the door.

"This will only take a short time. You are going to rediscover your earliest moments and you will have to explain how you justify the way you are living your life. Your track is full of opportunity and success, yet you do everything you can to avoid grasping your destiny. Unlike those who arrive here only by violence done to them, you arrived here also because you took a Sidetrack that denies you full access to happiness."

He talks like a computer. "A Sidetrack? What do you mean?"

"Your Life Track is predetermined. As you walk the track provided by the Processor, you have choices to make. Many other tracks intersect your own, bringing other people into your life. They influence you, and you influence them. Temptations and Opportunities come and go. Peyton Staley takes the Temptations, over and over again."

"I do? I work hard. I earn a good living. I have everything I ever needed or wanted."

"Do you? Deliveries do that for your bottom line?" Anthony touched the door.

"Come with me." Anthony said. "You aren't the only person who ever felt like an idiot at this moment." He laughed at me, and I laughed, too.

"Thank you." my anxiety faded away, replaced by a sense of calm.

"You'll be all right. Follow me," he said.

"Where are we going now?"

"You'll have to pass through the inquiry. Then you'll meet with Agents Two, Three and Four. Everyone goes through the same process. The Processor will provide your first three experiences. You will have to explain how they influenced you at certain points along your Life Track. Do you understand?"

"I think so. No, of course, not."

"No, of course not. Your mother died a few days after you were born, am I right?"

"No, I think you have that detail wrong. My mother is still living in New York."

"I'm sorry. Willa May Staley, the woman you know as your mother, lives in New York. Your birth mother died just after you were born."

Anthony led me into the FORMATION ENVIRONMENT. "You mean my mother isn't my mother." Absurd thought.

"That's right."

"I never did feel that I fit into the scheme of things. I lived in a shit hole little basement apartment with no toys to play with. My father worked two factory jobs, coming home only to sleep. Willa May was a sad woman, not much education and very naïve. She took me to the park almost every day, when the weather was good. The rest of the time I played with pots and pans, read books, and made toys out of junk I found outside around the apartment building. I could read by the time I was four. So I went to school."

Anthony and Peyton entered at the front of the build-ing. "We'll just wait in here for the tribunal members to arrive."

In the cramped living room, I touched certain things, but couldn't pick anything up. Everything was glued into place.

"It's just the way it was."

"Yes, that's so you can more vividly relive the event the Processor chose for you."

A young woman and two others joined Anthony.

"We will expect you to explain the significance to your life after each event. Do you have any questions?" she asked, her long, straight black hair heightening the stark contrast of her fair complexion and beckoning green eyes.

She's not bad looking, except for the missing eyebrows; she'd be better with eyebrows. "No, I don't, but I have to get back to my meeting—"

"There isn't going to be any meeting. Accept that. Now, prepare for your first experience."

The living room vanished. Standing on the front porch of the apartment building, I was only three years old. My blond hair, warmed by the midday summer sun and tousled from the wind, fell into my eyes. Willa May was leaving me with Carla Sue again. I hated Carla Sue. She smelled of stale tobacco and beer.

"Carla Sue?" my mother said, "I'll be back in a few minutes. It's a beautiful day for the park. Take Peyton to the park while I'm gone, will you?" Willa May asked.

"Yes ma'am, we'll leave in a bit," Carla Sue drawled, taking another drag on her nearly consumed cigarette. Willa May grabed her purse, kissed me on the cheek and hurried down the front steps. She was wearing a flower-print dress, which meant she had somewhere to go and someone to meet.

I stood on the porch, watching my mother walk as fast as she could toward the center of town two blocks away. Impatiently waiting for the baby-sitter to take me to the park down the street, I toddled into the kitchen where Carla Sue was sitting despondently at the kitchen table, smoking her last cigarette. I could see she was trying to control some kind of rage.

"I don't deserve this," she said, noticing me standing in the doorway. "I don't need to take care of other people's children for a living. I have my own. He can't have my children. He can't take them away to live out of state." She smiled at me in a way that frightened my three-year-old sensibilities. "So—I—made sure—he—will never get my boys," she said to me, drawing out the words in a peculiar manner. "Peyton! Come here, honey," Carla Sue stubbed out the cigarette butt in the overflowing ashtray. "Let's play a game!"

"I want to go to the park. Mama said we could go to the park! And you promised we could go to the park." My chin started to tremble. She always promised to take me to the park, and then broke the promise. I didn't like the games she wanted to play either.

"Let's play cowboys and Indians. I'll be the cowboy and you be the Indian. I'll catch you and tie you up. Then I'll let you go. It'll be fun." Carla Sue tried to make the game sound enticing.

"No! I want to go to the park!" I stamped my foot.

"You little creep. I'll show you who's boss here. Get over here!" She grabbed me by the arm. Her grip hurt.

"OOOwww! Let me go! I want to go to the park!"

"You won't be going to any parks—for a long time. We're going to play this game. Now sit down in that chair so I can capture you and tie you up." Carla Sue dragged one of the kitchen chairs into the living room.

"Put on the head dress and beads so you'll look like a real Indian chief." She tried to make her voice sound playful. I ran behind the couch, trying to get away from Carla Sue.

"No! I just want to play in the park. Please, let's go to the park." I began to cry.

"Shut up you little bastard!"

She reached over the couch and grabbed me by the shirt. She dragged me over to the chair and bound my feet and hands with clothesline from the laundry closet. She jammed a dish towel in my mouth and gagged me. She put several strands of cheap plastic beads around my neck. She took the drooping feather headdress from the toy box and placed it ceremoniously on my head.

"You're under arrest!" She was laughing. "I captured the big Indian chief! I'm going to get him!"

I whimpered in fear and confusion. She ran into the kitchen and pulled the large knife from the drawer, returning with it to the living room.

"Now I'm going to scalp the great Indian chief!" She raised the hand that held the knife and grabbed my hair with her other hand. I stared at her, shaking my head no. The front door opened, and my mother stood in the doorway with a policeman.

"Carla Sue Avery? Put the knife down! You are under arrest for the murders of three children." The policeman's voice stopped Carla Sue in her tracks. "Mrs. Staley came to tell us this morning how she was afraid for her son's safety. Your landlord let us into your apartment. We found your children in your freezer this morning," the policeman said calmly. "Now, put that knife down and come with me."

Carla Sue whirled around. She raised the knife higher. "You won't take me! I'm going to escape from you, just like all the others." She brought the knife down, thrusting it deep into her own abdomen. She crumpled to the floor, sobbing, gasping for air.

"I didn't deserve to lose them—I loved them—they were going —to take my babies."

Carla Sue fell forward and to the side, her hands still clutching the knife.

Willa May ran to me and freed me from the chair. She picked me up and held me, sobbing.

"You're all right? You'll be fine. We'll never let this happen to you ever, ever again." She repeated herself over and over. The policemen gently led us both crying from the scene.

I stood in the doorway, stunned. The black-haired young woman, in a very matter of fact way, motioned me to sit on the couch.

"Tell us how that affected you in later years."

"I don't know—I don't like big knives. But, I think I distrust women who tell me they want to love me and care for me. I keep my distance from women."

"Is that why you have divorced twice, and have a long string of lovers who mean nothing more than a night's sexual recreation?

Is that why you drink yourself unconscious on a regular basis?" the second woman on the tribunal asked.

"Is that why I have three women on my tribunal?" Anger exploded my emotional storehouse the way dynamite explodes a mountain. "Is this kangaroo court skewed to the female side for some reason? Unfair! A jury of my peers means men."

"Do you have a problem with women?" the black-haired woman asked, looking at me with a hostile glare.

"Of course not! I love women!" I recognized the disbelief in their eyes for what it was.

"I don't go for men, if that's what you're getting at! I love women. But—" still feeling the raw fear of the child I had been, "I do see how I must have been influenced by this event. Even though I don't actually remember it, anyone to experience that at so young an age would be hurt, you know, without knowing they were hurt."

The three tribunal woman nodded, reminding me of the judgemental adults of my childhood who always nodded in understanding, but rarely believed what I had to say about any particular situation.

"Was the result of this event good or bad?" the second woman asked. I heard the setup.

"Good or bad? What kind of question is that? From where I stand now, I couldn't answer anything but that it was bad."

"No, we mean, do you approach women differently than other men do?" Their faces were so expectant. I knew what they wanted to hear, so I gave them the obvious.

"No, like any man, I have trouble understanding women. In my experience, women are actually all about taking us men for everything we've got. They lie. They manipulate. They smother and squeeze you till you're about to explode."

"I see. And the drinking problem?" Again, the black-haired woman stared me down.

7

*S*uddenly, I was no longer in the apartment. The tribunal was gone, and I was bouncing a ball against the garage door of the second house in my childhood. I was about nine years old. I was new to the neighborhood of small cracker box houses lined up on the dirt streets and shaded by Chinese elms, the fast growing shade trees of sprawling over lower class suburbia. Across the empty lot there were several older boys playing stickball. They were clearly bigger than I was, and so I decided not to try to join in the game. They saw me too, and when they finished the second inning, the biggest one, the size and the demeanor of an ox, signaled to the others to follow him, as he walked toward my house.

"Hey! New kid! What's your name?" the Ox said, trying to sound tough through his southern drawl.

I caught my ball and turned to the motley crew of gangly twelve-year-old boys, not one of whom seemed comfortable in his skin. The Ox stared at me, squinting with intent to intimidate.

"Peyton Staley." My voice was reluctant to resonate. I cleared my throat in nervous self defense.

"Peyton Staley? What kind of sissy name is that?" The Ox laughed, and the others joined him in a burst of pre-pubescent, male-bonding laughter.

"Where are you from?" Another of the boys threw the hardball into his mitt for emphasis.

"South of here." I had learned a long time ago that less was more when you weren't sure of your adversary.

"South of here! Where's that?" the Ox said.

"Kentucky." I was feeling smaller with every answer.

"He's a red neck hillbilly!" They all laughed together. "What did you come here for, hill-bil-ly," one of them yelled like he was announcing my new title to the world.

"My dad got a job up here—at the factory."

I didn't know what else to tell them as they walked in a close circle around me slowly making it smaller and smaller. I succumbed to the knowledge that they were going to beat me up, or at least knock me around some.

"Let's find out how strong you are." Ox put up his fists to fight.

"I don't want to fight you," I stepped back. "There's no sense in it."

Ox moved toward me, punching the air near my head.

"You are a sissy—look at him fellas—he's a sissy!" Ox kept repeating his taunt, moving in a slow circle around me and trying to get me to fight.

No one but me noticed the curtain in the window of my house moving slightly to one side. Someone was watching, and I felt like my every move was being judged by the watcher.

"I think it's time to find out what he's made of." Ox shoved me hard, knocking me off balance. Another boy pushed me in the other direction where a third tripped me. I fell on my ass in the dirt. The pain they inflicted was not as great as the humiliation they intended.

"You don't want to fight? Huh, kid? You don't want to fight?" Ox kept taunting me.

"No, I don't want to fight." I stood up fast, using the upward power of my legs to guide my fist. "But—you do!" The punch landed square and hard on Ox's jaw. He went down. The others defended him, kicking and punching at me. I was fast and accurate enough to land a few more blows on several of the other boys and to duck most of their haphazard flailings. Ox shook off his dizziness and stood up again.

"I'm going to kill you!" He charged me. Two of the others grabbed my arms and held me. I struggled to get free, but Ox punched me in the stomach two or three times before I could get my feet up. I landed a kick on the Ox's groin that knocked him to one knee.

The curtain on the window fluttered closed.

"You're dead meat, hillbilly!" Ox shouted. "Let him go. I'm going to kill him on my own!" The boys let my arms go. I steadied myself for the Ox's attack.

The cannon-like gunshot shook the neighborhood. The boys stopped in their tracks. I looked up to the front porch of my house where my father was standing, shotgun in hand. His wrinkled wash pants, bare feet, torn shirt and day-old beard added credence to his wild-eyed gestures.

"You boys get out of here!" was all Aaron Staley said, flicking his hand like he was swatting at a fly. The boys scattered like buckshot, as he came down the steps into the yard.

"Listen son," he put his arm around my shoulders. "You did a good job against tough odds. But, sometimes we need a little help in this life. That's all can I offer you from time to time—a little help."

"You should have let me fight it out. Now I'm going to have to fight that kid again. He's not going to quit till I beat him," I was panting, trying not to cry.

"Maybe—maybe not. Just remember, you've always got your family. That counts for more than anything else in this life."

He shuffled stiffly back into the house, the scent of whiskey lingering on the humid air. I watched him disappear into the shadows of the porch. The screen door slapped shut, leaving me to face the boys who, I was sure, were regrouping behind the next door neighbor's house. I heard them return as soon as my father was gone, although I stayed facing the house.

"Okay, hillbilly. You're not as much a sissy as I thought. Want to play stickball?" Ox asked. Surprised by the sudden turn of events, I turned toward them.

"All right. I'll pitch."

The scene evaporated. I was standing with the tribunal members in front of the same house.

"What did you learn that day?" the black-haired woman said again, boring into my forehead with her eyes like she wanted to visually extract my brain.

"My father was rough on me. That afternoon was the first time I was sure loved me. He stepped in to help me only once or twice again before he died. For the first half of my life he was a hard man, always gone working two jobs, or drinking in front of the television, or sleeping. Sometimes in a rage, he'd throw things and terrorize us all. That's how I remember him. But that afternoon, things changed. Knowing he was looking out for me softened the pain of being the brunt of so much punishment."

"That's all? What about later on?" the second woman said.

"That afternoon stuck with me. Every time I got into a tight spot at work, I'd remember. That afternoon gave me the guts to fight things out in the workplace too. I didn't always win, but I won enough times to keep going. Mostly, I learned about respect—it's something you have to fight for, even when people are ready to fire you."

"Not bad, as explanations go." The woman smiled.

The third tribunal woman stepped over to my side. Her blue eyes twinkled from the web of wrinkles that defined her face and reflected the clarity of mind that diminished her elderly appearance. She took my hand as if I were a small child needing to be coaxed to go home from playing a favorite game.

"Come with me," she said very gently. "Let's take a walk." She led me outside.

8

I was standing in a crowd of strangers on the station platform waiting for the train to arrive. I was eleven or twelve years old. The distant sound of a train whistle an-nouncing its arrival split the frigid night air. The rush of sound and wind the locomotive made pulling into the station always thrilled me, and this night it would be even more exhilarating. Christmas Eve was rarely a joyous event in my house. Tight money and too many children usually made the celebration strained. But this year was different. My father had been lucky at gambling, and my grandmother was coming up from Kentucky for the holiday.

Nothing was more wonderful for me. She negotiated the steps cautiously, holding onto the railing, passing her small suitcase to the porter and accepting the conductor's outstretched hand for balance. Instantly, I ran to her. She wrapped me up in her arms, the slightest hint of lavender cologne escaping from her coat. I loved my grandmother. She taught me about music and how to grow vegetables. She gave me a sense of security and showed me what simple pleasure there could be in watching a sunrise. When she was in the household, nothing bad could happen.

The scene changed to the dining room on Christmas Day. My father and mother, my grandmother, my closest sister, Anna, and my three other younger sisters all gathered around the table. The platter of carved turkey had gone around. There was just a drumstick left. I reached to take it. As my hand grasped the bone, Anna took her fork and jammed it into the back of my hand.

"Shit! What did you do that for?"

"You're taking my drumstick!" She smiled with the outer corners of her eyes, a subtle movement I had seen hundreds of times before.

I shook my head. "No, it's mine. You already have your turkey."

Turning to the adults at the table, Anna screwed up her face and bawled. I didn't have to look at my father to know he was rising up like a grizzly bear. He slapped me hard on the back of the head, the blow knocking me to the floor. He grabbed my shirt, pulling me to my feet and shoving me hard toward the basement door.

"I'll teach to you be rude at the dinner table, you little bastard!" he roared, loosening his belt and pulling it out of the trouser loops with a snapping sound like a buggy whip.

Anthony and the others re-appeared. I started explaining as if apologizing for the events.

"The beatings were nearly always the same. I could still walk, but sitting would be hard for days. He never left a scar on me, but the bruises took weeks to disappear." My unspoken resolve to stay unemotional broke with a hollow clink like the tap on cracked china. "If I had deserved it, I wouldn't have hated that part of him so much. But I rarely deserved it, especially that time."

"That's true. But something was eating away at your father's soul. He let you believe that Willa May was your natural mother because it was just simpler. However," he paused to make sure I was listening, "your real mother died shortly after you were born—you are Willa May's adopted baby."

"No." The muscles in my face went slack under the weight of my tears.

"Willa May had been married as a young woman, but she and her first husband were apparently unable to have children. So, as time wore on, they adopted a son—you. The first husband skipped out on Willa May only a couple of months later, and Willa May was desperate to be married so the adoption agency wouldn't take you away from her. You were all she had to live for. Then she met the man you know as your father. Your future father and Willa May courted for a short time and married in a hurry. You were barely a year old, but your new father would have very little to do with you."

"No. My father loved me!" My voice was the voice of the child I had been.

"Perhaps, in a way he couldn't express, but he couldn't accept you as his son. He loved Willa May. And, even though he had taken you in when he married her, he couldn't accept you. You were just an adopted kid in his eyes. You weren't her natural child. He couldn't get over it, and his rejection of you drove her deep into depression, especially when your first sister, Anna, and then the other three came along, one right after another."

"I don't believe you!" The barren truth of their words shimmered in my brain the way a mirage emmanates heat from its illusory water hole, just as the desert conjures up its distorting and fragmented hope to the imagination of the tormented, desperate wanderer.

"All his life, your father's guilt over his inability to accept you and the toll it took on Willa May ate away at him. He began drinking, and after years of excess the liquor finally killed him. Don't be like him—don't let your guilt kill you," her words slipped into the silence like stones dropped in the still water of a lake, leaving rings that spread and in moments disappear.

"You aren't going to do this. I am not going to agree to any more of this."

"You have no choice. Now, how does knowing about your origins enlighten you?" the black-haired woman asked in a casual tone more fitting to asking a person's shoe size.

"Enlighten me? If what you say is true, it doesn't enlighten me. It disgusts me. I was just a baby, after all. Innocent. I must have somehow known I wasn't his or hers. Look how they risked my safety. And how they mistreated me! Now I understand why I didn't cry at my father's funeral, nor will I—now or ever! He's better off dead!"

I found myself back in the compartment, shouting.

"My whole life is based on lies!"

Anthony appeared, his face grave and unflinching. "No, Peyton. The road you were given to travel was littered with deception and abuse during the first years of your life. But your life was not based on lies. You made the choice to run from the truth. But you can never run far enough. With difficulty, you will have to face the realities of your life."

"But I'm dead!"

"Are you?" He vanished.

9

It's a miracle this guy is alive. When we brought him in here, I didn't have much hope for him," the young intern said to Detective O'Riley, who held the phone between his ear and this shoulder. "We'll wait for him to come around, and when he does, let's hope he can tell us who he is."

"We ran his license. Peyton Staley, from a small town near Detroit. But the address on this license is for one of those mailbox places. Might as well be a vacant lot. Call us when he wakes up. In the meantime, we'll try to locate relatives. Thanks for your help," he said, and hung up. Suspicious of any guy found shot in a naked woman's house and carrying a license with a mailbox as an address, Detective O'Riley was sitting at his desk, tapping away at his computer muttering to himself. Officer Brown sat down at the desk across from him.

"So, find anything?"

"No. He's a mystery. It's like he exists, but he doesn't. Even the IRS sends his tax stuff to the mailbox address. The Social Security number brings up nothing, except that he's got a triple A rating. His bank has only the bogus address. He doesn't work for anybody, yet has plenty of dough. But how? No employment history since 1985.

The credit cards are clear. Not even a traffic ticket. Nobody is this perfect—or this slick."

"How does he pick up his mail?"

"Maybe they send it to him here. Start with the mailbox place, and see what you can find out. I'm going to Barnaby's Pub."

"Barnaby's Pub?"

"Yup. He had one of their napkins stuffed in his pants pocket. I figure that's where he goes to let off steam. Maybe the the bartender will know something."

Barnaby's was a popular neighborhood hangout catering to mostly young singles and gays. At eleven in the morning, it was open, but deserted. Detective O'Riley blinked as he walked inside, squinting as his eyes adjusted to the dark interior. He took in the trendy decor and decided he was out of his element.

"Hello?" No response. He noticed a door behind the bar.

"Hello?" he said louder. The door opened as a woman in her mid-thirties stepped into the space between the door and the back bar.

"Do you want a drink—or do you want lunch?"

Her bleached blond hair, heavy evening makeup and long, intricately painted fingernails contrasted with the sloppy sweat shirt and stretch pants she was wearing. A blue sequined halter strap peeked out from the sagging neckline of the sweat shirt.

"Oh, I'm just interested in some information," Detective O'Riley said, sitting on one of the bar stools, one leg on the rung, the other braced on the floor. "I'm looking for anyone who knows a guy named Peyton Staley. Know him?"

"Maybe. Why?"

"Well, he's in trouble, and we're trying to help him out." Detective O'Riley smiled.

"The cops are trying to help a guy out? Ha!" She scanned Detective O'Riley, apparently sizing him up and simultaneously deciding he wasn't to be trusted. "I don't know any Peyton Staley."

"I think you do." He waited for a response.

"What kind of trouble?"

"He was found this morning, nearly dead from loss of blood from a gunshot wound. They're trying to save him at County General right now. But in case he dies, we have to find someone to notify. His identification is cold. We thought someone here might know him."

"Why here?"

"One of your napkins was in his pocket."

"So?"

"So, maybe he picked it up here one night while he was trying to get some action." He grabbed her wrist as she passed a wiperag over the counter in front of him. "Quit the games and tell me what you know."

The blond twisted free with the agility of a contortionist. Almost in slow motion, she slid a glass from the rack, filled it with ice and squirted some soda water into it. She plopped a lemon slice into the water, and then came around to the front of the bar to sit on a stool next to Detective O'Riley.

"Listen, Officer. You look like an honest cop. But I don't trust cops, not as far as I can throw them. Peyton Staley comes in here pretty often, drinks himself into oblivion and then leaves. Where he comes from, who he knows, who he is, I don't have a clue. Don't care to either."

"You're sure?"

"Sure, I'm sure. Now, I have work to do before the lunch crowd gets here." She turned to leave.

"Say, what's your name, in case I need to reach you again?"

"Angel." The door closed firmly behind her.

"She knows more than she's letting on," Detective O'Riley said to no one in particular as he walked out of the pub and headed down the street.

10

Peyton and I sat in silence on our recliners. The sensation was more numbness than comfort. The intensity of emotion and tactile stimuli seemed reserved for the environments. I was becoming anxious and felt a need for companionship.

I wanted to talk with Peyton, but he was shut down, just looking at the floor from the hunched over position he had taken with his elbows resting on his knees and his hands hanging limp between them. "This waiting for Agent Two is aggravating," I said to try to nudge him into a conversation.

Peyton ignored my comment as I stood up to move around. "Want to talk?" I approached him hoping he would respond.

"I'd rather not. I have to think things through."

"Your inquiry was hard for you, huh?" I put my hand gently on his shoulder, more to initiate human contact for myself than to comfort him.

"Yes. Now, leave me alone!"

Roughly pulling his shoulder away from me in a clear gesture of rejection, he walked over to the mirror and feigned concern for the condition of his face to avoid my glances. Without any warning, the train lurched and the lights went out.

"Peyton! Are you there?"

"Yes, over here—"

His voice was soft, calm, a quality I needed very much. I groped my way toward him, passing my hands through the darkness wanting to reach the safety of contact with the only other human being in this place. Gradually, I could see him and he gently took my hand.

"I'm sorry I was rude."

"I'll forgive you, just this once." I laughed at the absurdity of the circumstance. The train had stopped entirely, and the door to the compartment opened, as if on an automatic safety system.

"Come on, this is our chance." Peyton grabbed my hand and led me into the hallway stretching along the series of compartment doors. We hurried to the end of the train car, and pushed open the exit door. A rush of cool air blew up from below, and we clamored down the steps, jumping the short distance from the bottom tread to the ground.

"This isn't a tunnel for a train," he said.

"No, it's more like a cave."

An uneven wall, sweating in the humidity of the atmosphere and clearly carved in the ancient cave by water that no longer ran in rivers, shimmered in the half-light gleaming from far above us. Looking up, we could see that the wall was illuminated by fissures in the stone.

"That must certainly lead to the outside, somewhere," I said.

"Probably. What's this under our feet?" Bending down and picking up some loose pebbles, he handed a few to me. "Hmm. Just ordinary stones, " he said fondling the pebbles like he was trying to extract knowledge from their smooth surfaces.

"I remember stones like this in the caves of France. You know, near the southwestern border with Spain, where so many of the pre-historic cave paintings are? It's really very beautiful in those caves. Let's follow the wall till we get somewhere. It's got to lead either up or down. Up is better, though." I let my stones drop to the floor

"I suppose you're right. The path inclines this way. So, if up is better, this is the way to go."

Peyton offered me his hand, which I took with a growing sense of familiarity and comfort. Following the narrowing space of the tunnel, claustrophobic, shadowed and soundless, except for the crunch of our feet on the stones and the rhythm of our breathing, we walked in silence for the better part of half an hour until the path descended almost vertically into a vast, domed cavern, sunlight streaking from a fissure in the rocks overhead. Blinking helped our eyes to adjust to the comparative brightness and to focus on the imagery surrounding us on all sides.

"Oh my! Look at the walls—I wonder if these are the real thing." I ran my hand over the cold stone. "It feels real. It's cold, and moist. Can we make any sense of them—the paintings? It looks like the hunting lessons of the caves at Lascaux, only bigger. I don't understand why we're here." Suddenly chilled by a breeze from the tunnel, I shivered. "I don't feel right about this place."

"Wherever this is, the way out must be nearby."

Peyton and I backed up to each other, turning counter-clockwise to survey the circular walls, looking for an opening. He jabbed me in the ribs.

"Look," he said in a whisper. At the far end of the cave were two bald men, slender and very tall, dressed in bodysuits, one green, the other blue.

"Hannah Sebastian?" the man in green called out.

"Yes."

"I am Alex, Agent Two. Come with me." I stepped forward.

SIDETRACKS

"Peyton Staley?" the man in blue called out. Peyton anticipated his introduction.

"You must be—"

"Jeremy, and you're coming with me." Peyton stepped forward. The cave evaporated.

11

*P*anic jolted my nerves as I read the sign HANNAH'S CHOICES ENVIRONMENT on the door before me. The tightness in my chest accompanied a moment of rapid breathing, which I recognized as the onset of an anxiety attack.

"No Valium here. I'm on my own with this." The ringing in my ears annoyed me the way the dripping of water from an leaky faucet at night can drive the calmest person to insomnia.

"Just lean into this," I told myself, "relax, and lean into this."

"My job is to accompany you through your experiences here. The Processor insists you choose the most significant moment in your life when you might have taken a Sidetrack. Think about this. You must decide which choice you made in your life that could have taken you away from your original road."

Alex gazed in my direction, but was not actually looking into my eyes. The effect was unsettling, not a good thing for me just then. I was mentally counting the hundreds of times I had thought I might have made a different decision. "That's not so hard."

"Do not misunderstand. This is not an easy part of the Processor's evaluation."

I stifled the impulse to laugh at Alex's stilted, very melodramatic tone. He spoke like a stage actor from some Vaudeville play where quintessential Hero was about to save the proverbial Damsel in Distress.

"Humans amuse themselves by imagining how their lives might have been, but they do not actually want the knowledge. You are here to learn what your life would have been, if you had taken the Sidetrack, instead of the original road. You cannot avoid the Processor's demands. He wants you to know. It's as simple as that."

I considered the problem, trying to buy some time, and asked, "What was the cave all about?" as a stall tactic.

"Later. Now, the Processor will help you choose your Sidetrack. Watch the sign."

The sign on the door glowed. Three buttons appeared with identifiers on them.

The first button read: FORTUNES, GAINED & LOST. The second button read: LOVE, GAINED & LOST. The third button: RISKS, TAKEN & NOT TAKEN.

"So, do I press one of these buttons to see my choices?"

"That's right."

I pushed RISKS. Two buttons appeared. Button One read: TAKEN. Button Two read: NOT TAKEN.

I touched the button marked NOT TAKEN. The door slid silently open and Alex led the way into the CHOICES ENVIRONMENT titled RISKS NOT TAKEN.

"Paris! Oh thank you!" I turned toward Alex, but he was nowhere to be seen. Shrugging, I walked a short way up the street.

"I'm near the Opéra—there's Le Café de la Paix."

Thinking back in my own life, I knew what was coming next. I hurried to sit down at one of the small, outdoor tables. The warm June weather heightened every detail of sound and sight in the buildings, the trees, the people, the bustle of the traffic to a stark intensity I had only experienced in nightmares and dreams.

"Pardon, Mademoiselle. Vous désirez?" the waiter asked.

"Mais oui. J'aimerais un croissant et un café au lait." My French came back to me. A lovely surprise as I thought of real French coffee and croissants. It had been a long time since I had last enjoyed them. My college sweetheart and then fiancé would return from the men's room in a few minutes. Most of the other people sitting at the tables were reading newspapers or talking about the latest gossip in their lives. I noticed Alex sitting at the next table, alone. He was wearing a trench coat and beret.

"You don't look very French," I whispered.

"I know, but a green body suit would be outrageously obvious, don't you think?"

"Yes." I laughed with him. "Do you know who's about to sit down with me at this table?"

"Well, I know he's a very prominent businessman, destined to become Prime Minister in about ten years. Are we thinking of the same person?"

"Yes, we are. So, am I supposed to do the opposite of what I actually did in my life?"

"You're supposed to take the risk you didn't take at this moment in your life. Don't worry, I'll be watching."

"Okay." The waiter returned with my order. He moved with a precision honed from years of repetition. His gestures flowed from him with an ease that seems embellished with the theatrical flare reserved for tourists.

"Eleven francs, please." He winked at me.

"Thank you. And, here. Keep the change." I placed fifteen francs on the blue rimmed saucer atop the cash register tape.

"Merci, mademoiselle." The waiter smiled, taking the money

and going back into the café, swiftly slipping between the tables by swiveling his hips in a dance-like rhythm.

The morning rush hour traffic was moving slowly through the congested intersection in front of the Opera House. A white Citroën sedan pulled up and stopped at the curb near my table. As the hydraulic lifts lowered the rear of the car, the door opened, and M. Jacques André-Bouchard stepped out. Tall and distinguished in his black pinstripe suit, he was every bit the image of a renowned Bordeaux winery owner from an aristocratic family. His career had reached a new pinnacle with his election as political leader of the most prominent conservative capitalist political party. His face appeared on the cover of every news magazine and smiled from every kiosk and news stand in Paris. His entire life of privilege, his military service in World War II and the time he spent as a prisoner of war had groomed him for the success he currently enjoyed, trying to undermine the strong leftist elements in the French Government. The patrons of the café pointed him out nodding in recognition to each other. He stood for a moment, scanning the tables. Three years had passed since he had last seen me. I was certain he had forgotten my face. Then he saw me, he raised his hand to wave and his pace increased as he came toward me.

"Hannah! Hannah! Comment allez-vous? Ça fait trop longtemps que je ne vous vois pas!"

I waved, smiling, and noticing from the corner of my eye that the people around me were looking me over. The dark blue leather mini skirt and tight knit top I was wearing were the height of fad fashion. My long straight blonde hair and chunky high-heeled gold suede sling backs lengthened my short stature and made me feel confident. Nothing like being worth a bit of gossip

"Hello, M. André-Bouchard. I am very happy to see you again."

The same waiter hurried to the table, to make sure he didn't miss his chance to be seen serving such an important person.

"Would you like something to drink, Sir?"

"Un café noir." Jacques André-Bouchard dismissed the waiter. "And I'll take a little time with this beautiful American woman," he said, picking up my hand and kissing it gently. "What have you been doing to keep busy since we last met?"

Trying to grow up was all that came to mind. "Oh, I spent two years on government assignment in a small West African town, up country from the coastline. I was teaching English there."

"In West Africa? Did you know that I was the French ambassador to Benin eighteen years ago? What a beautiful country!"

Small talk first. Of course. "That's the country next to where I was stationed. We can share our impressions of Africa, one day." Some coincidence.

"Would you like to visit me here in Paris? Maybe you could teach me English. I could help you find the means."

He spoke in the familiar usage of the language, which is chosen either as a compliment of friendship or as an insult of class control. "Do you know why I am using the familiar form of the verb?"

I was thinking about the directness of his question and what he was implying.

"I want to tell you that you could stay here—you alone, without the fiancé you mentioned on the telephone yesterday. I could offer you several students among people in big business and in the government. Does that interest you?"

"Let me think about this." I let my mind absorb the possibilities. His voice was quivering. He was nervous to even suggest the idea. I remembered how the first time I had pretended not to understand his offer and simply responded that I was going back to the United States to get married.

Alex looked at me over the top of his newspaper and nodded. Inside the café, my fiancé reappeared. My heart was pounding. I saw only Jacques André-Bouchard. Why not? This was the moment I had always wanted to change.

"Yes, Sir. I would like very much to teach you English, and the others as well. But, I will need two or three days to end my relationship with my fiancé. You understand the situation."

"Certainly." His smile drew a firm line across his face, but I could not decode the glimmer of discomfort in his eyes.

As my fiancé arrived at the table, all the broken dreams I had lost in an unhappy marriage flashed across my mind. "You're history this time, honey. See you in my next life." The idea formed and evaporated with the breeze.

"Matthew Winters, I'd like to introduce you to M. André-Bouchard."

M. André-Bouchard stood up and shook Matthew's hand. "Hello, Mr. Winters. It's nice to make your acquaintance." The formality of his greeting seemed appropriate to Matthew, but the choice of words implied so much to me. The stand-off-ish use of formal language meant distrust or lack of friendliness, which in the more relaxed times since World War Two was a clear message. I followed through with the conversation, much as it actually had transpired the first time. M. André-Bouchard knew exactly what to do.

"Do you have a tourist map of France?"

"Yes, we do have one in our rented car. Matthew? could you go get the map for Mr. André-Bouchard?"

"Okay, Hannah. But, remember that we don't have a lot of time before leaving for Spain. The train leaves in an hour and a half, and we have to get our suitcases from the hotel."

This time I saw how Matthew was jealous that his fiancé was sitting with a powerful man as if she had known him all her life. He had always hated how I was so at ease with people only because he was so uncomfortable. He took off at a jog to get the map. He was angry. Was that all right?

"Listen, dear. When he comes back, I will invite you both to visit my home and winery in Bordeaux. It's much closer to Spain, and it's very easy to get there after you visit Spain as planned. Accept the invitation. Bring him to my home. That way, I can help you to convince him that it will be better to go home to the United States without you. What do you think?"

Too easy. Too simple. Too unsettling. Jacques André-Bouchard tried to read my reaction. He couldn't possibly know how my mind was racing. Last time, after our visit to Jacques André-Bouchard's home, Matthew and I returned to the United States, married in a hurry, and as the years passed, lived a downhill, dead-end emotional life. Our marriage ended with a whimper and was followed by a nasty divorce. A life of financial difficulty for me and my two children defeated me, until I pulled myself together and made my own fortune in marketing. Like an instantaneous movie, I imagined how a life in the privileged realm of Jacques André-Bouchard might provide the unique opportunity to achieve my highest personal ambitions.

He would work in his aristocratic offices, directing the ebb and flow of great wines into the world markets. I would spend the years tutoring ambassadors and prime ministers, captains of industry and the highest ranking socialites in Parisian cultural circles. But when his work was done, he would meet me and take me alternately to the finest five star restaurants and the most intimate hidden bistros, tucked away in the quiet back streets of the city of lights. We would travel the world for both business and pleasure, and we would fall in love. We would have two children, a boy and a girl. They would go to the finest schools. He would grow up to be powerful in business and she would become accomplished in the arts. We would live the definition of the good life, growing old together, still holding hands the way new lovers do as they walk along the banks of the Seine. I would survive him by many years and finally pass away, leaving three generations of progeny to carry on the legacy of the life we had made together. This possibility, the surreal image of how life ought to play out, obliterated the harsh reality of the life I had already lived. Could I do this, turning my back on what had been to discover what might have been?

"All right. As you have proposed, I will accept your invitation, and I will break up with Matthew at your home." My heart was pounding, thrilled by the prospect of this adventure. I glanced over at Alex's table. He was gone.

12

The trembling moved upward from my hands to my arms. I recognized the symptoms: anxiety attacks are terrifying. I could always find a way to put an end to the trembling, but here, standing in front of a sign that reads PEYTON'S CHOICES ENVIRONMENT made that possibility very remote. I needed just one drink.

"My name is Jeremy. As your Agent Two, my job is to accompany you through your experiences here. The Processor insists you choose a significant mistake in your life. Think about this. You must decide which choice you made in your life that took you away from your personal goals." Jeremy was all business, listing the rules in a very matter-of-fact manner.

"When are you going to lighten up? I've made so many mistakes, I don't know where to begin. What the hell difference can it make anyway? I'm dead." Couldn't he see me shaking? I needed something to calm my nerves. A couple of beers would do just fine.

"Make no assumptions. You are not dead yet. This is the Processor's evaluation and you must comply. Maybe you can't even imagine how your life might have been, but you are going to learn what your life would have been, as if you had taken the Sidetrack, instead of the original road. You cannot avoid the Processor's demands. It's as simple as that."

"All right, I'll play your game, but there are too many mistakes to choose from." My teeth were chattering, and I could hardly control my body. I needed a drink, a valium, a chocolate cake, something, to stop this quaking.

"In that case, the Processor will help you choose your Sidetrack. Watch the sign on the door and follow my instructions." I felt the tremors subsiding as he put his hand on my shoulder. "Do you have these physical responses often?"

"I think too much. I sometimes get the shakes. It's not unusual you know, anxiety attacks are fairly common."

"Well, you should feel better in a few minutes," he said, not removing his hand as the sign on the door began to glow. Three buttons appeared with identifiers on them.

Button One read: FORTUNES, GAINED & LOST. Button Two read: LOVE, GAINED & LOST. Button Three read: RISKS, TAKEN & NOT TAKEN.

"Now, press one of these buttons to see your choices."

"Hmm, interesting categories." I pushed FORTUNES. Two buttons appeared. Button One read: GAINED. Button Two read: LOST.

I touched the button marked LOST. The door opened and Jeremy led the way into the CHOICES ENVIRONMENT called Fortunes Lost.

"Why did you bring me here?" I looked around the empty corporate conference room. "What fortunes did I lose here?"

Jeremy seemed puzzled. "You don't remember this day? This is the day you had the opportunity to move up several rungs on the corporate ladder at HIGHLAND TECHNOLOGIES, Inc. All you had to do is reveal the incompetence of your boss, Harvey Biehl. Remember him?"

"Oh—yes, I remember. I didn't tell top management about his blatant verbal abuse of several of the male workers in the department and his overt sexual advances toward several of the women. I didn't tell them about his heavy drinking at lunch meetings with clients and his habit of sleeping it off behind the locked door of his office. I didn't tell them how I covered for him, finishing his reports for him, writing his evaluations and basically doing his job. The number of times I put him in a cab and went back to those lunch meetings, dutifully making excuses for his departure, is astronomical."

The anger of those days rose to the surface as I remembered the humiliation and lack of recognition I suffered every time Harvey Biehl took credit for my innovations and creative advances in the IS department. Memory of my resentment of Harvey Biehl's tight fisted control of my pay check and the insulting raises he forced me to accept ignited my emotions. Most aggravating of all was Harvey's cavalier attitude about the backstabbing tactics he used to discredit his competitors within the corporate walls and in the open market. The ancient imaginary wars I waged to rise above him, to conquer him passed through my mind. I had been such a fool to let him take me for all I was worth.

"So, I'm only supposed to tell all and reap the rewards. Right?"

"That's right. You'll get to relive your life the way it would have turned out. All you have to do is forget about the personal code you preserved that day. Be ruthless in getting what you want for yourself."

"Do I have any choice in this?"

"Yes, you can go through this meeting again and live it the same way. Or, you can do what your instincts tell you to do. But if you repeat this Sidetrack the same way as before, you will have no to chance go back to living your life any differently than you did before. You will be forever trapped in the troubles you inflicted upon yourself to get here. How you handle it is up to you."

Walking to the window to take in the panorama of the city below where the rooftop mosaic extended to the visible horizon, planes taking off and landing in the distance caught my eye. From the fiftieth floor, lofty thoughts of power and wealth come easily. I have always feared exposing the misdeeds of unethical men. Fear had cost me advancement many times in my career. This meeting provided a chance to act on my inside knowledge and to reveal Harvey Biehl's incompetence. Doubt is an insidious enemy, eating away your insides, leaving you hollow and helpless. Did I have enough unspent courage left to act, or would I keep silent?

"Will I—" Jeremy was gone.

The door at the far end of the conference room opened. "Time's up. Here goes."

"So, there you are! I've been looking all over for you, Mr. Staley." My secretary, Andrea Cartwright chirped at me. "I have your notes and the charts you wanted for the presentation right here. I'll just put them on the easel for you." She fluttered through the room the way a butterfly flutters through a garden of flowers, lighting for only a few seconds, just long enough to gather the nectar and spread the pollen. "Is there anything else you'll be needing?"

"Yes, Andrea. I left a confidential memo on my desk, actually two memos: one for the CEO, Dr. Hollingsworth and a copy for the President, Mr. Andersen. Would you bring them to me, immediately? I want them to read the information in the memos before this presentation."

"Oh, certainly, Mr. Staley. I'll take care of it right away. You have only fifteen minutes until the others will be here. I cleared your calendar for the rest of the day."

"Thanks, Andrea, you're the best."

Picking up the packet of papers I scanned through the main points of the presentation, surprised at how I recalled so many details. The first time, I did not send the memo to Hollingsworth and Andersen. I wrote it, but I shredded it. Andrea returned with the envelope containing the memo in hand. I opened it and re-read it.

CONFIDENTIAL MEMO: EYES ONLY

TO: Dr. Jeremy Hollingsworth, CEO
Mr. James Andersen, President and CFO
FROM: Mr. Peyton Staley, Senior Vice-President, IS
RE: Mr. Harvey Biehl, CIO

Dear Sirs:

Due to recent events that may threaten to derail upcoming merger negotiations, I am forced to bring to your attention the serious concerns I have regarding Harvey Biehl and the unethical practices in which he engages during client contacts and in his day to day oversight of the IS Department. As CIO, his actions seriously compromise the performance of the team members, and by participating in these practices he brings disrespect to the HIGHLAND TECHNOLOGIES, Inc. corporate doorstep.

Attached, please find the sworn affidavits of several employees within the IS department, including exit interviews from team members he fired without cause, and the allegations of improper sexual advances made to several women, who were let go or left on their own, along with their signed assertions that they plan to file suit against HIGHLAND TECHNOLOGIES, Inc. Add to these the chronology I maintained over a period of a year to document his flagrant drunkenness and unseemly behavior during client lunch and dinner meetings, and the letters of complaint I have received from several of our most important clients expressing outrage at his unprofessional conduct in public, and I believe you will share my concerns. In addition, I have attached an extensive listing of files pertaining to the most sensitive aspects of HIGHLAND TECHNOLOGIES' business that Harvey Beihl has copied and taken into his possession, for what purpose is anyone's guess.

Thank you for your attention to this memo, and its confidential status. I underscore the serious nature of the information contained herein. I expect you will need time to consider the information contained herein, but, as always, I remain ready to answer your questions, and to assist in any manner possible to bring resolution to this problem.

Sincerely,

Peyton Staley, Senior Vice-President, IS

I returned the documents to the envelope and handed it to Andrea. This time the documents would arrive on their desks fifteen minutes before the presentation. She took it and returned in five minutes.

"You would not believe it, Mr. Staley. I rushed into the secretary's station and told Gerry how I've got to deliver your documents to her bosses A-S-A-P. She says to me 'Oh, I can do it for you. They're in a short meeting, getting ready for the big presentation.' And I say to her, 'Could I just take them in to them? Personal delivery is critical. Eyes Only kind of thing. You know how Mr. Staley gets if I don't follow his directions to the letter.' Then she says 'Sure. But you know how they hate to be interrupted.' And I have to say, 'I understand this is information critical to the presentation that they must have before it takes place. Gerry, I am just doing my job,' just to get past her. Gerry always wants to read memos before delivering them, as she does so many of the confidential papers, to stir up trouble by controlling the timing of my bosses' receipt of information. It gives her a feeling of limited power. This time, I was determined to circumvent her tactics. So, she says to me in this snippy voice, 'Well, I suppose I can let you take it in. Why you won't let me do it is beyond me.' I bark back at her, 'Just have to follow Mr. Staley's orders to the letter.' So I swish past Gerry's desk and into the meeting room. 'Excuse me, gentlemen. I apologize for interrupting, but Mr. Staley instructed me to deliver this information personally. It is very important to the up-coming presentation,' I say to Mr. Hollingsworth and I handed him the envelopes. I told him that you wanted him to read the enclosed materials immediately. I left as fast as I could and hurried back here."

Andrea sat in her chair like a crow perching on a branch over road kill. "They seemed all right with getting the memo at the last minute."

"That's good. We'll know how they really feel about it when this presentation begins." My ingrained fear of being exposed began to affect me. My palms turned clammy. Nervous churning gurgles in the pit of my stomach. I retreated to the window again to gaze at the city. Again, and as always the impressive panorama calmed me. Either I would be praised or I would be fired. There was no option between these extremes. I came to grips with finality of my actions. Winner take all epitomizes the corporate system of ethics making revenge all the sweeter than in any other realm. The doors to the conference room opened wide, and all the corporate power brokers filed in like sentinels gathering on the castle wall before a battle. Dr. Hollings-worth stood, dominating the room with the militaristic demeanor of a supreme commander, or like a mythical king who knew he had control over life or death, real or political, for everyone in the room.

"Gentlemen and Ladies. Welcome to this important meet-ing. I must say, the acquisition proposals before us from MACRO-WORLD, Limited are impressive. We have our work cut out for us today, as we consider the short and the long range implications of this merger and what our acquisition by MACROWORLD will mean to our company. But first, I must address some disturbing information that has been brought to our attention. We have it on good authority that one person in management has, unfortunately, committed some serious indiscretions—"

I kept my eyes fixed on Hollingsworth's face. I knew the coming commentary would be scathing. I hoped it would not be directed at me. My ingrained insecurities began to kick in again, blocking the sound of Hollingsworth's voice for a few moments. I sure could use a drink.

" —and so I must ask Mr. Harvey Biehl to step out of this room. You are instructed to clear out your office immediately. Also, I hereby put on you notice that the allegations against you will be pursued to their conclusion. A security guard will accompany you to assure that you take nothing other than your personal effects with you."

The silence in the room crushed even the sound of breathing. Harvey Biehl stood shakily, his face drained of color and his eyes moist with tears of humiliation. He tripped on his chair as he turned to leave, adding to his embarrassment. No one moved a muscle as he rushed to escape the room.

Dr. Hollingsworth glanced around the room, pausing a moment to make eye contact with every person in turn. He fixed his gaze on me for a split second longer than he had with the others. A very subtle smile passed across his lips that told me Hollingsworth approved of my action. I slowly allowed myself to breathe again. I pondered how my future at HIGHLAND TECHNOLOGIES might play out as the merger meeting droned on. At ten o'clock, the meeting broke for a short recess. Dr. Hollingsworth and Mr. Andersen retreated to another conference room and sent for me.

"Sit down a moment, Peyton." Dr. Hollingsworth's broad grin spread wider as I entered the room. "I—we want you to know that we think your action in providing the information you gathered on Harvey Biehl took uncommon courage. The allegations in that memo, well documented as they are, provide us with the proper materials to make certain that Biehl will be brought to justice."

"Thank you, Sir." If you only knew.

"We appreciate the risks you took in gathering the information and in giving it to us. Going over Biehl's head was the only way you could have handled this. Irregular as that breech of protocol may be, you could not have succeeded as you did without stepping out of line at that particular moment in your career."

"No, Sir." Panic button. "Yes, Sir."

"I am sure you realize we will reward your courage in substantial ways. We also must be certain of your loyalties. You may have won this battle. But you will not win all battles, not even when ethics and righteousness are with you."

"No, Sir. I realize that. It was to my mind something my job required me to do, as I saw the problems persist and expand out of control. I could not keep silent any longer." Straight jacket.

"Nor would we have asked you to do anything otherwise. So, to fill the void Biehl's departure creates, we are appointing you the new CIO. We will work out the details of your contract by the end of the week, but we'd like to reassure the others in today's meeting, and the officials from MACROWORLD, that your tenure begins immediately. Would you accept our offer of this promotion?" Dr. Hollingsworth nodded at Mr. Andersen for his agreement.

As if belonging to someone else, my head wagged in mild disbelief, then nodded in agreement. "Yes, I will accept the position on the condition that the terms be worked out by the end of this week and no later." Could he hear the blood rushing in my ears?

"We'll provide our offer in writing by this afternoon, and you will have a few days to make any changes you'd like to the proposed terms. Ethical men like you are rare in business, and we'd like to keep you with us for a very long time. Welcome to the top management team."

Didn't he see me shaking? "Thank you, Sir."

While still shaking hands, we all stepped into the corridor to walk down the hall together and return to the merger negotiations.

"Excuse me a moment. I must check in for messages," Dr. Hollingsworth disappeared into his office.

"I'll see you in the conference room. Excuse me a moment." Mr. Andersen stepped into the men's room.

I turned the corner to see Jeremy leaning against the wall by the elevators.

He nodded for me to follow him. "Come on, we have something to do before that meeting resumes," he said. I followed, no questions asked.

≈≈

13

≈≈

*L*ynn Hargrove was in Hannah's office at her desk taking her personal phone book out of the file with all her letters. She turned to the M section, found Lenny's listing and squinted at the scribbling in the margin.

"Funny she only has business phone numbers for Lenny, like she tried to forget him, to get away from him." Taking her glasses from her briefcase, she put them on. "That's better—dating back twenty-five years. I guess I should call the last number under his name. 1988—more than ten years since Hannah wrote this number." She plugged the tape recorder into the cradle, picked up the digital handset and punched in the numbers.

"Dayton-Holland Industries. To whom may I direct your call?"

Lynn took a deep breath. "Lenny Miller, please."

"Just a moment while I connect you." The receptionist paused. "May I say who's calling?"

"Yes. I'm Lynn Hargrove, Hannah Sebastian's attorney."

"Just a moment please."

"Dayton-Holland Industries—the name on the cell phone."

Lynn said in a whisper, flushing with nervous energy as she waited for someone to come back on the line.

"Yes, Ms. Hargrove? This is Lenny Miller. What can I do for you?"

"Um—I need to let you know first thing that this conversation is being recorded, Mr. Miller." She checked the recorder to make sure it was operating.

"Lenny's better. Go on," he said.

"Well, Mr. Miller, your sister, Hannah, is in the hospital, recovering from surgery after a serious accident, that could cost her her life." She paused to see if he would respond.

" Please, call me Lenny. Go on."

"Well, Mr. Miller, it seems she was injured in a fall in her bathroom, and she and the man who came to her rescue were shot. The doctors say they both will probably survive, but they also contend that if Hannah does survive, there will be permanent physical difficulties to overcome, and possibly mental ones as well. It is miraculous that she survived at all."

"I see. Why are you calling me about this?"

"Mr. Miller, I am your sister's attorney and her friend. She is in dire need of the support of her family. You are one of the two relatives she lists in her personal phone book. Your sister Donna is the other, but that number is disconnected."

"So, your point is—what?"

"Hannah told me you control her portion of the estate your parents left."

"I do."

"I understand she receives nothing from her portion."

"She will when she's sixty-five years old. I have been managing all the funds for retirement purposes. I manage my own and Donna's as well."

"Hannah's medical costs are going to be astronomical. She needs money now to pay for her survival. Is there some way—"

"No, there is not. The terms of the inheritance are quite clear. She will not receive a dime until age sixty-five, and then only in payouts of interest. She will never see the principle."

"Is your portion subject to the same restrictions?"

"Of course not!"

"And Donna's portion? Is hers restricted as well?"

"No. But I don't see your point. Hannah insisted she be written out of the will after a particularly heated exchange with our mother. At the time, Mother thought she would go back on her demand. When her letter arrived telling Mother she would give her portion away if she was forced to accept it, well, let's just say it is lucky she'll get anything at all, considering the pain and anguish she caused our mother at the time."

Lynn paused to gather her reserves. "I'm looking at Hannah's copy of the terms in the original version of the living will. It mentions that she could at anytime ask to be reinstated to the will. I notice that less than two months later there is an addendum that precludes her from receiving her inheritance. But I also notice that the addendum was mailed by certified mail two months after the expiration of the time allotted for her to change her mind. In effect, she was notified of the change in her option for reinstatement two months after the date she could be reinstated. How do you explain that?"

"I don't understand what you mean."

"She did not have a chance to be reinstated to the will, because she didn't get the notice that she could be reinstated until two months after the deadline she needed to honor to be reinstated. You and your attorneys did not inform my client of her options until it was too late for her to act upon them."

"Well, I'm sure you have that wrong."

"Not according to the certified receipt on the enve-lope in which the addendum was mailed. That is a legal document. Someone apparently wanted to prevent Hannah from receiving her rightful inheritance. Do you know who that someone might be?"

"No. To my knowledge, the papers were sent in plenty of time. In fact, she had to sign the document showing she had read it. I have that in my possession. So, your argu-ment is just so much water over the dam, isn't it?"

"No, it isn't. If you have a signed copy, I suspect the signature was forged. I advised Hannah not to sign anything more from you and your attorneys when it came in the mail after the deadline. I am filing suit on her behalf to release her inheritance, with interest and damages for the financial hardship inflicted by denial of the money that has been rightfully hers all along. You will receive the papers shortly."

"You can't do that! She doesn't deserve one cent of that money," Lenny was shouting into the phone, his anger getting the better of him.

"Who thought that? Your mother? Your father? Or you? And —I question your motives. Don't you stand to receive her portion if she dies? Or, is it going to a charity of her choosing, or will you contact her children?"

"No, our mother requested it be divided between Donna and me in the case of her premature death."

"I see. And what happens to your portion and Donna's portion in the event that she survives the two of you?"

"The money then goes to our spouses and our children. That's simple enough, isn't it?"

"And what happens to Hannah's portion? Does it go to your spouses and your children, too?"

Lenny's silence answered the question.

"We'll talk again," Lynn said in an icy tone that could freeze

Hell over. "You will be required to produce a complete and full accounting of your management of the funds, and for the payments you receive as executor of the estate. I would suggest you put your books in order, Mr. Miller. I am sure it will be important. Remember, even the dead can talk."

Lynn hung up the phone, holding back to keep from slamming it down, and then she turned off the recording device. She was shaking with rage. She wanted to scream at him. But, she had already done the screaming, in a more professional way, to be sure.

"What a jerk! He withheld Hannah's inheritance, not her mother. Little old ladies who love their sons more than their daughters, tend to do as their sons tell them, especially in matters of finance, and especially if their husbands handled the money all their married lives."

Lynn walked in slow circles around her office, talking aloud.

"What could possibly have angered Hannah so much that she would have insisted on forfeiting her share?"

She stopped pacing to punch the intercom button.

"Marjorie? Cancel the rest of my calendar for today. I'm going to Hannah's house to look through her personal papers - you know, legal letters and things like that. I have to figure out how to free up her inheritance. If I get any really important calls, you can page me."

"All right, Ms. Hargrove. Shall I start to gather the necessary forms for filing the suit?"

"Yes, that would be a good idea. And call the police to tell them I'm going into the crime scene to find some of my client's papers. I'll be in touch." Lynn escaped from the office building in her Lexus.

Lenny Miller was fuming. He was surprised that Hannah had an attorney. He thought she was too unsophisticated for that. He punched the intercom button.

"We have a problem. Get Hannah's file and bring it to me."

14

Jeremy led me into a small conference room with a large monitor, wall-mounted, normally used by the top brass for teleconferencing with overseas clients. He touched the screen. It glowed a bright blue before the image of a man, lying in a hospital bed came into focus. Detective O'Riley peeked into the hospital room and then left.

"Hey! You! I'm here! Come in and talk to me." I shouted, pointing at the screen.

"Pointless effort," Jeremy said. "He can't hear you, and you won't break through to him until we're done with your evaluation. Whenever feasible, we show our clients how they look in their real world. It has proven to be a good motivator. By the way, your chances are about fifty-fifty for survival right now. "

"What the hell is this? Let me out of here! I refuse to stay here anymore. I've got so much to get done today. I can't waste anymore time with this!"

"Mr. Staley! You must calm down. I have explained to you, there is no going back there until the Processor has finished with you. If it is any consolation at all, the process is about half over already. You'll be joined by Agent Three when you return to the conference room to finish the meetings you were attending."

"Listen here, you!" I grabbed Jeremy's arm with the intent to intimidate, do harm, get my way. "I know I'm supposed to do what you tell me to do, but that meeting in there is just so much bullshit. No one can relive their lives to see how things might have turned out if they had made different choices. You're messing with me here. I refuse to cooperate any longer! Do you hear me?"

Jeremy redirected my attention to the screen. "Watch this. You'll learn a few things."

After the darkness of Barnaby's Pub, Detective O'Riley squinted in the afternoon sun as he retrieved his sunglasses in the car. The police band crackled. He picked up the microphone and checked in.

"It's O'Riley!" the dispatcher shouted to Officer Brown, who grabbed the dispatch microphone, knocking the dispatcher backwards in his chair.

"Hey, O'Riley!" Officer Brown's excitement bordered on the unprofessional. "He woke up. But—" his voice came down rapidly, "Staley's got total amnesia. He hasn't a clue as to who he is."

"I'll go back to the hospital and see if they'll let me talk with him."

"No, you don't get it. He can't talk. He can't feed himself. He can't write. He stares into space, not even blinking. He's fried. The loss of blood pickled his brain. He's a veggie omelette at least for now."

"For now? Meaning they think he'll get over it?"

"Who knows? The doctors certainly aren't placing bets on it. They'll keep him a few days, and then they'll send him to one of those state funded, long term care clinics. Poor guy."

"Maybe he'll come out of it."

Detective O'Riley's voice was flat, without conviction, reflecting his helplessness in the face of the enormity of this information.

"Maybe. But, we did get a little something to go on. The guy at the mailbox place has an address of his second ex-wife. She was co-partner in his business until they split up about five years ago. If she's still there, then we've got a chance to help him out in one way or another."

"Get hold of her. I don't care what you have to do to find her, and I want to see her. Get on top of this lead before it gets cold. I'm still going to the hospital to talk with the doctors about his prospects."

Jeremy nudged me to break the locked gaze I had acquired to watch a spider building a web in the corner. I looked back at the screen as Detective O'Riley signed off and swung the car around toward the hospital. A few minutes later, he put on his most cheerful attitude and sauntered up to the hospital information desk at the main entrance.

"Hello there. I'd like to visit a patient named Peyton Staley?"

The rotund volunteer at the desk looked up from her paperback and smiled. "Just a moment please while I find his room number." She pulled a clipboard from under a pile of ladies magazines and dragged her sticky index finger down a list of names. "He's in room 266. You'll have to follow the hallway to your left to the end. Take the E wing elevators to the second floor, and turn right out of the elevators to follow the corridor to the nurse's station. Check in there."

She picked up her paperback and reached for a half-eaten doughnut at the back of the cubicle. "You'll have to wait until three o'clock to see him. Visiting hours begin then," she said, opening her cavernous mouth to take a huge, sugary bite of the doughnut. Powdered sugar puffed into the air as she spoke, mouth full. "You can still go up there to wait, if you want to."

Detective O'Riley's face betrayed his disgust to the nurse receptionist on the second floor. "You met Dolly, huh?" She chuckled. "Pretty strange way to welcome people to the hospital, don't you think?"

"Yes, very bizarre, she is. I'm here to see Peyton Staley. It's a police matter," he added for clout as he showed her his badge.

"I'm afraid you'll still have to wait till visiting hours begin. It's only fifteen minutes or so. The lounge is at the far end of the hallway."

"I don't want to be too much trouble, but I also need to confer with the doctor tending to Mr. Staley regarding the prognosis. We're trying to locate his family and need to have something of value to tell whoever it is we find." O'Riley smiled at himself and maintained his calm demeanor.

"Well, that's going to take a lot longer. Dr. Wilson left the hospital an hour ago to meet patients at his private practice. He's not planning to return till tomorrow."

"Has he got a phone?" O'Riley's voice tightened as his patience evaporated with frustration the way water evaporates from a boiling pot.

"Yes," the nurse said. "But it's unlikely he'll talk with you during office hours."

"Police business, remember?" The veins on O'Riley's temples were bulging.

"Yes, I remember. But you'll have to use the pay phone downstairs to call them, unless you're carrying a cell phone, which you'll need to use outside—hospital regulations."

"Thank you. And the number is—?"

She wrote the local number on a post-it note and handed it to him. "The lounge is down the hall," she said, pointing to her left and turning her back on the boiling explosion she saw foaming before her and returning to her paperwork.

O'Riley walked down the hall toward the lounge. About half

way he came to room 266. The door stood ajar just enough so that O'Riley could almost see into the room. He pushed the door open a bit further to look in and found no one but the patient in the room.

The sight was unsettling. The man was me. I was lying flat on my back, staring with unseeing eyes at the ceiling. The IV dripped slowly. The tomb-like silence, broken only by the steady beeping of the heart monitor. O'Riley shuddered. I realized that the chances were slim to none that the doctor would have anything encouraging to say.

O'Riley glanced around at the windowless, faded hospital green lounge. It was inhabited by a blaring television tuned to a violent talk show, three sagging plaid couches and a couple of scarred end tables with mismatched table lamps of doubtful usefulness. The raw fluorescent light bleached the room to a flat, shadow-free space.

"Sure is 'County General'," O'Riley muttered. Never one for rules and regulations he pulled the cell phone from his pocket and punched in the doctor's phone number.

"Doctors Wilson, Whitehall and Johnson. How may I direct your call?"

"I need to speak with Dr. Wilson regarding a Peyton Staley. This is Officer James O'Riley. I'm with the Chicago Police Department." He slipped his free hand into the pocket holding his cigarettes, fondled the packet of a second, and let it go, knowing the time he must wait was going to be too long.

"I'll put you through to his nurse. One moment, please."

The innocuous music that clicked on as she put him on hold, irritated him. It cut off almost instantly.

"Hello, Officer. This is June Mason, Dr. Wilson's nurse. How may I help you?"

"I need information about Peyton Staley's condition. We are attempting to find his family, and any news about him is better than no news. I'm here at the hospital to see him, and they told me Dr. Wilson was his attending physician."

"The doctor is with a patient. But I'll let him know you're waiting on the line when he comes out of the treatment room. It shouldn't be too long."

"Thank you. I'll hold," O'Riley said with a forced politeness. He looked around the lounge. He patted the pack of cigarettes in his shirt pocket again and sat down on one of the couches. He tightened his lips in denial of the fact he was longing for just one drag.

"Detective O'Riley?" The male voice on the phone startled him. O'Riley stood up, like he was greeting a woman he had never met before.

"Yes! Dr. Wilson?"

"That's right. You're needing information about Peyton Staley?"

"Yes. We're in the process of locating his next of kin, and I thought it might help to motivate whoever we find, if we had your opinion of his situation."

"Yes, yes. I understand. Well, Detective, the situation isn't good. He's essentially in a vegetative state as a result of the blood loss he suffered last night. He may come out of this state over time, but we don't know how long a time that will be. That's really all I can say at this moment. I know it's not much."

"Did you keep the bullet from the wound?" Detective O'Riley asked.

"Yes, I assumed you'd want it. It's at the nurse's station on his floor. I've given them instructions to release it to the police, which now means you."

"Can he hear what people say to him?"

"Probably, but he may not be able to process what he hears. It very likely is just sound to him. We don't know for certain. It can't hurt to talk to him, but it's best to say good things, though. Weather, encouragement, the sports scores, things like that. You understand, nothing that he could misinterpret if in fact he can process your words."

"I'd appreciate it if you'd page me the moment there is a change, doctor. Is that all right with you?"

"Of course. But I must get back to my patients now. Thank you for calling. Give your pager number to my nurse. I'll switch you back to her. Goodbye."

"Hello? Detective O'Riley?"

"Yes, my pager number is 455-555-2367. The doctor said you'd call if..."

"I'll call call you immediately with any news," Nurse Mason said.

"Thank you ma'am. Goodbye." He closed his phone and walked quietly back to my room. Realizing that visiting hours had begun, he entered the room and closed the door. He stood immobile next to the bed looking into my face.

"Can you hear me?" I shouted at him with everything I had. Jeremy stared an exaggerated bug-eyed stare, very clearly communicating his disgust for my actions.

"Listen, buddy. I know you don't know who I am. I'm sorry for the mess you're in. We're trying to find your family and who did this to you. I want you to hang in there. Try to fight to come back. It looks like you're in good hands, at least for a couple of days. I'll come back—soon."

Detective O'Riley left my room for the nurse's station.

"Dr. Wilson left a bullet here for me. May I have it?"

"A bullet?" the distracted young nurse asked. "Let me check with my supervisor." She disappeared for a moment and returned with an older woman.

"Yes, Officer, I have the bullet." She handed him a plastic bag with a small, misshapen black nugget rolling along the bottom seam.

"Thanks."

"Can you hear me?" I shouted again. I was back in the conference room, sitting in my chair. Everyone in the room was staring at me in surprise.

"Do you have something to say, Mr. Staley," a clearly perturbed Hollingsworth asked me coldly.

"Oh—uh—no, Sir. Excuse me, Sir. I didn't mean to say that. Just thinking out loud. Pardon me." I felt my face flush with embarrassment.

"It seems our new CIO was daydreaming," the socially conscious Hollingsworth joked. "I can understand that. We just increased his salary five fold. Planning how you're going to spend it, Staley?" Hollingsworth was smiling at me.

"Oh, no, Sir. I mean, yes Sir. I mean, well—I will, Sir."

Everyone chuckled politely and smiled, and then they applauded. "Welcome to the ranks of top management, Peyton. We're glad to have you with us," Hollingsworth said sweeping his hand broadly to indicate the entire assembly, and then clapped his hands with the others.

15

*H*ey there! Where were you? It seemed like an eternity you were gone."

Peyton shook his head, as if not sure why he was suddenly feeling safer back in the train compartment.

"I don't know where I was. This is a weird place. I saw myself. They told me I had a fifty-fifty chance of survival. Then I was in a meeting where I was promoted to CIO of my old company. I know I could have been a success like that. But at the time, I really had trouble ratting on my boss. So, instead, I ended up taking the fall when his department went under scrutiny. He framed me with all the dirt and incompetence. He did to me exactly what I had been unwilling to do to him. And he was the one who deserved the dismissal. He was responsible for the downward spiral of the department. But because I couldn't imagine him on the streets trying to get a job, with his five children going hungry, he ended up destroying me. I let him do it."

Peyton's shoulders dropped visibly, his head drooped between his hands.

"I think I can understand. I have been betrayed by people I trusted too. Want to talk?"

Peyton nodded, looking up at me and placing his arm around my waist. His hug begged for comfort. I placed my hand on his back and rubbed it. We embraced in silence for a few minutes, allowing our feelings to surface. Peyton took several deep breaths to master his emotions.

"If we both get to go back, I'm going to find you. I want to know you," he said.

"If we both get to go back, I'll be looking for you, too." I just had to smile.

"But I think this place isn't what it appears to be. The impossibility of the Processor's premise, that we could relive our lives and change our destiny, while we're somehow trapped in limbo in the real world, doesn't make sense. I just don't think it's going to end up the way they present it. I don't think we're supposed to just sit back and go through the motions here. I'm thinking we're going to have to fight to get out of here."

"A bit distrusting are we? I'm ready to see it through, at least for the next experience."

"Time's up." A voice boomed from nowhere. I turned to see two women standing at the compartment door to the train's corridor. One was dressed in a very conservative business suit. The other wore traditional Spanish peasant clothing. She spoke first.

"Hannah, it's time for the next Environment. I'm your Agent Three, Carmelita. Come with me."

I obediently walked toward her. Glancing back I winked at Peyton and smiled.

"See you when I get back."

"Peyton, come this way," the other woman said. "I am Claire and you have a date with destiny."

Peyton hesitated. "Hannah, be sure you come back," he said, watching until I left. "All right, Claire, I'll come with you, but my destiny is not with you, it goes with that woman."

16

*M*atthew and I walked down the corridor of the train in tense silence. The first compartment we came to in the third car was empty. Wanting to keep it that way, Matthew put our tickets in the clip holder, pulled the window shade on the door and scattered our luggage on the seats, as if to show others have already taken possession of them. The ruse was successful. Other passengers occasionally opened the door to see if there was space for them. Every time he shrugged his shoulders and smiled, a universal gesture of "Sorry, these seats are taken." He lit a cigar and let the smoke fill the compartment. I tried not to cough as I lowered the fold-down table. First, taking the ripe Camembert, a baguette and a couple of enormous apples from my backpack, I then opened the non-descript red table wine with our folding corkscrew. The cork crumbled as I turned the handle.

"Looks like we're going to be able to keep this one to ourselves," Matthew smiled as he sat down across the table from me, reaching for the bottle. "Here, allow me."

"Okay, I guess." This was going to be a long ride. Spain was several hours away. I tried to decide how to suggest we return to France by way of Jacques André-Bouchard's home in Bordeaux. Matthew was still grinning at me. I smiled half-heartedly back at him and the train lurched into motion.

"Great! Now no one will bother us," Matthew said. "I always wanted to make love on a train."

"Let's eat a little something. By the time we're out of Paris, I'm going to want to see the countryside." Ignoring his comment, I offered him a hunk of the bread spread with a slice of the soft Camembert, which oozed deliciously from the sliced wheel of cheese like honey from the comb.

Matthew poured wine into the clever telescoping travel cups he kept in his backpack. They were a gift from his father, who was an avid camper and who was always finding unusual thingamajigs to try out. He tried to find something to say that would melt my reserve.

"You know, when we get back to the States, we should get married right away. I'm sure it won't take too long to get the blood tests and the license taken care of. And, if we invite only a few close relatives and friends, we don't have to go to much trouble for the wedding itself. What do you say?"

"Oh, Matthew. How can you bring that up right now? Let's enjoy our ride to Spain. We may never come here again, and I want to see everything I can and live it up without thinking about the future before we go back home. We can make plans after we get back."

A cloud of anger darkened his face as the youthful smile evaporated and the skin on his cheeks sagged inward, adding years to his expression. "What's the matter, Hannah? You've been so distant ever since we met with that politician. I don't know why you're being so hard to get along with. Tell me what's on your mind."

"I don't want to ruin our time in Spain."

"Tell me what's bothering you. I won't let it ruin anything."

Trying hard to keep control of his suspicions he fidgeted as I nibbled another piece of bread and cheese, buying time to think before answering him. Reluctant to begin, I paused, lengthening the delay, which irritated him even more. The voice I heard was soft, hesitant, frightened.

"I'm just not sure we should be getting married just yet. We've spent all these years together, and I feel like I haven't known enough people—men—to be sure I should marry you."

Matthew's voice hardened to an edge like a wedge of stone. "Where is the problem? I thought we were happy and ready to make a commitment. What could you possibly need to know that you don't already know?"

"I expected this." I let out long a sigh. "I know it's hard for you to understand. It's hard for me to understand. There's just this thing in my head that tells me I'm not ready. You aren't either, Matthew. There are too many other women who turn your head. Elisa, back at school—Jeanette, in Africa —and I'm sure there will be more. It don't think we're really as committed as we say we are. Doubt is a warning. I have doubts, that's all. It's a warning."

Matthew was silent for a minute or two contemplating the turn of events. "Look, if you have doubts, then let's not talk about getting married for now. Let's just have fun while we're here. We can deal with the rest after we get home."

He decided to go easy on me and not try to change my mind. I was glad for that, but the problem wouldn't take care of itself. So, I opted for detachment to let my nerves settle and to give him time to get used to my point of view.

"Okay. I need to think. Let me watch out the window. That's really all I want to do." I turned away, relieved to be looking out the window instead of at him. We didn't talk again for hours. I let the countryside occupy my thoughts. He picked up the paper and read every article. As we entered Spain, Matthew broke the silence.

"You know, I see here that the running of the bulls in Pamplona is tomorrow. Why don't we get off there and see what it's all about. I've always wanted to do that, since reading Hemingway."

"Aren't you afraid of getting hurt?" Matthew hated athletic activities of all sorts.

"No!" he said mocking my concern. "I could do that." The bravado in his voice betrayed his motives.

"You don't have to prove anything to me."

"No, I don't. But I want to prove to myself that I can do something dangerous and have fun. No one has been gored in years. If all those young Spaniards can do it, so can I! What do you say? Let's go to Pamplona."

"I suppose so, if you really want to, I won't stop you."

I walked into my new corner office. Andrea followed me with a cup of coffee and the newspaper.

"Andrea, some of our normal routines are going to change. I won't be reading the paper at the office anymore. And, I expect there will be plenty of late nights. Are you ready for this?"

"Of course, Mr. Staley. I was so proud of you and honored, when you wanted me to move up with you. I'll do whatever it takes to help you make a success of this. Congratulations! Nobody deserves this promotion more than you do." Andrea was blushing like a school girl who just got a perfect score on a math test, proud yet humbled.

"Thanks, Andrea. Now, let's get to work. Call two staff meetings, one for ten o'clock tomorrow morning, the other for two o'clock tomorrow afternoon. I want to outline the next project for the managers in the morning, and I want to meet with the rank and file programmers and inspire their confidence in the afternoon"

"Consider it done. I'll reserve the small conference room."

"No, we'll have the meetings right here in this office. I want to set a precedent that I am accessible to everyone. No closed doors and no fake protocol."

"All right. Should I have any refreshments sent up?"

"Yes, that's a nice touch. As always, you remember the social details. Now, I'm going to need some time to lay out my strategies on paper. Can you hold all my calls for the next couple of hours?"

"Sure, boss!" Andrea saluted me as she closed the door.

I looked into the city through the bullet-proof plate glass windows. The same sensation of power washed over me. I loved the adrenaline rush just thinking about the future infused into my system. The money would make a big difference in my lifestyle. But most of all, I enjoyed the prospect of being in control.

"Yes, power is all. Now I understand. I understand why it is winner takes all." A ruthless surge of energy flowed through me like lightning down an antenna—safely directed to the underground, but awesome in its potential for destruction. Sitting down at my desk, I began to outline my plans on the simple yellow legal pad I was accustomed to writing on. Someone was watching me. Looking around the room, my eyes sharpened by the adrenalin rush came upon tiny holes in all four corners of the office. I looked back to the legal pad and wrote 'Surveillance'.

The morning in Pamplona dawned warm and humid. Matthew and I got up from the lumpy hotel bed, dressed in a hurry and rushed to the main plaza in Pamplona. The young men were gathering, and heading toward the starting gates at the cul-de-sac end of one of the little side streets. Matthew took me in his arms.

"Listen, Hannah. I love you. Whatever happens here, I love you. When we go home, we're getting married. There will be no other women. I can't imagine life without you. So, just kiss me, and let me know you'll be waiting in the arena when I get there." His eyes filled with tears.

"Of course, Matthew, I'll be waiting. You go ahead and do this. I think you're crazy, but I guess that's one of the endearing parts of you."

Matthew's kiss said more than "see you in a little while". I returned the passion.

"Bye." He casually trotted down the side street with the others.

I followed the crowd into the old roman amphitheater that served as the bullring. Brilliant red, blue and yellow banners hung over the solid dark green fences, encircling the arena. The kaleidoscope of colors of the crowd undulated as a throng of happy spectators gathered to fill the bleacher seats. I remembered how similar the seating was to the ballparks back at home, but more compact and circular in form. The peccadilloes began the pageant of equine dressage to entertain the audience. The announcer came over the loud speaker. I couldn't understand what he was saying, but the crowd exploded in cheering. I turned to the man sitting next to me.

"Excuse me, do you speak English or French? Parlez-vous anglais ou français?"

"Why, yes, I do," he answered in a strong Australian accent brightened by his white toothy smile that beamed from a craggy, leathery, dark brown face.

"Can you tell me what's going on? I've never done this before and I don't speak Spanish."

"Well, the announcer just said the bulls were running. There would be only a few more minutes to wait until the first runners and bulls come into the ring. We're to watch that doorway over there." He pointed at the largest opening in the fence, directly across the arena.

116

"Thank you, I really don't understand why this is such a big sport."

"No need to understand. Just watch." He smiled at me again, looking me up and down before I turned away.

The few minutes of an eternity passed. Then a cheer went up from the crowd.

"Olé! Olé! Olé!" The crowd roared. A small calf trotted into the ring. The laughter was deafening. I watched, beginning to feel worried.

"It's a corny joke. They send in a calf every time—just for fun." My Australian sportscaster had decided to keep me informed of every nuance of the game.

"Olé! Olé! Olé!" The crowd roared again. I stood up to see the first bulls charging into the arena. Then a few young men, running and stumbling, try to get out of the way of the pack of bulls behind them. The dust rose into clouds as more men and bulls ran into the ring. They tried to avoid the bulls by running for safety behind the barriers placed at intervals around the ring. Another pack of bulls thundered into the ring. I strained to see if Matthew was in the clumps of runners. His red hair would be easy to spot among all the dark-haired men. I stretched myself as tall as I could to squint and search the throng of more than a hundred runners. I couldn't see Matthew.

"Excuse, me. Are you looking for someone special down there?" The Aussie laughed as he asked the obvious.

"Yes, my fiancé was going to run the bulls with the others. He has very red hair. I'm sure we could see him from here. Do you see a redhead down there?"

The man peered into the crowd the way a submarine periscope peers at an approaching battleship. We both scanned the confusion, looking for one person with red hair.

"No, I don't. But I'm sure that means nothing. He probably couldn't get into the pack of runners. Or he stopped back on one of the side streets. Only about a sixth of the runners actually come all the way through the course to the arena. Most of them stop before getting this far."

His attempt to explain made no difference to my sudden fear that something had gone wrong. I was frantic to leave the arena, and he grabbed my arm as I stood up to leave.

"You can't go yet, they lock the entrances until the events are over."

I didn't like that he was touching me on the arm. I pulled away and called on all the power I could muster to leave no doubt in his mind. "I'm going. I'm not waiting. I have to find him."

Running down the stairs, I jogged almost without my feet touching the risers of the ancient steps. I made my way through the tunnel that led to the outside of the arena. The guard tried to stop me, but I ran past him and squeezed through the wide bars of the grilled gate that block the exit. Being small and slender paid off at times like these.

I arrived at the mouth of the barricaded street where the bulls had passed. Carmelitia was standing alone, leaning on the second barricade. The look on her face betrayed her. Something was terribly wrong. I was distracted by a commotion two or three blocks down the street. When I glanced back, Carmelita was gone. I slithered through the barrier and ran as fast as I could in my sandals. The siren of the ambulance shrieked in panic as it rounded the corner. I reached the cluster of people standing along the edges of the narrow street with expressions of fear freezing their faces into a panorama of horror. Two bodies were lying in separate pools of blood on the time scarred bricks of the uneven roadway, one a young dark-haired boy. The other was Matthew.

〜〜〜

My phone rang. Dr. Hollingsworth's voice sounded restrained. "Peyton, could you join me for a moment? I have some questions to ask you."

The abrupt silence one the other end bothered me. I entered Dr. Hollingsworth office a minute or so later to find him seated with Mr. Andersen.

"Our CFO, George Arthur, will be here in a minute. The terms of your contract are really his domain. I'm sure you will find the details of interest. While we wait, lets go over the main items, shall we?"

"Sure." I chose the middle of the three chairs in front Dr. Hollingsworth's expansive mahogany desk and sat down.

"First of all, you'll receive a yearly salary of five hundred thousand dollars, with a ten percent increase each year for five years. Full health benefits in addition to dental and disability coverage are customary. Your 401K will be fully vested after only six months. We want to be sure you're well taken care of upon retirement. After that, your monthly contribution will be matched two and half times by the company, after our initial lump sum contribution. Of course, you'll have use of the corporate jet for business travel, and you will receive six weeks paid vacation each year. The company will pay for your travel expenses wherever you choose to go to rest up. The contract will remain in full force for five years. After that time it is re-negotiable. We expect all our top executives to own their own homes. To that end, we've retained a realtor on your behalf to find suitable lodgings for you. Would you prefer a high-rise condominium or a suburban single family dwelling?"

"A high-rise condo would be fine."

"Overlooking the lake, I presume?"

"Sure. Why not?" I was growing more suspicious by the minute.

"There is a buy out clause that permits us to release you, but we'll be required to pay all your remaining compensation including increases in a lump sum. The 401K would remain in force until your retirement, even if you leave us. You can take it with you. In return, we require six months notice of your intent to leave, should you ever decide you wanted to leave. In that case, you'd forfeit your 401K, but we'd still pay one year's salary in advance to make sure you can live while you seek other employment. Health benefits go with you, if you choose to take advantage of the COBRA provisions. You could buy the condo from us, or simply relocate, no strings attached. Any questions?"

"Yes, this is an extremely generous package. I feel it may be too generous for a simple sixty hour work week. Is there some condition that hasn't been mentioned?"

"Condition? You mean, an obligation to HIGHLAND TECHNOLOGIES?"

"Well, I guess I mean, where's the catch?" Sitting back I folded my arms in an unconscious gesture of self-protection.

"There is no catch. We simply expect the best you can give, in time, creativity, leadership and loyalty. Just as we expect from all our top men, you will be essentially on call, twenty-four hours a day to manage the growing information needs of HIGHLAND TECHNOLOGIES. The job description is simple. Be your best, and we'll be getting our money's worth." Dr. Hollingsworth smiled and looked to Mr. Andersen.

"So, what do you say?" Mr. Andersen leaned forward to emphasize his question.

"I'll accept your terms with just a couple of additions. Remove the surveillance cameras from my office, and eliminate any bugs you have installed. The phone is not to be tapped, and I am to have full and complete decision-making power in regards to the design, function, personnel and day-to-day operations of the IS Department. Otherwise, the terms are fine."

"Done. Call in George and tell him the details, would you, Mr. Andersen? Mr. Staley and I will be going to lunch."

I looked into the crowd of shocked and sobered celebrants. As I bent over Matthew's body, nothing but red scarves and legs closed in around me. Trying to focus through my tears, looked back one last time at Matthew, hoping he would just sit up and laugh at me, telling me this had been a sick joke. He didn't. Carmelita beckoned to me. I felt numb, following her to a small restaurant down another narrow side street. We sat at a window table and refused service. I was sobbing out of control.

"Listen, Hannah. We know you would not have wished this to happen to Matthew for anything. But this is what would have happened. You are reliving your life as it would have been, remember that." Carmelita said, trying to calm my hysteria but I wouldn't let her.

"No, I can't remember that. These emotions are too real. He didn't deserve to die in Pamplona. Last time, he was waiting for me under the shade trees outside the arena. This time he's dead. I can't accept this. Peyton is right. We're going along with this all too easily. Send me back. I don't want to finish this road. I want my old one. I'll accept any consequences the accident caused me. I can't see this through!" I was screaming by the time I stopped talking.

"Well, before you wish for that, I have something for you to see. Look at the television in the corner."

I walked over to the small black and white television sitting on a wrought iron and glass table. The image blurred as I stared at the screen. Slowly the picture came into focus. A woman was lying in a hospital bed. Bandages covered some of her face. The tubes and monitor wires suspended from her body made her seem like a puppet laid away for safe keeping.

"That's me! Oh, my God. I look dead!"

Another woman entered the scene and sat down next to the bed, taking the patient's hand.

"Lynn! What are you doing here?" I gasped as Carmelita stepped close to my side and placed her hand on my shoulder.

"Hannah, it's me, Lynn. I have some good news, and some bad news. The good news is, we have a strong lead on who did this to you. The bad news is, the lead points to your brother as the one who hired the attacker. The doctors say you're doing better, but it will take time for you to recover. Oh, Hannah, try to wake up. I need you to help me."

"Lynn! Lynn! I can hear you! I'm trying to wake up! Lynn don't give up! I'll be there as soon as I can be." I put my hand on the screen, as if to touch my friend's hand. Then I turned toward Carmelita. "I won't continue this way. Take me back to the train. NOW!"

"I'm sorry, that is not possible," Carmelita said, no inflection in her voice. "You will continue this road. You have no choice. The Processor is in control, not you. Rest assured that Matthew's body got back to his family. You took the next train out of Pamplona."

Without being aware of movement, suddenly I was sitting on a bench at the tiny train station at Saint-Vincent-de-Tyrosse. I smelled the scent of the Atlantic Ocean. The pines waved in a gentle breeze, their scent mingling with the salty perfume of the sea. Sadness and confusion over Matthew's death hung heavy on my mind, while I sorted through the afternoon's events and listened for some familiar sound to enhance the endless view of water and sky from the platform of this tiny seaside town. A yellow Jeep outfitted with sand tires bounced over the road, oddly unfamiliar with tarmac and gravel, and clearly designed for the soft dunes that lay beyond the trees. Jacques André-Bouchard waved heartily with a healthy vigor that conveyed joy where I wanted gloom.

"Bonjour, Hannah! How was the trip in Spain?" Jacques shouted from the car. He got out of the Jeep and walked up the steps to the shadows of the station where I was still sitting. "What is it? What's wrong?"

"Oh, Jacques, Matthew is dead—killed by a bull in Pamplona. Dead—like that—in the street. I didn't see it coming, his death. It was horrible! I don't know what to do - go back to the States or stay here." He heard the helplessness of my words and saw the uncaring abandon in my eyes.

"Stay here a few days. We will be better able to consider the possibilities. You have to rest up a little before deciding what to do. No one can decide anything just after such a loss. Come. Come to my house. You will have the chance to better reflect near the ocean. The sea air will be good for you."

The calm and convincing tone of Jacques' words drew me in his direction. My resistance to his offer faded by the end of his last sentence. I let him lead me to the Jeep, buckle me into the black leather bucket seat and take me to the seaside home he loved.

Waking in my condominium bedroom, the early morning light filtered into my eyes through the half-closed blinds. By the softness of the light, I could tell it was barely dawn. I sensed that I had been living in the luxury condo for a long time. But it seemed very natural to be getting up here to start my morning routine. I stumbled into the bathroom to shower and shave. In the mirror an older version of the young man I was accustomed to being in this recycled life stared back at me.

"Hmm. I see I've been here quite a while. Looks like the job has been pretty good to you, old man." The changes time had made to my face showed wrinkles creasing my temples near the edges of my eyes. The deep furrow at the start of my left eyebrow testified to how much I frown. Though not yet deeply etched, the lines on my forehead were pronounced enough to mark the years effectively. I wore a mustache that almost perfectly matched my gray and receding hair.

The phone rang.

"Peyton? It's Andrea. You've got to come into the office right away. Hollingsworth is on a rampage. The Board of Directors just fired him and Andersen. He says they're after you."

"I'm on my way!" A quick shower and in fifteen minutes I was sipping coffee in my limousine while on the phone to my broker. "Harper! I want the controlling shares on my computer when I get in. You're sure the hundred thousand shares are secure?"

"Yes, Mr. Staley. We're poised to buy every share of MACRO-WORLD available, even against our better judgment. You'll have more of that flounder than anyone else."

I hesitated for a moment to absorb one glaring detail in Harper's comments: MACROWORLD. The old HIGHLAND TECH-NOLOGIES must have been absorbed by MACROWORLD as originally planned. I realized my gamble was even bigger than I had anticipated. I was going to take over all of MACROWORLD, not just HIGHLAND TECHNOLOGIES. I liked the ideas and possibilities that burst like seltzer bubbles in my mind.

"Good going, Harper. I'll call you back later. Hang on tight - it's going to be a hell of a ride!" Laughing as I closed the cell phone,

I picked up the Wall Street Journal where a small announcement under editorial comment caught my eye:

"MACROWORLD stocks closed down again after a continuous two month slide. Stock value has dropped from one hundred thirty-four and seven eighths to two dollars a share. Industry analysts predict the total collapse of the once all powerful microchip developer by week's end."

The end is in sight, or so most of the financial world believed. All overt efforts to save the company had proven useless. For months the stockholders had been up in arms and sold out in droves. Hollingsworth and Andersen's jobs had been at risk since the first sign of trouble. Not even the Chairman of the Board had tried to weather the storm. Resignations from the Board of Directors pared the committee down to only a couple of hangers on. Doomsday for MACROWORLD seemed inevitable. I indulged myself with a wicked smile.

None of the executives at the top of the MACROWORLD food chain had been informed as to what was happening. They all thought we still developed breakthrough super-microchips that were still malfunctioning. Capitalizing on my advantage as CIO, I created the company's fictional decline on paper over a period of months, turning MACROWORLD into the worst risk in technology stocks by manipulating the content of available information about development progress. The destruction was now nearly complete.

"Information is everything. They won't even know what hit them."

Only Orson Stillwell, Director of Research and Development and I knew of MACROWORLD's enormous advances in biomolecular computer and biochip technology. The corporate executives still believed our electronic super- microchips were sinking in a developmental quagmire. They were told nothing of the secret success of

Orson's revolutionary developments. Of course MACROWORLD stock declined as other companies announced their own, supposed technologically superior advances, undercutting MACROWORLD's fictional effort to be first in the marketplace with the latest super-microchip design. Orson and I would announce the production of advanced biomolecular computers—which we called BMCs—and biochips that operate software and store data on the double-helix of DNA, once I was in control of MACROWORLD.

In only minutes I would be taking over. When the New York Stock Market's bell sounded, I would own the controlling interest in MACROWORLD. Its reorganization would begin, with Peyton Staley at the helm. The power base was in place. My competitors for control were all gone from the board room. I admitted to liking the mental image of myself in total control of MACROWORLD.

I entered my office through the back entrance.

"Andrea! Get Orson up here right away."

Andrea opened the door to my office. "Dr. Stillwell has been waiting for a while, Sir. Is there anything else you need?"

"No, Andrea, just keep the barracudas at bay. Don't let anyone disturb us. Not anyone." I smiled at her before turning to my computer and accessing the encrypted development files. Shy and socially withdrawn, Dr. Stillwell walked haltingly into my office, his rumpled clothes hung loose, his long, greasy, thinning hair uncombed and matted. Stillwell's outward appearance masked his visionary, intellectual brilliance. Placing his body askew and crossing his feet to expose scrawny bare ankles that protruded from misshapen brown leather loafers, he sat awkwardly in one of the chairs facing my expansive, uncluttered desk.

"And so, Orson, our time has arrived. As soon as the meeting begins, I will announce the reorganization of MACROWORLD. I have control of the stocks. You'll get your portion as soon as our

BMCs and biochips are announced worldwide, as agreed. The contracts are in order."

"I trust you to handle the details, Sir. But, I've been having second thoughts about this. What happens if the Board votes against you and our BMCs and biochips? What happens if they dissolve the corporation?"

"Not a chance of that, Stillwell. I have taken precautions to prevent even that possibility."

Andrea opened the office door. "The Board members are waiting, Sir." The furrowed brows and down-turned mouth that creased her face betrayed her concern.

"Is something wrong, Andrea?"

"I don't know, Sir. It's just that there are a number of people in the meeting room whom I've never seen before—mostly Asians, Sir."

Orson and I exchanged glances. "Thank you, Andrea, that's all."

The MACROWORLD challenge to the established technology superpowers was already beginning. I alone knew why unknown people were in the board room. They were my new team of allies from up and coming Asian and Israeli companies that employed the most creative renegade inventors in BMC and biochip technology. Essentially, I planned to eliminate my marketplace competition by absorbing the best and the brightest minds into MACROWORLD. I had been waiting for this moment since I began my thirty year career in computers and as I opened the conference room doors, the sense of power invigorated me as nothing else ever had.

"Ladies and Gentlemen, welcome to the new MACRO-WORLD—"

17

*W*ithout being aware of the change, Peyton and I found ourselves in the train compartment once again.

"Do you think we have a chance of getting out of here?" I whispered to Peyton without moving my lips in an effort to remain motionless and yet communicate, the way children do when they are bored in church.

"I don't think so." Equally interested in appearing to ignore me, he whispered back, "At least, not from here, not right now. I'm working on it."

I gave up the pretense and spoke in a normal tone. "I am really not interested in anything that's coming next. I'm sure I made unwise choices in my natural life, but they weren't anything like the unwise choices I've made since coming here. The strangest part is, for me, I can't remember why I'm here anymore. It feels like this is real, and I can't remember any other time in my life."

"I don't know what you're talking about. I was enjoying the feeling of power I got from being in control of the whole corporation."

"Try to be completely honest. Don't you feel like it's too good to be true?"

"No."

"I feel like I'm losing my mind. I have no reason to pursue the road I chose."

"But I do. I have the control I want."

"But, can you explain what brings us back here? Matthew is dead. That is too intense for me. And, whether you are comfortable with your sense of power right now or not, it's going to go bad. I just know it. I can't shake this feeling that we should get out of here."

I turned my recliner around and gave his a shove bringing him around to facing me. "I'm not going to wait here for Agent Four," I said to him with a wink and a smile, I filling the tone of my voice with youthful bravado. "You can come with me, if you want to. I'm going to find my way out of here."

Peyton looked at me hard and long, as if wrestling with his desire to keep his new-found power against his hunch that I was right about how events might take a turn for the worse in his corporate heaven. Then with an abrupt change of pace, he paced the room, periodically kicking the walls with his feet, again searching the corners for cracks.

"There must be a way out," he said knowing he would find none. He inspected the windows for any structural vulnerability at all. They were solid. Suddenly, I saw an inflaming frustration push him into a frenzy of futile action. Grabbing his recliner he pounded it with his fists until he was winded from the exertion. He finally sat down on his recliner.

"How's that for a show?" he said to me between his teeth, playfully raising his brow a couple of times and winking for my benefit.

"Peyton. Get hold of yourself," I said to him in an overly loud voice, realizing my complicity in his ruse. "There is no going anywhere. No doors, remember? No exit of any kind." Speaking more calmly, I pretended to try to help him relax. "Just relax, my friend. We're in this together."

"Yeah, I guess we have no choice but to wait for Agent Four," he said without energy.

We both sat back in our recliners and reached across the space between us to hold hands, soldering the bond between us with the molten metal of fear and anticipation of freedom.

18

Lynn pulled in front of Hannah's brownstone and turned off the ignition of her Lexus. A lake fog blew inland from Lake Michigan in minutes and transformed the sun and bright blue sky to a gloomy gray. A bank of low clouds led the cool front in from the eastern Great Lakes. The bone chilling change in the weather caused Lynn to pull her coat tighter around herself as she walked through the gate.

"Could he hate her enough to try to have her killed? What could be his motive for such a thing? He's got money. He's a wealthy man. Her portion of the inheritance was only sixty-five thousand dollars in stocks, bonds and cash from the sale of the parents' home. It's just not enough financial motive for a rich man to kill his sister."

Lynn stopped at the junction of the walk to the front door and the wrought-iron gate and gazed at her friend's brownstone for a couple of minutes. The windows were dark. Forlorn in its unkempt state, the yard seemed as if it were mourning the absence of its inhabitants. Walking toward the front porch, her emotions boiled over. Tears ran unchecked down her cheeks.

Blinking hard to see the lock, and pushing aside the yellow crime scene tape strung by the police to keep out intruders, Lynn used Hannah's house key to enter. She slowly opened the door inward, as if expecting to see a ghost as she stepped into the front hall.

The smell of neglect had already set in. She looked at objects in the space again taking mental pictures of the scene. Lynn's sniffling punctuated the disarray left behind by the attack and the evidence gathering by the police. Fingerprint powder coated every flat surface and smeared the edges of the walls. The sight of the still wet carpet, the gate, leaning useless against the wall, the memory of that morning overwhelmed her. The dried blood droplets the police left untouched upset her even more. She went into the kitchen to find something to blow her nose on and dry her eyes with.

"Get a grip!" She stared into the mirror above the sink. "Think for a minute about where Hannah would keep her papers." The sound of her own voice appeared to make her feel more at ease. Lynn kept on talking to chase away the silence. "I'm sure she kept them in the office. Probably in a file cabinet. I'll go up there first."

She headed for the stairs up, but glanced toward the spot where Sandy's bed, food and water bowls still waited for the dog to return. The cheese bone she had enjoyed that morning still sat unfinished in the corner of the landing. Feeling light-headed, the sudden loss of muscle control in her legs forced Lynn to sit down on the floor as the tears flowed again.

"Oh, my God, why did this happen?" Her grief expressed itself unchecked. When the tears finally stopped, she breathed deeply to regain composure and harden herself to her goal.

"I've got to find the answers in Hannah's files." Her single-minded purpose gave her the strength to stand and go up the stairs to the office, holding onto the handrail as support. She turned on all the lights in the office. The mahogany wood of the armoire and filing cabinets warmed to a bronze glow in the light from incandescent lamps. Lynn regained her composure in the coziness of the room and set about searching every file in the numerous filing cabinets.

Most of the files pertained to Hannah's failed business dealings: client files, old order forms, sales and promotional materials, unpaid invoices, and the fattest file containing copies of all the papers. Lynn paused to read the list of unpaid creditors.

Most of the vendors were galleries, auction houses and shops, and credit card companies. Lynn sat back to consider the information. It was the first she had heard of Hannah's business troubles, her financial instability, and she was baffled by her complete ignorance it all. It was clear that Hannah had started her own business, as an art and antique dealer.

Lynn's muttering broke the silence. "All of these suppliers lost thousands of dollars in unpaid invoices and an incalculable loss of face with their own contacts when Hannah had just closed her accounts and walked away without a word. I wonder if they just kept on going, or if this effected their business."

"Now, as I think about it, Hannah had told me her accounts were in trouble financially from the huge influx of competition by the growing impact of international competition. Their specialty lines of art and antiques and high priced boutique items had been selling less and less. Hmm . . . Hannah's love for antiques and art had helped them keep their business afloat. But had her failure hit them hard enough to hurt them?"

Lynn dialed her cell phone. "Hey, Marjorie. See if you can find out what has happened to Smith & Carlson Antiques since last year. I think there might be a connection between Hannah's attack and them, if their company was hit hard by lost business. It's just a hunch."

"I'll see what I can do, Lynn. You should know the police called to say they had identified the fingerprints from the discovered Dayton-Hollands cell phone. They belong to a small-time hoodlum named Antonio Cordoba who moonlights as a hitman when he's not making crack deals. They're looking for him now and say the word on the street is he's disappeared."

"Huh! Why am I not surprised? I'll be here a good while longer. I've still got to find her personal papers. I got sidetracked by the list of unpaid vendors and the thought that one of them might be real angry at getting stiffed by her. Call me if there's anything else, and get that info on Smith & Carlson as soon as possible!"

Lynn closed her phone and went to the next file cabinet. Pulling open the top drawer, inside she found a box of old family photographs.

"Oh, no! If I start looking at these, I'll never get to the papers. Keep going, girl. Don't get sidetracked now. What's this?"

Behind the box is a large manila envelope. She pinches the wing clasp together and opens the flap. Reaching inside, Lynn's fingers touch three packets of bound up letters. She pours them out on the filing cabinet.

The first was a batch of letters Hannah had written to her parents and their responses while she was overseas as a young woman. The colorful stamps and the thirty year old postmarks intrigued Lynn as she carefully thumbed through the envelopes to look at each one.

The second packet was some love letters from her first husband, bound in blue ribbon.

"Why did Hannah keep these?" Lynn shook her head.

The third packet was a mixture of letters Hannah had written to and received from Lenny and Donna. Most of the postmarks in this batch of letters went even farther back than the others. But, the most recent postmarks were less than a year old.

Lynn carried them over to the antique wingback chair in the corner near the window next to the small, round and certainly rare three-legged table. She untied the red yarn that held the letters together, letting them fan out on the tabletop.

"Hm, Donna's last letters are less than a year old." Lynn opened the most recent one and read aloud.

March 11

Dear Hannah, my silly little sister,

It's the Ides of March, and my luck is running badly. The doctors have said my episode was caused by an irregular heartbeat. This getting old thing is for the birds. But don't worry, Lenny has arranged for me to go to a hospice, where they take care of people like me. I should get better with a couple of months of rest and be back home in time to plant May flowers and vegetables in my garden. While this sounds worse than it is, just remember, Lenny will always take care of you when you need his help. I'll write when I get settled in the hospice. Just so you have the address:

Donna Miller

c/o LITTLE HOUSE HOSPICE

#12 Route 5

Snohomish, WA 98290

Don't worry about me. Just keep that little side business of yours going. I'll try to make sense to Lenny about your inheritance as soon as I'm feeling better. I think his resolve is cracking. My tenants will take care of the house while I'm gone. So, don't feel you have to come way out here to do anything.

Keep smiling and laughing.

Love, Donna

Lynn flipped open her phone and dialed national information.

"National Information Directory. What city and state, please?"

"Snohomish, Washington, please."

"Yes."

"I'd like the phone for the Little House Hospice on route five, please."

"Just a moment—here you are."

The computer voice gave the number. Lynn wrote it down as the auto-dial service punched in the numbers. Someone answered on the second ring.

"Little House Hospice. May I help you?" the pleasant female voice asked.

"Yes—I'd like to speak with one of your residents, Donna Miller, please. I'm a friend of her sister, Hannah Sebastian and need to give her some important information regarding her sister." Lynn tried to stay calm.

"Oh—Donna Miller—I, um—I'm sorry. She died just over a month ago. She had a heart attack just a few weeks after coming here. I'm sorry. I thought her sister knew."

"No, she was not notified. Can you tell me who was notified of Donna's passing?"

"Yes, a Mr. Lenny Miller—her brother. He instructed us to dispose of her remains, and we did. I'm sorry. That's all I can tell you."

"Thank you. I'm sorry too." Lynn closed her phone as her adrenalin kicked in. "That bastard!" She shouted her rage. Lynn tried to catch her breath from the emotional outburst. Getting back to the work of sorting out the motives that kept rising to the surface from the meager evidence she had to go on, she carefully turned each letter over, looking at postmarks, names and addresses and built a teetering pile in a few minutes.

"If I know Hannah at all, manipulation by money would enrage her beyond reason." As the last words passed her lips she picked up Hannah's letter to her father. Lynn began to read.

October   *My Journal Homework COPY*
Dear Daddy,
How can I begin? The second millennium has begun. It's fall again and I am fifty-three and you would be ninety-four. You've been gone for

*ten years now, longer if we count the years when you had forgotten who
I am. I miss our late night heart-to-heart talks. I miss the hugs and pats
you gave me to keep me going when things were hard. You always had
just the right word, or just the right look to let me know you loved me,
in spite of the hurt and hard times that I attracted. Now, as I journey
into my fifties, I have to tell you how things have turned out. Can you be
patient with me one last time as I talk with you about it all now?*

"Oh, my God, she put it all down in writing. Where did she
send it?" Lynn picked up the envelopes and certified receipts, and
shuffling through them, checked the postmarks and delivery signa-
tures against the dates on the letters.

"Her fifty-third year—October—that's this year, she sent this
out just a week before the attack." Lynn stopped to think. "The certified receipts! There must be one for this October." She dealt them
out on the desk like the playing cards of a winning poker hand. She
spread them out, com-paring the dates.

"Here it is. She sent this to Lenny Miller. Why am I not surprised?" Lynn picked up the letter and went on reading.

*"The weekend you died, my true place in the fam-ily became clear
to me. Because I couldn't be with Mother on Saturday, I called her to see
whether or not I could arrive on Sunday. Mother told me that Lenny
and Donna had just arrived and that she really didn't want me to come.
They would handle things and grieve together. I wasn't needed. You were
cremated and scattered at sea, and I was excluded from even the smallest
gathering of the family. I couldn't talk to any of them for a long time. The
scar that rejection left me has never healed.*

*You taught me that the rough spots in the road make a person
strong. Oh, Daddy, I have had lots of rough spots. The saddest part of
all for me in all of this is that after you were gone, Mother, Lenny and*

Donna turned against me. Mother became very hostile as she aged. You remember things were never smooth between her and me once I turned sixteen. You should know how she handled things after you were gone.

To Lenny and Donna she played up the martyred mother role perfectly. But she told me that she would cut me from the trust if I didn't "straighten up" and start living my life "right." But that wasn't the end. I told her that if the money was more important to her than I was, then I didn't want it. Lenny agreed with me, that I had to do what I had to do to communicate with Mother on this issue. Donna supported my position too. I know now they saw the money flowing their way. But once you were gone, my right to be included in the family dissolved simply because I couldn't be bought."

"That a girl, Hannah! Keep your dignity. Don't let them get to you," Lynn is talking to the room, gesturing with her free hand. Lynn continued reading aloud.

"Lenny lied to my children, telling them that he tried to talk me out of my position. He never once did that. Nor did Mother. Nor did Donna. In fact, the ink wasn't even dry on the legal exclusion papers before they made sure I could never have control of my share of your gift to me. You taught me to be truthful and to keep my word. I have kept it. I am still not willing to be bought. You would never have allowed such a thing.

Daddy, none of them even know my children's birthdays. All the years they were growing up, no one ever once called any of my kids to just talk, to get to know them. My children have seen them perhaps five times in their lives, if that. Their names are misspelled throughout the trusts. What is this scrim curtain of personal relationship? What is Lenny hiding from my children? What was Mother hiding from me?"

"Control, Hannah. It's all about control. You need to have yours back. You have to survive to let me help you fight this."

"The result of all this is that now my children won't have anything to do with me. That hurts more than anything else. But, the reality is, Lenny's trying to get all the inheritance for himself.

When they broke up your house, I kept the furni-ture and pictures and memorabilia—Mom's sheet music from the twenties, her old stock certificates and her old costume jewelry. They kept the house and sold it for a couple hundred thousand more dollars.

Daddy, aren't family and blood forever? Would you tell me my crime? Would you explain how Donna could be the prodigal daughter, putting the family through ten years of hell and now be considered a valued family member? Is she really? Yet, I was the "alpha and omega" of her family in the letter she wrote to me so she could get back together with Mother and you?"

"That explains everything. Donna didn't deserve the money either, but Lenny used her just long enough to make sure Hannah was powerless. Then he got rid of her." Lynn went on reading the last of the letter.

"So, Mother died, and I never found out the an-swers. The wall was too high. The time was too short. The mileage was too great. In all my life, I never did hear her say she loved me. Did she love me, Daddy? Or was I just the accidental child who got in the way? I still want to know.

Death is immutable. Silence is forever. Secrets are kept by the Devil. Love is all there is. So, after thirty years this is who I have become. I did and still do what you taught me to do. But last year, my husband died in a car accident and everything changed. I prefer my solitude now.

Rest in peace. I loved you so. We were friends. Only my husband brought me that same warm kind of friendship. I have to believe I'll see you both again someday. I know that is true.

Forever, your loving daughter,
Hannah"

Lynn was sobbing as she stuffed all the letters back into the envelope and fumbled turning off the lights. She ran down the stairs and slammed the front door on her way out. "I'll read the rest of the other letters later. He's got all the money now. But not for long—I'm going to see to that!" Lynn backed out of the parking spot and drove into the rush hour traffic, hardly looking where she was going.

"I hope Marjorie has something to tell me by the time I get back to the office. Get out of the way, asshole!" Lynn's driving was erratic and aggressive as she cut in and out of the barely moving traffic. "Her situation is impossible. There is no one but me between Lenny and her, and I am going to win this battle if it kills me. Who do you think you are, cutting in like that. Creep!" Lynn pounded on the horn and swerved across three lanes of traffic to make her exit.

Marjorie picked up the phone and dialed the number for Smith and Carlson Antiques and Arts.

"Good morning, Smith and Carlson. How may I direct your call?" The receptionist's stilted greeting fell dissonant on Marjorie's ear.

"Yes, uh—Mr. Carlson, please"

"Our vice-president of marketing, Mr. Jack Carlson is in. May I tell him who's calling?"

"This is Ace Collections." Marjorie said.

"Just a moment please."

A slightly warped recording of Barry Manalow singing "Mandy" droned in Marjorie's ear for at least a verse and a chorus before cutting off mid-phrase.

"Hello, this is Jack Carslon."

"Yes—Mr. Carlson, I represent Ace Collections. We specialize in retrieving lost receivables for companies like yours."

"And what makes you think we need to collect anything? Our clients are solid corporations. We don't need your services."

"Your annual financial report to the antiques and fine arts industry indicates your company had a substantial burden of uncollected receivables," she interrupted him, trying to keep him on the line. "For example, the art and antique dealer, Hannah Sebastian. We can get you that money."

"Oh, that was nothing. Hannah's bankrupt and her little business with her. Nothing to do about that. Besides, our losses were minimal. We don't need your services. Good-bye."

Marjorie hung up the phone. Seconds later, Lynn swept through the door like a whirlwind blowing in from a desert, hot and gusty. "Marjorie, got anything on Smith and Carlson?" she blurted out without stopping on her way past Marjorie's desk. Marjorie followed her into the inner office, unaffected by Lynn's high energy.

"No, not really. It appears they absorbed the loss without much difficulty and went on about their business. The fellow I spoke with, a Jack Carlson, vice-president of marketing was quite blasé and cool. I posed as a collection agent willing to track Hannah for them. The cover worked pretty well until I mentioned her. He shut down and essentially just hung up."

"Well, we can let that sleeping dog lie for now. Lenny Miller is Hannah's biggest problem. Her sister, Donna, died in the hospice where Lenny sent her to recuperate from heart trouble, all her money passed to Lenny. Hannah was attacked and nearly killed by an intruder. If she dies, all her money will pass to Lenny. Smell anything?"

"Rotten eggs?"

"Worse. Leaking gas. This guy is a bomb waiting to go off. When he blows, he's going to take everything he can with him. But why a rich guy like him? He's got more than his share of everything. I can't figure his motive for trying to get hold of the paltry inheritance money. Compared to his own net worth, Donna and Hannah's money combined amount to nothing but measly pocket change. What is he after?"

"Revenge? You know how sibling rivalries can get out of hand when it comes to inheritance money. Even the rich hate their brothers and sisters. I had a cousin who—"

"Save it for later, Marjorie. We've got to get the suit filed and go after Lenny. He thinks he's about to win the pot, and we've got to protect her. Hannah's not dead yet, and if we can find out who really tried to kill her, then maybe we can keep her alive. I'm going to the police for more information on that Antonio Cordoba guy. Hold down the fort."

"I'll finish putting the papers together for the suit." Marjorie's words fell unheard as Lynn slammed the door. Minutes later she walked in the door of the police station and identified herself to the staff sergeant at the desk.

"I'd like to talk with Detective O'Riley."

"Certainly." The sergeant led her among the labyrinth of desks, each buried in mounds of unfinished paperwork and inhabited by an array of haggard looking patrolmen and women, typing on ancient typewriters instead of computer terminals. Toward the back of the room sat Detective O'Riley, reading the Chicago Sun-Times and swallowing the last of his customary Ho-Ho, Ding Dong and coffee snack.

"O'Riley, Ms. Hargrove is here to see you." The sergeant turned on his heels and left Lynn looking down at Detective O'Riley, who remained engrossed in the newspaper.

"Excuse me—Detective O'Riley?" Lynn said as if she didn't want to interrupt him.

He looked up. "Oh! Ms. Hargrove. Hello, how are you? I was just reading this article about Antonio Cordoba."

"I only know he's a hit man for hire when he's not selling crack.

"Yes, that's him. But he's not working anymore."

"Pardon me? He's out of work?"

"Not out of work, not working. Big difference. Listen to this," he said, folding the newspaper open to a short article.

"A body was pulled from the Chicago River early this morning. Police have identified it as that of Antonio Cordoba, a small time hoodlum and drug pusher. A one time hit man for the mob, Cordoba was brought up on charges in several murders and attempted murders over the years, but was never convicted in any of the cases. Cordoba's body was bound hand and foot, and there were gunshot wounds to the temple and the torso. Police speculate his mob connections explain why Cordoba was killed gangland style but have no reasonable motive for the killing."

"Not exactly the best farewell, huh?" O'Riley chuckled. "I guess that puts things in perspective for you, right?"

"I don't follow you. Cordoba nearly kills Hannah and the delivery guy, and then turns up dead as front page news. Motive?"

"Money from someone who wanted her dead," O'Riley said.

"Payoff?"

"A bullet in the brain and the bottom of the river as a gravesite. Not hard to figure."

"Maybe not, but at the crime scene, we found his fingerprints on a cell phone that belonged to Dayton-Hollands Industries. Hannah's brother runs that company. Any conclusions to draw there?"

"Sure, the brother hired the hitman, then had him killed too."

"Or, killed him for a botched job. Isn't this a little too convenient? Something bothers me about how easily we've pieced together a fairly plausible scenario in less than five minutes." Lynn studied Detective O'Riley's face, raised her eyebrow and looked at him quizzically, expecting a response.

"Sometimes the evidence is clear. That's a good day in this business."

"But this time it's too clear," Lynn objected. "Lenny Miller is getting away with attempted murder, maybe even murder, and he's cashing in on a sum of money that is too small for a decent motive. I can't buy it. Can you help me get to the bottom of this?" Lynn spoke directly.

"Detective O'Riley at your service, ma'am. But, I have to go to Michigan to meet with someone before I can give you more of my time. Will you give me a couple of days?"

"All right, but not much more. I've got to move quickly to sue Lenny Miller for the inheritance and tie him to the assault. The recent death of his other sister, Donna, is suspicious to me as well— another part of the picture that needs to be exposed. He sends her to a hospice to get well. Instead, she dies of a supposed heart attack which translates to unexplained causes. He has the hospice dispose of her remains—like a dog—no funeral, no notification of Hannah, just a dead sister and more money in his pocket. Did I mention? He's the executor of the estate—so, the inheritance."

"Promises to be interesting," Detective O'Riley mumbled. "But, I have a flight to Detroit in an hour. Gotta go. Leave me your phone number et cetera. I'll contact you in a couple of days." He picked up his briefcase, threw on a jacket and left Lynn standing alone by his desk.

"Not much for manners," she said as she wrote her information on his calendar and left a couple of her business cards on his desk.

19

A light rain mixed with mist and fog, more reminiscent of London than Detroit, greeted Detective O'Riley at Detroit's Metro airport as he stepped from the terminal and hailed a taxi. A short ride into the city, and the cab pulled up to a tidy Depression Era bungelow in a tidy Depression Era neighborhood.

"Wait for me, I'll only be a few minutes," O'Riley said to the cabby, and then ambled slowly up the walk to Beverly Staley's front door. He took in the details of her house, dark brown brick, fresh white trim, new roof, tidy yard with the last of the summer's flowers just giving up the ghost to the cold nights. He stood uncomfortably in his suit and tie, waiting for her to answer the bell. A couple of minutes passed. He rang the bell again, this time pushing longer to make it insist that someone answer. He turned away from the door, considering the prospect that she was not home and whether he should leave or not. The bolts scraped back as Beverly opened the door.

"Yes?" She blinked rapidly, as if trying to clear a speck from her eye.

"I'm Detective O'Riley—from the Chicago Police Department. I've come here to talk with you about Peyton Staley - your former husband. May I come in?" He smiled, hoping to encourage her compliance.

"Peyton? I haven't even thought about him for a long time. How can I possibly help you? I don't know anything about him that could be of any use." In the moment of silence that followed her comment, her obvious discomfort succumbed to her curiosity. "Is he in trouble or something?"

"May I come in?" Detective O'Riley said a second time and held his badge out for her to look at. "I think you might know some things I need to know." Caution and reserve flickered on Beverly's face as she considered his request.

"All right." She opened the screen door and stepped back for him to enter. She waved her hand toward the living room. The couch, harvest gold wrapped in plastic, was in like-new condition, but styled for earlier times. Every pillow, vase, lamp, knick-knack and curtain vibrated harvest gold. Beverly Staley had clearly stopped moving forward in the mid-nineteen seventies. She wore a dated, brown corduroy jumper over a harvest gold turtleneck pullover. Her long dark hair, tied back by a wood and leather barette, was streaked with gray. The strained formality of her words and actions suggested to O'Riley that she handled unexpected situations with reluctance.

"Please, sit over here." She gestured to a chair backed up against the stairway to the second floor. O'Riley waited for her to take a seat. She chose the straight backed chair near the window. He smiled briefly and letting the smile evaporate, went to work on her.

"Could you give me a rundown on Peyton's life—as you knew it? A few days ago, he turned up beaten, shot and left unconscious in a woman's bathroom where she lay close to death from a fall in her tub. We don't know why. Maybe knowing something in his past will help us find who did this to him."

Beverly's wide eyes blinked nervously at Detective O'Riley, like she was keeping back surprise or shock, even though her face reflected a hint of caution mingled with disbelief.

"I—uh, only know that while we were together, he allowed his entrepreneurial urges to drag us into bankruptcy. When we lost the house, the cars, the success—he lost himself. The drinking started, and not long after that the gambling losses broke him. It was like Jekyll and Hyde—the man I knew was happy and successful. The man he became was obsessed and enraged."

Beverly breathed deeply, as if purging herself of fear and then sat quietly, observing a bird figurine, perched on a twig as if it were about to take flight.

"He left for Chicago three years ago with a job offer in a big firm. He liked the title, the expense accounts and the power the new job provided. But, I heard from him less and less frequently—soon not at all. After another year of silence, I finally filed for divorce and with nothing more than a piece of paper stating our marriage was ended, he disappeared from my life. That's all there is to my connection with Peyton Staley."

Beverly sat deeper into the harvest gold pillow at her back, not smiling, barely breathing. Her lips trembled and taking a deep breath to cleanse her tension, she wiped one tear from the corner of her eye.

"What kind of business did he have—and what was the firm he joined in Chicago? I need some details, if you have them."

Lowering her eyes to the floor and studying the pattern in the worn oriental carpet, Beverly was not going to be hurried. She chose her words carefully, and then she spoke in measured phrases.

"He's a genius, Detective O'Riley. He's a computer wizard with low self-esteem. His small computer based business blossomed and grew so rapidly, he couldn't keep up with it. He had huge corporations standing in line for his services. He's a great salesman but not a businessman. He's a genius in getting computers to think in ways that—well, let's just say he's ahead of his time and has been for twenty years."

She crossed her ankles, smoothed the wrinkle-free skirt over her knees. Then she looked into Office O'Riley's eyes, searching for a glimmer of understanding.

"The sad part is, that when he failed, it was more like he died. He couldn't pull himself out of the depression that set in. When Dayton - Holland Industries hired him, it was like a transformation took place. He had regained some of his former hope, but I guess something went wrong there too, because, like I told you, soon I didn't hear from him any more. He disappeared from my life." Beverly relaxed into the chair. The tension flowed from her muscles until she seemed deflated, hardly breathing.

"Dayton-Holland Industries?" he repeated, writing the name in his notebook.

Beverly shifted her position. "They're a big firm in Chicago—they have a whole building in the heart of the Loop."

"Did you ever know the name of his boss?"

"Yes, let me think—Lenny, uh, Lenny Miller. I think that's it. A real jerk, that man. I met him only once. Self-centered bombastic creep." She stiffened, and breathed in sharply as if catching her breath.

"Excuse me?" Her description caught O'Riley off guard. Her change of tone and the choice of words jumped out at him. His face couldn't hide his surprise.

"Oh, I'm sorry, Officer. I can't help it—the name resurrects some anger for me." Beverly flushed, embarassed by her mood. "Lenny Miller is a very sinister man, Detective O'Riley. He's the kind of person who can be most charming, when he wants you to like him, very engaging. Then, he can turn into a cold, calculating, heartless rogue, someone who could kill with his bare hands. The night he flew Peyton and me to Chicago for a meeting was the only time I met him."

"Could you elaborate for me?"

"Yes, but not much beyond that night." Beverly stood up and walked to the bay window, gazing into the fog, again organizing her response. "I never saw him again, and soon I lost Peyton to him. We went to dinner at one of the finest restaurants in—The Frenchman, I think it was called. Anyway, as the evening progressed, he drank too much wine and began to tell about his company, all the while referring to his employees as his 'little slaves.' If you can imagine it, he made that appellation sound like a joke, but he meant it." She paused, turning into the room, staring at Detective O'Riley with an intensity that could have cut steel. "Peyton looked past the obvious, choosing to see and hear only the salary, the unlimited expense account, the vacation time, the freedom he'd have to do his job his own way."

"Sounds like a corporate protocol to me, and, you know, talking that way isn't a crime."

"No, but after Peyton was working there, in the beginning he'd call to tell me the job wasn't what he'd thought it was. He was unhappy, but the money was so good, he couldn't quit. He uncovered a number of questionable company practices that lined Lenny Miller's wallet and cheated the stockholders. He told me he thought he was being watched, and that because he was doing so well, Lenny had begun to feel insecure."

Beverly stepped into the small kitchen to the left of his chair. "Coffee, Detective O'Riley?" She had passed a threshold, her restraint melted away.

"Sure, black, please. Lenny Miller was insecure?" he said, drawing the conversation back to his purpose as he stood up to stretch his legs.

"Yes. You know, threatened that the new guy would take away

the glory and eventually take over the power base from within the corporate hierarchy."

"I suppose that's not a good thing." He inspected the framed photos on the wall. None of Peyton.

"No, and in fact, the last time I heard from Peyton, he said he had been accused of substance abuse on the job, philandering with the female employees and embezzlement." She returned from the kitchen.

"And?" His question begged an explanation, as Beverly handed him a flowered, porcelain teacup and saucer.

"Well, the substance abuse might have been possible. Philandering—unlikely. Embezzlement—impossible."

"Impossible?" He sipped the burnt tasting java and returned to his chair.

"That kind of criminality is not in Peyton's gene pool. It would be impossible for him to engage in that kind of illegal act. He was the kind of man who made sure his employees were paid, even from his own pocket, as his little company failed. We lost the house, the car, everything because he couldn't hurt the people who were counting on him. No, Detective O'Riley, Peyton was a lot of things, but dishonest? Never."

"What about Dayton-Holland Industries?" He blew on the steaming liquid and sipped again.

"Well, I'm sure Lenny Miller still runs it. But, be careful. He's a vicious soul. He'll stop at nothing to get what he wants." She set her cup on the lace covered table top next to her chair and sat down.

"Do you know where Peyton is living now? We only have a mail box address."

"No, the last I knew he had a studio apartment on Division Street in Chicago. I don't think he even owned a car. He didn't need one in the city, I guess." She unconsciously twisted the ruby ring on her right hand. "Please, don't ever let anyone know you've spoken with me. If Lenny Miller ever knew I had told you what I did, he'd be after me. He's that insecure under the bravado." Her fear was palpable.

"Of course, and thank you, Mrs. Staley." Detective O'Riley put his cup down and stood up. "Could I call upon you again if need be?"

"You're welcome—and no, I'd prefer you not—well, yes, if there's anything more I can do—just let me know." She crossed the small room to the entrance, turned the lock and pulled open the heavy inner door.

"I will, for certain. And thank you again." He stepped onto the small porch, pulled his jacket closed and left her house as quickly as he could, grabbing his cell phone as he reached the curb. "Officer Brown, please." O'Riley stepped into the taxi as Officer Brown responded.

"O'Riley? Any luck?"

"Oh, yeah, and plenty of trouble is brewing for Peyton Staley. I'm catching the next commuter flight back to Chicago. I've got to connect with Lynn Hargrove, that lawyer who came to see me this afternoon. Her number is probably on my desk, check the calendar. Get hold of her. I'll be back in a couple of hours. Okay?" He clicked the phone off, not waiting for an answer.

Lynn was sitting at her desk, trying to sort through a stack of paperwork without much success. Her mind kept returning to Hannah. She startled at the first ring of her phone.

"Hello?"

"Ms. Hargrove?" The male voice on the other end of the line sounded vaguely familiar.

"Yes?"

"This is Detective O'Riley—um, I've got to talk with you—uh, face to face. Could you meet me at Barnaby's Pub in half an hour—it concerns Lenny Miller."

Lynn's attention focused instantly on his tone. The excitement he clearly was trying to conceal left his words edgey and hurried.

"Lenny Miller? Hannah's brother?"

"Yes, I know it sounds improbable, but Peyton Staley—the deliveryman, remember?—worked for Lenny Miller. Isn't that the guy you mentioned at my office?"

"Yes, that's the guy."

"That's all I can tell you over the phone. Will you meet me?"

"The Barnaby's Pub on Division?"

"That's the one."

"All right, I'll meet you there in thirty minutes, give or take for traffic."

Lynn's lethargy disappeared as she pulled on her London Fog trenchcoat and rushed out of her office and to the garage where her Lexus was waiting. Twenty-two minutes later, she stepped into the darkness at Barnaby's Pub and chose a window seat to wait for Detective O'Riley. Only a moment passed before he sauntered through the doorway, squinting into the somber atmosphere to see better.

"Hello, again, Ms. Hargrove." He took the seat across from her. Providing illumination from only one side, the light from the window accentuated the rugged details of Detective O'Riley's face, showing his age and the years of neglect, over indulgence and genetic moles filling some of the ancient acne craters that gave testimony to the ravages of his teenage years.

"Hello, Officer. I've been trying to imagine what possible connection the deliveryman could have with my client."

"The trip to Detroit—remember? I had to go see someone?"

"I remember you left me standing at your desk."

"Yeah, I'm sorry about that. I'm not the best at social graces."

Lynn squeezed a smile and a sarcastic nod in his direction.

"I went there to meet with Peyton Staley's ex-wife. She told me that he once worked for Lenny Miller, and that Miller is a dangerously insecure fellow—one of those genteel charmers with murder lurking just below the surface, ready to explode any second. He hired Staley three years ago, but then destroyed his reputation, professionally speaking, and fired him. I'm thinking there is some kind of link between the attack on your client and the attack on Staley. This Cordoba punk—the one who turned up in the river—is a small time dope peddler, who probably had a gang of other even punkier punks working the streets for him. I'd lay money on that. The slug the doctors took from Staley's chest and from Hannah's thigh was for a .22 caliber—probably an automatic. That's small arms for street punks—more like what a lady would carry."

"Do you have any leads on where he would get such a firearm?"

"Not yet. I'm waiting for ballistics to get back to me. As you know, Hannah's office has been dusted for fingerprints, and we're trying to I.D. what turned up there. I don't think we'll get too much for our efforts. Usually, these gangs leave the breaking and entering to kids who haven't been booked yet—they're getting younger and younger every year—and who are trying to prove themselves to the gang leaders. Our job is harder, since tracking babies is pretty tough."

"Babies?"

"Yeah, kids without records. These are the nameless ones you read about in the papers, or see on the nightly news, who turn up dead in ditches and deserted fields when their usefulness is over. Cordoba rose through the ranks of gangs like that. He very likely used the same process he was taught as he came up in the organization. So, logically, there should be some young kids roaming the streets who know what happened. With Cordoba dead and retribution from him eliminated, we might be able to convince one of them to tell us more about Cordoba's activities."

"Are you saying someone else had been in Hannah's home office before Cordoba?"

"Does—did she ever walk her dog?"

"Yes, now that you mention it, every morning, early, at or just before dawn. That day wouldn't have been any different."

"What's to say that the real break-in happened on the same day as the attack?"

"Suppose the kids were there earlier, even a couple of days earlier, and got the stuff Cordoba wanted, but didn't turn it over."

"Or, they didn't find what he wanted, and he had to come do the job himself."

"How do you find these kids?"

"Informants. Surveillance. Sneaky stuff like that. We usually can collar a kid within a couple of days if he stays in the area. Some of them get scared and split. They're harder to find, but we have a nationwide network trying to locate ordinary runaways—sometimes we come up with fugitive gang members too."

"Time frame?"

"That all depends. I have been lucky and found kids inside of a week. Other times, it can take months. Sometimes, we never find them—alive at least."

"Excuse me, can I get you guys something to drink?" Angel placed one hand on her left hip and shifted her weight to her right foot, clearly a gesture of impatience.

"Hello, Angel." Detective O'Riley raised his eyebrows as if asking Lynn to order.

"I'll just have a Coke, please," Lynn said on cue.

"And, I'll have a cup of coffee, no cream, no sugar."

Angel's face showed curiosity as she shifted her eyes back and forth between her customers. Slipping behind the bar to fill the order, she kept an eye on Lynn and Detective O'Riley. She returned with a small tray in hand.

"Here you are." The glass of ice, the Coke and the mug of coffee took up most of the space on the table.

"Angel? Could I impose on you a second?"

"I suppose so, Detective." Her nails silently tapped on her crossed arms.

"A few nights ago, when Peyton Staley was in here— you know, we talked about it the other day—the night Peyton Staley was in here, did you see anything out of the ordinary— any people he spoke to that maybe seemed out of place—or something?"

She looked upward for a moment, mentally tallying that night's clientele. "No, not really. He had a long conversation with some woman who sat down next to him at the bar, and after that—hmm. Well, later, a couple of young creeps came into the bar, but they didn't talk with him for long. They seemed to be having a dispute of some kind, and then they left. Of course, nobody could have talked with him after he fell asleep."

"Did he fall asleep before or after they left the bar?"

Angel looked up at the ceiling again as she tried to remember the order of events. "After, I'm about ninety-nine percent sure."

"Did either you or the bartender see him on the street in front of the bar—I mean, at closing, when he left?"

"Jack was annoyed with him and essentially threw him out. He told me later that Peyton had fallen down, but Jack isn't the soft-hearted type. He just left him on the sidewalk and came back into the bar to finish cleaning up."

"Did anyone hear any gunshots?" Lynn took a sip of the Coke and wiped the condenstion from the sweating glass.

"If I heard some, I'm sure I thought a car was backfiring—we only get the old, rickety kind in this neighborhood after one or two in the morning. The gangs are out then, and the decent people have all gone home. We hear all kinds of noises that would be strange any other time and think nothing of it."

"So, it's safe to assume you don't know any of the gang members?" Detective O'Riley was leading her.

"You could assume that." Angel's face hardened, like a clay mask drying instantaneously in the sun.

"What about Jack?" Lynn asked. "Bartenders know just about everyone who even passes by their establishments."

"You'd have to ask Jack. I learned a long time ago not to try to speak for him."

"Is he here?" Detective O'Riley glanced toward the door behind the bar, hoping he wasn't fishing in a dry pond.

"Comes in at nine PM. You could ask him then." The phone rang, calling her away from their table. "But, he's not too easy to talk to, unless you're buying and crying in your beer." Angel said as she headed toward the phone. "Typical bartalk bartender." Angel disappeared through the door into the kitchen, leaving the bar phone untouched.

"I'll be back if you will be," Lynn said.

"At nine, then."

"I'll do it this time. Think she'll be insulted by the tip?" Lynn waved a ten dollar bill in the air and dropped it on the table.

"No."

They stepped into the sunlight. "Can I drop you somewhere?" Detective O'Riley asked, blinking in the bright light and shuffling through his pockets for his sunglasses. A soft sigh of relief escaped him as he settled the dark shades on his face.

"No, thanks, I've got some shopping to do. See you tonight," she said as she headed for the sidestreet where she had parked her car. She made sure Detective O'Riley was gone before changing direction and hailing a cab. The garish yellow of the taxi intensified in the ruthless sunlight. The black interior of the car was stuffy and smelled of sweat. "The Dayton-Holland Building, please."

20

Hannah Sebastian?" The voice filled the compartment. "Follow Agent Four."

I tossed a glance in Peyton's direction.

"Peyton Staley?" Another voice spoke. "Follow Agent Four."

We walked toward the farthest end of the hallway outside the compartment. Agent Four was one and the same person, twinned in perfect replication. Tall, lanky in stature he reminded me of a basketball player ill at ease with his height. His brown hair fell in unruly curls to his shoulders and he walked with a slouch as if accustomed to ducking under doorways and low tree branches. We submitted to the system, which we had come to accept as unavoidably in control of their time, to begin living the next level of our sidetracked lives. The train's hallway evaporated, leaving us standing in a train station, feeling the echo of the train's horn more than hearing it.

"This way, please. I am Javier."

Peyton's Javier copied everything my Javier did, although he didn't speak. We walked together for a short distance from the station to an opening between the very large rocks facing the station.

We entered the opening and assembled as a small group in the center of the same cavern we had been in before.

"You will experience the most intense reality of your time with us. What occurs next is called your Final Sidetrack. It's the culmination of what might have happened if you had not followed the original road of your lives. How you handle the events to follow will in great measure determine the outcome of your evaluation. You are free to choose how you handle what comes next. We will return here upon comple-tion of this life sequence before your Final Decision Sympo-sium. Any questions?"

"Yes, just one," Peyton said. "If we are free to choose how we handle what comes next, what is the point of even going through with this life sequence?"

"You are free to choose within the context of the life sequence. You are still confined to this realm until the Processor allows you to pass onto the next level—to return to your original life or to die and receive a new road."

Peyton and I exchanged glances. I understood his meaning as I reached for his hand. Just as he reached to touch mine, he was gone and I found myself again in France.

21

I awakened in a luxurious bedroom in the home of Jacques André-Bouchard. From the window, sand dunes sprawled sensuously into the Atlantic, almost as sensuously as the naked and near-naked bodies of bronzed men and women reclining on blankets and cavorting in the gentle surf. Anyone would immediately fall in love with the Impressionist imagery of the coastline vista, and feel intoxicated by the famous and cultured Jacques André-Bouchard. That he was married, prominent in French business and politics and a ravishing and distinguished fifty-something gentleman of world importance mattered very little to me. I was myself, young, beautiful and irresistibly vulnerable to his whimsy. Sorrow and regret no longer had a place in my life here on the western seaboard of France. The summer was passing quickly, helping me to forget Pamplona's losses and to capture a new life, far from my Midwest American roots.

At first, I slept as late as I could every morning, at minimum until noon nearly all the time. But, by mid-July, I was getting up with the first birds as dawn softened the night sky. I dressed in shorts and a tee shirt, put on a pair of tennis shoes and wandered the labyrinth of tree-lined streets around the André-Bouchard summer home. Weeping willows hung heavy with age, incongruous with the conifers and rhododendrons, the bougainvillea and overgrown bushes that camouflaged the secluded living quarters of every family in the town. I soon became familiar with the dogs and cats that populated the alleyways and side streets. I gathered shells from the water's edge and picked wildflowers from their habitats scattered along the edges of the beach.

Jacques was gentle and caring, respectful of the peace I required to re-establish my personal equilibrium after losing Matthew. He traveled between Paris and Saint-Vincent-de-Tyrosse, attending to his political and business duties during the week and spending the weekends with me. At last, one Sunday in August, I entered the breakfast room to find him reading Le Monde and drinking his café au lait at the wrought-iron table nestled in the glass enclosed alcove that gives out on the ocean.

"Bien dormie, cherie?" he asked, as he always did to be sure I had slept well.

"Yes, of course. Anything of interest in the newspa-per?"

"No, not really. How would you like to come to Paris with me this evening? I've been invited to a gala opening of a new art museum, and I need someone to accompany me."

"Why not Madame André-Bouchard?" During the months of my stay, I had often wondered why her name was never mentioned.

"She's out of the country, partially on official busi-ness, partially to get away from me." He laughed boyishly to make light of his comment.

"Won't people talk? I mean—you are a prominent person. I'm just as happy to wait here until you return."

"No, people won't talk. Unlike in the United States, people here accept other women in the lives of men like me. My wife and

I share a marriage of convenience—the habit dates from the time of the monarchies in Europe. The aristocracy and royalty often married for political or financial reasons. Love was never part of the bargain. I want the world to glimpse the woman I do love. Come with me."

A thrill of excitement sizzled through my being. "But—I don't have anything to wear."

"You are in France, my dear. I'll have a few dresses sent over for you to try. Size eight American, right?"

Dresses for me to try? Is he kidding? Size eight American? Sent over? "Oh, Jacques, have I died and gone to heaven?" I hugged him like a child about to open an unexpected present.

"No, darling. I just want you to be your most beauti-ful. Let me spoil you. You deserve to be the most beautiful of the beautiful."

He looked down at me with tenderness in his eyes. He kissed me long and deliciously. I succumbed to the temptation. I let myself flow through the next few months without concern for the future. The present was delectable and irreverent, a smorgasbord of parties, trips, limousines and unending revelries, until the one evening when the superficiality of my relationship with Jacques André-Bouchard turned ugly.

"Arnaud!" Simone Andre-Bouchard shouted from the kitchen of her Paris three-flat where she was preparing a small plate of pâté de fois gras to use with the remains of the morning's baguette. "Arnaud! Bring me the wine from the cellar, now!"

"Yes, ma petite chouchou, I am coming. I am coming. I have it right here," Arnaud said catching his breath as he entered the room from the cellar door. The stairs leading up from the cellar were nar-row and steep, rutted from the unknowable thousands of footsteps that had for centuries carried wine up from its cool dark cave to the dining room overhead.

"What took you so long, Arnaud? I was beginning to think you had forgotten." Simone's voice lilted with the sudden coquettish playfulness of a schoolgirl.

"I could never forget you, or anything you want. I am yours, your slave, your servant forever." He kissed her cheek.

Simone's eyes betrayed a dark excitement as she carried the plate and two glasses into the eating area on the balcony outside the dining room. Arnaud followed her obediently, dusting the ages from the wine bottle and pulling the corkscrew from his back pants pocket. He deftly uncapped the foil with the point of the screw, and easily turned the tool into the center of the cork. With a quick twist and a short tug, the cork pulled free from the neck of the teal blue bottle, and Arnaud poured the first taste for Simone to judge. She swirled the red fluid with a simple motion of the wrist, coating the sides of the goblet and watching the wine grow its legs. She sniffed the bouquet, sipped a small taste, and drew the air back into her mouth over the wine to test for its maturity.

"Excellent," she half whispered. "Pour us some of this lovely nectar, and then join me, my darling, for a fine moment in our simple lives."

Simone spread some of the pâté on two of the diagonal slices of bread she had cut, and offering one to Arnaud, captured his eyes with hers.

"It is time to bring Jacques to his senses. She must be put to work! He knows it, and we know it. But in the process, this time, I want to cause this new mistress of his some real trouble." She took a bite of her hors d'oeuvre, and with it a sip of the wine.

Arnaud speared a cornichon with the small two-pronged fork and laughed to cover his confusion.

"You mean go yet a step further than last time?"

"No, I only mean to corrupt her to her soul."

"Oh, Simone, why this constant obsession to humiliate his mistresses? Why can't you live and let live? You have me—remember?"

"Because he destroyed me, and don't you ever forget it," she said with a flash of rage. Then, quickly gaining control over her emotions, Simone continued. "She's a tutor for his influential friends in the government. She has contact with some of the highest-ranking members of the Assemblée Nationale. When the right time presents itself, we will invite Jacques and that little American tart he has taken up with, and we shall enjoy getting to know her better."

Arnaud stared over the top of his wineglass, sinking into the heady sense of well being the claret imposed upon him. "I am not sure of your meaning, cherie. Why would you want to spend even a moment with them, when it will cause you such pain?"

"She is too much in love with him. We must destroy that love— use it to destroy him. I am not willing to sit by and allow him to love her."

"He doesn't love her. He's only infatuated by her," Arnaud said.

"No, no! She is different from all the others, some-how. She is too perfect: sad, yet joyous; innocent, yet worldly; pure, and not yet soiled. We can make that work for us. We can change it all to eliminate her from his heart. Better yet, we can tear him from hers."

Arnaud began to nod his head. A smile without a joyous foundation formed on his lips. "I think I understand. You, Jacques and I will convince her to help his career—just as we have done with the others—when he brings her up to Paris."

"Yes, yes. That's right. We'll all be very pleasant. We'll take her to a restaurant and then we'll all three convince her to do what is best for Jacques' career." They both lifted their glasses in a silent toast.

"To his career!" they said and drank the champagne to the last drop.

"I would like to book a round trip ticket on an international flight, please." Prime Minister, Pierre Alain Duclos spoke slowly, his English thick with the dipthong laden southern French accent common to Provence in the south of France.

"Good! Good!" I encouraged him. Then playing the part of the airport ticket agent, I said, "Where would you like to travel, sir?"

"I would like to travel to New York, please."

"What dates would you like to travel?"

"I would like to leave on May third and return on June tenth."

"First class or coach?" I looked up when Monsieur Duclos hesitated.

"Qu'est-ce que c'est 'coach', Mademoiselle?"

"Seconde classe, Monsieur."

"Oh, non, pas seconde classe. Not second class, Miss," he said switching to English in an effort to keep me happy. "I would prefer first class, thank you."

My cell phone vibrated in my dress pocket, distracting me from the lesson.

"Yes, sir. I have a flight departing at four-thirty in the afternoon," I said, as I slipped the phone from my pocket and checked the number calling. Seeing that it was Jacques, I smiled at Monsieur Duclos. "I am afraid I must take this call—je dois décrocher, Monsieur—que je m'excuse un instant?"

The Prime Minister nodded and smiled in a conspira-torial way. "C'est Jacques, n'est-ce pas?"

I laughed. "But of course—mais oui." I stood up and moved quickly into the corridor, gently closing the door and nodding at one lawyer who passed me on the far side of the marbled hall. "Jacques, what do you need? I am giving Monsieur Duclos his English lesson."

"Meet me at La Tour d'Argent for dinner at eight o'clock. Simone and Arnaud want to dine with us this evening." He tone was crisp, as if he was in a hurry to make plans and get on with something else.

"Jacques? Is something wrong?"

"No, darling. I just want to get Simone off my back about meeting you. I hate to spend time in her company. I hate even more time spent with Arnaud."

"Hate is a strong word, Jacques. Why does she want to meet me? I can't possibly be of any interest to her."

"Well, as unpleasant as it is to acknowledge, you are not the first woman I have known outside my marriage to Simone. She has taken the habit of meeting the women I am seeing, especially if she thinks the woman is anything special to me. I indulge her to get her to leave me alone, which she usually does."

"You are sure we should do this? I have no interest in meeting her."

"Trust me. This will be the only time, and we can go on as we have. Please, darling, let's get this behind us."

"La Tour d'Argent it is, then. At eight."

"At eight." Jacques hung up without his customary kiss into the phone. I closed my phone just as Monsieur Duclos opened the door to his office.

"Miss, I must stop our lesson," he said, clearly trying to keep to English. "There is an important meeting—an unscheduled meeting—I must attend. Can you forgive me?"

"Yes, of course." I entered the office and crossed to the magnificent Louis XV desk that stood proudly on the edge of the Gobelin carpet in front of the enormous, ornately carved white marble fireplace. I jotted something on a page in the Prime Minister's tutoring notebook. "That is your devoir, Monsieur. Please practice for your next lesson."

"But of course," Pierre Alain Duclos said, smiling as he opened the door to the corridor. "Until next time, Miss."

"Yes, until next time." I hurried down the curving staircase that led from the offices in the Elysée to the main foyer. I winked at the guards standing at the open doorway. "Au revoir!" I said to them. I walked quickly along the peripheral sidewalk, avoiding the pea-gravel of the courtyard, which had a habit of getting inside my shoes.

Monsieur Duclos was my last lesson of the day, and I had to get ready for the dinner that evening. I hailed a taxi, and returned to Jacques' apartment to bathe, dress and arrive at La Tour d'Argent without a minute to spare.

Jacques was standing with Simone and Arnaud, as my taxi pulled in front of the world-renowned restaurant. He opened the door for me and helped me get out of the taxi.

"We'll manage this just fine," he whispered in my ear as he kissed me on both cheeks. "Let her have her way—it is better for everyone if she is not upset."

After introductions, Jacques and I followed Arnaud and Simone into the entrance foyer of La Tour d'Argent. Simone took control of the moment and chose a magnum bottle of Moët Chandon from the menu of the sommelier, instructing him to chill the champagne to icy perfection. Having done so, we took our apéritifs in the bar, as we waited—however briefly—for our table. The sommelier gracefully poured four flutes and placed them at just the right distance from the other wine glasses. His stoic face, graced by curious eyes that seemed to be taking in every detail of the way the rich and famous dined, showed no emotion as he went about his duties.

SIDETRACKS

I had heard of and had even studied about La Tour d'Argent while still a graduate student. I knew the history of the restaurant, which has endured since 1582 as the finest culinary experience in Paris. The several story building takes in three addresses along the Quai de la Tournelle on the Left Bank of the Seine just across from Notre Dame and not very far from the Champs Elysée. Since the Middle Ages it has catered to the culinary delight of kings, queens, powerful politicians, the most successful business leaders and famous glitterati from all over Europe. Mingling with the well-heeled upper classes are the under-foot tourists—mostly Americans and Japanese—who know enough to search out this gustatory delight, but not enough to recognize who is sitting at the tables around them. Rarely do Parisian waiters pay much attention to the bits of conversation they hear as they come and go, serving the every need of their clients, but ours was clearly an exception to this indifference. He lingered a moment too long, or returned a minute too early, interrupting our conversations with useless inquiries as to our needs.

I felt an odd uneasiness as the waiter returned to our table with a message for Jacques.

"Sir, you are wanted on the phone," he said. "You may take it in the small meeting room to the left of the entrance, sir."

"Certainly." Jacques acquiesced. He brushed his lips against my cheek and whispered, "I'll be right back, darling. I am sure this will take no time at all."

The call must have been important, beyond the usual requirements of his duties, for him to take the phone and leave the table so easily. It put me ill at ease. I did not want to spend time alone with Simone and Arnaud.

"Garçon!" Simone snapped her fingers with authority, a sharp crackle, so like a twig breaking under the weight of a hunter's heavy boot as he moved stealthily through the forest in search of prey, invisible yet deadly. The waiter responded with obedience, as if without a will to do otherwise, robotic yet humiliatingly congenial.

"Oui, Madame?" He half-bowed with the air of a conscripted slave.

"More champagne. Again Moët Chandon. Your best."

"Oui, Madame."

"I think our meeting requires a bit of celebration," Simone said, too sweetly, too gratuitously. "It isn't every day that Jacques and I can sit at the same table with our significant others and achieve the appearance of sociability."

"I would say it is more than that." Arnaud's words in-terrupted her, accompanied by an intense stare that flashed from his odd expression, which quickly transformed into a clown-like masque of frivolity. "We have so much to learn from this lovely young woman, don't you think, my dear?"

"Yes, we do." Simone's words fell from her lips like pebbles dropped from the hand of a child who had decided not to throw them into the pond, one no longer curious about what might radiate from the gesture.

"Let us take this into the cellar. We'll have dinner brought down to the secluded dining room hidden among the historical bottles of great wines far below the streets of Paris."

I heard the words, but did not understand their mean-ing. I knew La Tour d'Argent had a world-renowned collec-tion of wines, and that favored guests were occasionally allowed to dine in the cel-lars. But I felt the hair crawl on my neck as the waiter stood behind my chair to assist me in getting up.

"What about Jacques? Shouldn't we wait for him?" I felt myself succumb to the tension of fear creeping up my spine.

"Oh, that's not necessary. He'll follow along in a few minutes. The headwaiter will inform him of the changes. Come along. You'll see one of the wonders of Paris."

Simone and Arnaud stood swiftly, leading the way to-ward the elevators. I had no choice but to follow, so unfamil-iar with the rules, so insecure without Jacques at my side, and so sure the patrons of the restaurant scrutinized our every move as we moved across the room.

The waiter managed the century-old elevator with care, slow-ly closing the wrought iron doors, slowly turning the handle that lowered the cage two or three stories below the street level into the depths of the caverns below. The musty air flowing into the elevator from below was tinged with a floral scent, as if to cover the smell of decay. When the doors again opened, before us was a softly illumi-nated octagonal foyer, with several recessed cases holding aged and rare bottles of cognac, each with a small plaque indicating the owner, year, vineyard and other historical information. There was a small round table in the center of the room, set for dinner for four. I read the plaques with a feigned fascination, trying to delay any further dis-course with either Simone or Arnaud until Jacques could join us.

"Your champagne, Madame," the wine steward said, as he en-tered the foyer from the only door, other than the elevator. We each took the glass handed to us. I sipped the bubbles and savored the flavors of the liquid, watching Simone and Arnaud move about the room from my peripheral vision.

"This is delicious champagne," I said in a feeble at-tempt to make conversation.

"You know, Hannah, Jacques needs to have influence over cer-tain powerful members of the government," Simone began.

"No, I didn't know," I said, suspicious of the conver-sation's leap from champagne to government officials.

"You could be quite helpful to him in this regard," Arnaud continued.

"Me? How is that possible?"

Simone and Arnaud returned to their places at the table, just as Jacques returned from the phone call. His eyes searched the room as he pulled in his chair. I looked to him for a signal, some sign that all was well. It was not to be.

"Hannah," Jacques said, handing me a slip of paper. "These are some new students for you. They are very impor-tant people who can influence the legislation I need to be able to expand my holdings around the world."

I glanced down the list. I recognized the names of the ministers of commerce, agriculture and international trade. There were several names I did not recognize, but that seemed unimportant as I looked at Jacques, Simone and Arnaud.

"You know, I was the first to help Jacques—early in his career—to succeed in the expansion of his winery. I worked hard to see that those who could make his success a reality were well treated, didn't I, Jacques?"

"Yes, Simone, you were the first."

"Others have been instrumental in their turn, and now it is your privilege to participate in his expansion into global markets."

"I don't understand how I can possibly help. I know nothing about wine or international commerce. I tutor English. How can that be helpful?" A long silence greeted me as I considered the juxtaposition of the list of new students and my work as a tutor.

"Well," Arnaud said, quietly breaking the silence and the thread of confusion in my mind. "Actually, tutoring would be only a part of your job."

Again, an uncomfortable silence settled on the cellar. I saw Jacques, Simone and Arnaud considering my reactions the way a trio of musicians might consider an unrehearsed work by Mozart. I felt them silently absorbing my responses, preparing for the first remark I might make.

"You could simply agree to go to dinner with any one of these gentlemen, if and when they invite you to accom-pany them," Simone said with a haughty tone in her voice.

"And, you could accept their gifts of flowers and jewelry, which will certainly follow your time with them," Arnaud continued, nodding and raising his eyebrows to imply some-thing more than dinner would transpire.

"But, if you refuse, I would have to remove you from my employ," Jacques said, "and that would be very regrettable."

"Your employ?" I was astonished. "You consider me to be working for you, Jacques?" I searched his face for an answer to my question. Finding none, I considered my situation. I was in love with Jacques André-Bouchard. I depended on him for my life. I was afraid of life alone, even incapable of surviving without him, in the way I imagined abused women feel they must go on in horrible marriages in spite of the brutality they suffered. I had given up my family ties, my fiancé was dead, I tutored English to men who were unlikely to ever learn it—given their advanced years, and I sat at a table with the wife of the man I loved and her live-in playmate, as they all were trying to convince me to service members of the government in ways that had nothing to do with tutoring English.

"Essentially, cherie, you can help me achieve the next plateau of my success. You be good to these gentlemen, and because they will be good to me, I will be good to you." Jacques spoke firmly, the way a parent speaks to a child, leaving no option for a contradictory remark.

I knew I had little choice but to agree, out of my love for Jacques, my fear of abandonment, and the words that Simone spoke next.

"I was the first. There have been many. And you won't be the last. Jacques married me for the convenience it provides in his business. Men like him are married. But, never happily married. So, they have mistresses, and they share these women with each other—doing favors that have no financial recriminations in the paper trails of banks and brokerage houses—but influence peddling, nonetheless."

"It was a shame what happened to the last one," Arnaud said, shaking his head. "She was so beautiful before the accident."

I looked from one face to the next, trying to grasp the sense of what I was hearing.

"Yes, the fire in her cabana on the Riviera was tragic. At least she escaped with her life." Simone's eyes smoldered with hatred. "Even though she has had to undergo so many reconstructive surgeries to restore even a semblance of a face, at least she didn't die, like the girl before her. Such a shame to trip while walking across a glacier in the Alps and fall into a bottomless crevasse when the footing gives way."

"Jacques?" My question evaporated into the air as I saw the look in his eyes: Do this or die.

As I first awoke, I could hardly see the room around me. I looked for anything familiar. There was nothing familiar in the room. I could tell it was morning from the soft glow around the curtains. The candles had burned out. The room smelled of sweat, wax and sweet perfume. I licked my lips, trying to moisten them, but tasted only the salty stickiness of blood. I was lying naked in the tangle of rumpled sheets. The sensation of isolation gave way to pain. My groin was throbbing. My hands and feet ached. I felt scratches all over my body. I soon understood why it was hard to see. Swollen nearly shut, my eyes and my cheeks wouldn't move when I tried to squint. A migraine-like agony pounded inside my head. Then the door swung open.

"Good morning, cherie. How are you this morning? Feeling a bit under the weather?"

"Simone, you bitch. Let me out of here!" I screamed in my mind because I couldn't form the words. My mouth was a mass of bulging flesh.

"I can tell you want me to leave you alone," she said. "Here, this will make you feel better—I apologize, your companion was a little rough with you," she admitted as she injected me. "I promise tonight your guest will be a little gentler."

"Tonight? No! Nothing will happen tonight!" I could only think my words. The drug worked fast. "Don't do this!" I tried to struggle, but my body let go of itself as I drifted into a stupor.

The same sequence of events was repeated day in and day out. I would go to tutor my students—there were perhaps ten on my list—and I would see two every day on a rotating schedule. In the evenings, I would meet one of the men I had tutored that day for dinner. Then, when we would arrive at the arranged hotel, usually in a darkened back street in the seamier parts of Paris, Arnaud or Simone administered the drug in increasingly larger doses, until I could not last the hours between injections. Eventually, I was no longer tutoring. I stayed in a room in some nameless hotel. The drugs weakened me, until food, clothing, water, and companionship no longer mattered. All I wanted was for one of them to give me my drug. I couldn't escape them at first, and later I didn't want to leave. Then one morning as he entered my room for the first time in months, Jacques spoke to me.

"Hannah," he said, "I want you to please a couple of my friends who are coming over to see you. They will be here in a short while. So, go over to the armoire and choose a dress to wear. These are very important people, and I want you to look your best."

I tried to sit up. I was too weak.

"Here, let me help you," he said, taking my arm and pulling me to a sitting position. He was not gentle with me, but he clearly wasn't trying to hurt me either. He scooped my feet together and pulled them over the edge of the bed. I fell sideways. He pulled me up to a slouch and then took my hands to pull me forward to my feet. I collapsed on the floor.

"Stand up! Get to your feet, whore!"

I managed to roll over on my hands and knees. My head fell downward. I couldn't hold it up.

"Get up, bitch!"

Reaching up to him for help, he laughed at me.

"Crawl, tramp, crawl to get your clothes."

I crawled toward the open armoire. I reached it. I pulled myself up, using the shelves as leverage. The nearly transparent red chiffon dress hung from a single wire hanger in the armoire. My balance was returning as I lifted it off the wire and over my head to let it slither into place on my body. The mirror reflected my every move. I watched with dazed eyes as my image sharpened in the glass.

"Oh, my God!" My mind screamed. I turned around to see Jacques leering at me. I looked back at the mirror. Still visible bruises, though on the mend, scattered across my face and upper body like patches on a tattered coat. My arms and legs were stick-like, barely defined by any muscular curvature. My skeletal torso, visible through the cloth, matched the dark-circled eyes staring from sunken sockets. My once radiant complexion emitted a grayish pallor that suggested dust and decay. I touched the veins on my forearms, protruding dark and web-like from the effects of the needles and the drugs.

"Oh, my God! You've destroyed me." I began to cry. I cried until I could hardly breathe. Jacques held a handkerchief out to me. I tried to wipe away the tears and the slobber. Anger infested my heart.

"Hungry?" He held a tall glass of white liquid out to me. I nodded.

"Will you be good?"

I nodded a second time. I sucked pathetically on the straw to drink the thick, milky liquid. The gritty texture tasted like ground vitamin tablets poorly mixed into melted ice cream. At least it was sweet, and the sugar infused me with energy no one could have known I would derive from such a concoction. When I was a child, sugar made me hyperactive. As an addict to the drug Jacques André-Bouchard, Simone and Arnaud had used on me, sugar provided me just enough sustenance to regain control of my thoughts.

I was glad I couldn't clearly remember many details of my encounters with Jacques' influential friends or how long a time I had been working as a call girl. I was vaguely aware that the drugs were to prevent me from struggling against their depraved actions with my body.

I was glad I couldn't remember the beatings that showed on my reflection in the mirror. I imagined the marks to be the remains of the rages these men expressed at my expense. I was sure I should have been thankful I cried too hard to talk. I imagined I would have been killed for what I might have said.

The absence of the drug caused unbearably painful muscle spasms when one of them withheld an injection. They denied me the drug periodically to remind me of the control they had over me. Jacques timed his arrival, or Simone or Arnaud's arrival, to coincide with beginning of tremors and sweats.

"I see you are ready for me," Simone would always say, as Arnaud stood at the door with a lecher's smirk on his face.

In his turn, Jacques would taunt me. "Let's see how long it takes for you to beg for relief."

I always shook my head in response. If I screamed at him, he slapped me and threw me against the wall. If I cried, he raped me. If I remained unresponsive, he left me to the ravages of early withdrawal, watching the progression of tremors and sweating bloom into muscle contortions, until I writhed on the floor in agony. If I shook my head with a pleading look in my eyes, if I projected true compliance and begged only with my facial expression, he took pity and injected me. Most of the time, I had no control of which response my body would make. It took all my strength to scream. It took all my courage to shake my head and plead.

I began to have thoughts of escape. These thoughts were my only solace and came to me only in the few lucid moments just after eating and before the injections. I noticed the visits from Jacques' friends were becoming less frequent. Simone and Arnaud stopped coming to the room as well. Jacques appeared only once in a great while. He ignored me except to relieve his urges. A large woman with enormous, masculine hands brought me the drink and the injection, five or six times a day, always just as the drug was beginning to wear off. She watched me drink and then she injected me. The routine was simple. I was always compliant.

One night, as the nameless woman arrived at my door, I decided to act on my thoughts. She set the drink on the table, and I picked it up. I drank most of the liquid as quickly as I could, watching the thick white substance dimin-ish as I drank. Just as I had planned, I threw the glass at the window, shattering both. She came at me. I bared my teeth like a wild dog and, drooling white foam from the drink, I screamed at her. She backed away as I hunched my back and raised my hands like claws, lunging in her direction, screaming again. This exertion took a toll on my strength.

"Monsieur! Madame! She is crazy! She is rabid—like a mad dog!" The woman bolted from the room. The counter-balanced door swung shut. I had only a few seconds to grab a long shard of the windowpane and to wrap one end of it in a pillowcase so I could hold it. Holding it close to my side, I turned myself so it would not be immediately visible to anyone entering the room. Only another few seconds passed until the key turned in the lock. The door opened. Pausing only a moment to assess the damage to the window, Jacques entered the room.

"Hannah, you won't get away with this. I heard the window. I know what you're thinking. Now, hand me the shard of glass."

I couldn't move, though the sweating had begun and I was beginning to shiver. I shook my head. Jacques stepped forward. I bared my teeth and growled a warning. He stepped forward until he was just one step away from me.

"Hannah, hand me the glass," he said, slowly raising his hand toward me.

The heat of adrenaline infused a long forgotten sense of power into my body. For a few brief seconds, I at last had the upper hand. The shard of glass slashed his wrist as I brought the weapon upward from my side. He grabbed his arm in pain and bent over to slow the blood spurting from the deep gash. I thrust the shard deep into the muscles at the back of his neck, as I brought it down with all my strength. I made sure to sever his spinal column. I hated to make it easy for him, sparing him the pain of dying like this. I couldn't avoid the anger of knowing he felt so little agony before falling to the floor.

I had killed the man I had once loved. I killed him for all the abused women in the world. I killed him to save the others who might have come along and fallen for his charm. I killed him for the daughters I had never had. I killed him to liberate my soul from the prison of the heart I had built in the name of love.

I knew my time was short. I pulled a sheet from the bed, wrapped it around myself and staggered through the door, not knowing where I was or which way to go. The hall led toward a stairway. Not having walked anywhere in months, I had to negotiate the risers with the ache of moving my legs helping me to stay conscious and using the banister as a crutch to descend the stairs. Exhausted, I arrived at the bottom, where a large foyer yawned before me toward a heavy oak door on the opposite side.

Tremors took control of me. I had to get across the foyer and out the door. I was shaking in spasms as I hurled myself toward the door. My hand could hardly grasp the handle. Locked! Oh, God, no! The windows on each side of the door begged me to break them. A chair on the facing wall mocked me. It would break the window for me. My strength was going. I had only to drag it and then lift it. I would never know how I made the chair fly through the window. Not stopping to consider that I had nowhere to go, I climbed out the jagged opening, cutting my feet on the shattered glass as I ran from my prison into the streets of Paris.

I stumbled from building to building, pounding pathetically on windows trying to get help. No one answered. I was losing what little strength I had left flailing uselessly against the barren walls of a dark and deserted side street in the city of lights. The tremors and contractions took permanent hold of me as I reached an intersection. The lights and bustle of the Champs Elysée burned my eyes and ears. Where there had been no one, now there were crowds of late night revelers, chatting and laughing as they strolled up and down the great boulevard.

They saw me! They would help me! I fell to my knees, shaking and reaching out for help. They walked a safe distance around me, their faces shocked and disapproving of my condition. My sheet was bloody and filthy from dragging through the gutter. I couldn't speak. I could not see myself as they did—a wormy scab from the underside of society. They could not see me as I did—a helpless young woman, battered and depraved by drugs administered against her will.

"Au secours! Au secours! Help me!" I seethed at them through my chattering teeth. They either chose not to understand me, or they could not. I'll never be sure which. But, as I fell onto the pavement, writhing in agony from the advancing drug withdrawal, a gentle hand touched my shoulder.

"Soeur Amélie, it's a young, lost woman." The two nuns leaned over to determine what was wrong with me.

"She needs medical attention to save her. The withdrawal is strong."

Sister Amélie stood upright and walked resolutely toward the next gentleman she saw.

"Monsieur? You will stop and help us."

The man stepped back to try to avoid Sister Amélie's request.

"God is entrusting you with a soul," she said, touching his arm as a gesture of kindness.

"Yes, Sister." He realized he must act within the confines of the French Good Samaritan laws that require the passers-by to help the sick and injured.

"What do you need me to do?"

"Lift her up and carry her to our cloister. It is just around the corner. We can see her through the next hours and days it will take to rid her of the drugs that have crazed her."

"Yes, Sister."

I looked into the stranger's eyes as picked me up into his arms. I felt as if every tissue in my body would tear apart and yet for the first time in over a year, I felt safe. He looked into my eyes and saw nothing familiar there.

Agony came in waves. The sisters and he managed to carry me into the small cloister as the tremors subsided for a few moments. He laid me on the cot and stepped from the room, embarrassed to be inside the living quarters of a religious order.

"How will you tend to her?" the man asked.

"It is our calling to minister to the drug afflicted children of God. We know the cures and have help from doctors when we cannot make the cure ourselves. Now, please feel free to go."

"But who will pay for the treatments?"

"We receive donations at the Cathedral of Notre Dame. The priests provide us a small budget."

"Let me augment their help." The man reached into his coat for his portefeuille. He removed ten one-thousand-franc notes and handed them to Sister Amélie.

"Use this for her needs. Provide her the cures and a future. Let me know if you need anything more for the others you tend." He placed the money in Sister Amélie's hand and left. Sister Amélie held the money out for Sister Anna to see.

"Oh my!" Sister Anna said. "Can you believe your eyes?" She picked up the card. "Monsieur must be very well to do."

"God provides for those he loves. This girl must have much more to accomplish in her lifetime. We have been entrusted with her recovery. We are blessed and so must she be."

Sister Amélie and Sister Anna represented the last of the order of the Sisters of Notre Dame de Navarre, a little known sect, which originated in Germany in the 1200's and blossomed in France in the early 1800's. The original ministry served orphaned children and the poor. They continued the work of their predecessors, Sister Mary Joseph and Sister Mary Margaret, who tried to answer the needs of the present day by rendering care and cures to the drug addicted poor of Paris. Like so many of the old religious orders, their numbers had dwindled to near non-existence. From the moment the gentleman helped them bring me to their cloister, their donation box filled to overflowing every Sunday at the noon Mass in the most famous cathedral in the world.

These two gentle middle-aged nuns spent their time and the stranger's money nursing me back to health. They made no attempt to bring me into their order, no attempt to convince me that my mistreatment at the hands of Jacques, Simone and Arnaud somehow required me to seek seclusion from the world in devotion to God. Instead, they purified my body, fed me, and allowed me to talk in complete confidence about the events of the previous months.

One morning, Sister Anna brought me the newspapers she had saved and let me vent my anger as I read how the news media made much of the mysterious death of Jacques André-Bouchard. There was no clear explanation of who might have killed him. Inevitably, no one could guess that he had been keeping a sex slave, and predictably, none of the men who had abused me came forward to confess any knowledge of the events that had taken place in that Paris hotel.

The authorities finally decided that he had somehow fallen against the window and that his death was accidental. Of course, he was given a grand funeral, with a long cortège that wound its way through Paris to the Cathedral of Notre Dame. His body was then returned to his hometown of Saint-Vincent-de-Tyrosse. Only the nuns and I knew the truth of the matter. I decided not pursue a course of retribution, choosing instead to spend my days in silent meditation.

As I was sitting on a bench in the courtyard of the cloister, taking in the morning sun, Javier appeared. I knew he had come for me.

"So, Hannah, you have lived your Sidetrack. It is time for your Final Decision Symposium."

"I want to leave the nuns a message—I can't just disappear."

"No, they are not actually living beings, remember. All of this was a Sidetrack. You have no choice." The courtyard evaporated, and I was standing alone in the cave where Peyton and I had last seen each other.

22

I looked around the oval table at the faces of the few remaining stockholders and my new Asian and Israeli allies. The absence of Hollingsworth and Andersen fueled my energy.

" —We are gathered here today to witness the complete restructuring of this great corporation."

The silence from the stockholders and the unchang-ing smiles of the Asians and Israelis allowed me to continue.

"I have taken it upon myself to weather the storms of disaster and to guide our beleaguered business through the choppy waters of despair. We have lost the confidence of the Market. We have lost the majority of our financial backers. We have fired the faint at heart direction that brought this corporation to its knees. Orson Stillwell, our genius organic chemist who has created a revolutionary and viable biomolecular computer, brings you news that will restore your confidence in MACROWORLD and in your own choice to sustain your hope for the future of our biomolecular technology. Orson?"

I waved my hand toward Orson as if introducing a vaudeville act. Orson stood at his chair, hesitant to speak. Clearing his throat several times, he finally addressed the group.

"In recent weeks, our competitors have flooded the market-place with super-microchips that contain electronically store data at exceptionally high capacities. I am here to announce and MAC-ROWORLD will withdraw from the production of electronic super-microchips and why."

There was a gasp from the audience. Orson shifted his weight as if centering himself for what he was going to say next. He looked to the farthest back wall to avoid catching anyone's gaze directly.

"I am announcing the beginning of production of MACRO-WORLD's microscopic DNA computers that will be able to course through human veins and arteries and which are capable of diagnosing and treating an infinite variety of ailments at the molecular level. Our revolutionary biochip confines millions of snipped DNA strands on its surface instead of the millions of electronic circuits on conventional computer chips, microchips, or super-microchips. They store as much information as one trillion—yes, I said one trillion—compact disks on one gram of DNA. One gram of DNA equals the size of an ice cube. And, they consume very little energy while producing no heat to cause malfunctions so common to their electronic predecessors."

A low grumbling rose from some of the stockholders, all of whom were shaking their heads in disbelief, as Orson shuffled back to his place. The Asians and Israelis were still smiling. I gathered my courage and stood again to speak.

"Thank you, Orson. I am sure your words have stunned our guests. But, I must assure you the information you read about in the press regarding the failure of our super-microchips was true. I know the skeptics will speak loud and long against us, but in the next few weeks, the actual demon-stration of the developmental quantum leap our BMCs and biochips represent to the medical community will silence them all. Hang on to your stocks. They will be worth fortunes in short order. I am now going to adjourn the meeting with the full confidence that you will have all your questions answered in due time."

I motioned to Orson and we disappeared into my office before the others could respond. We could hear the cacophony of voices pouring into the hallways as the stock-holders began to express their discomfort to each other.

"Great job, Orson." I pumped Orson's hand vigor-ously. "We did it! Now all that is left is to inform the world."

"Sir? I need the contracts. I think to wait any longer is fool-hardy." Orson said.

"We agreed you would receive your contracts as soon as the BMCs and biochips entered production." I patted him on the back and laughed in a collegial way.

"Well, I've changed my mind," he said without humor and drawing away from me. "I will not release the bio-engineering specs nor the complex of drawings and details for production until my contracts are signed and registered. The patents must be issued in my name only, and I will negotiate the exclusive rights to their use to MACROWORLD. These conditions must be met within the week, or I will take my work elsewhere." He stood straight and rigid.

"Orson, you can't get away with this. Our agreement is in writing. Our partnership is in writing. You can't go against that." The vertebrae in my back loosened as I spoke.

"My attorneys say otherwise. Your part of the agreement is contingent on mine. If I will not disclose my work, then you have nothing. I am not beholding to you, Peyton. I am not tied to you. There are hundreds of compa-nies in the world that would jump at the chance to produce my BMCs and biochips and could do so every bit as well as yours can, and you know it."

Orson's uncharacteristic stubbornness shook my confidence.

"But, we've opened our mouths. The news is out. The stockholders, the international team of developers, the financial backers all know what you have created." I was sure my face showed utter disbelief. "You and I agreed to enter into the restructuring of MACROWORLD together, as a team. I trusted you."

"And, I trusted you. All I am asking is that the contracts be signed and registered before I release the work. That's in my own interest. You cannot screw me over if the contracts are signed, sealed and delivered. It's a simple thing, Peyton. Make good on your part of the deal and I will too. Easy."

I quickly calculated the consequences of manipulating Orson's holdings. My early morning buy up of stock to secure majority control would certainly be revealed.

"Orson, is there something you want that I don't know about?"

"Yes."

"Well?"

"Control."

"Control of what?"

"My work, its development and exploitation. My ideas and the wealth they will earn."

"You already have that."

"No, Peyton. You do. Or—I should say, you would have had."

"What are you telling me?"

"That I know about your stock buy up. I know why you wanted me to wait for the contracts until after the production of my BMCs and biochips."

"Why?"

"So you could eliminate me from the equation."

SIDETRACKS

"Eliminate you? I couldn't have developed MACROWORLD without you."

"That's right, but once the BMCs and biochips are in production, you might have no more need for me. Remember what you said at the meeting."

"I said what we had planned to say."

" 'I know the skeptics will speak loud and long against us, but in the next few weeks, the actual demonstration of the developmental quantum leap our BMCs and biochips represent to the medical community will silence them all. Hang on to your stocks. They will be worth fortunes in short order.' Remember? And, we both know that once in production, further substantive development is impossible. What about the talented international team members of the meeting? What is their role? Not invention. To develop application after application for one use after another. The originator would not need to be available to them even for consultation. No, Peyton, you would find a way to eliminate me."

"Orson, how can you think? "

"Because you eliminated so many others and drove the stocks and MACROWORLD into the ground just to gain control. You have no scruples, Peyton." Orson's fists clenched. "I see that now. I didn't see it before. So, produce the contracts for signing, or I go elsewhere. I'll give you until four this afternoon to add this condition to them and make them available. It will only take a week for the lawyers to transfer the patents to my name. Only then will the exclusive rights of production go to MACROWORLD."

Orson stood up from the chair and ambled toward the door, slowly opened it and stepped into the hall, turning back to face me.

"I hope you'll do the right thing. It could be such a great adventure."

He closed the door and was gone.

SIDETRACKS

I sat motionless for a moment, stunned. "Who would have guessed?" I pushed the intercom button.

"Andrea, bring in the contracts for Orson. Notify our attorneys that we need an addendum to sign the patents over to him before he'll release the work for production. He's given us a week—I want it done this afternoon."

I opened the bar and poured an Irish whiskey. I guzzled it and poured another.

Who would have thought the geek could be so gutsy as to demand his rights before production? No loss. I'd just fix the damn contracts to give him what he wants, at a price of course. My thoughts were running away with me. The phone rang. I stared at it, took a couple more swigs on the whiskey and on the fifth ring, I answered. It was my attorney.

"Staley, here."

"Peyton? It's Allen. What's this about the contracts and patents?"

"Orson wised up. He wants his work protected in his name only before production. He'll give us exclusive rights, of course, but he's not going to release anything until he's got what he wants."

"I don't think this is wise. Corporate control of the patents is essential. Otherwise, there is nothing to prevent his leaving at any time in the future—when the rights agreement runs out—or even before—what then?"

"You know and I know that once our BMCs and biochips are in the marketplace there will be plenty of attempts to make clones and knockoffs. Someone will eventually figure out the secrets of Orson's vision. But no one will be able to reproduce it. He's made sure of that with the biocodes and micro-bioinfusers. What are we afraid of? That the genius will take over the business? No, Allen, he'll get his due, that's all."

"It's my advice to you to try to prevent the patents from slipping away. He doesn't trust you, and now, you'll never again be able to trust him."

"Trust has never been a part of big business, Allen. He's got us in a vice. Make the rights agreement for a hun-dred years or some-time frame that extends beyond all our lives. Then there will be no problem." I took a long draft from my whiskey glass. "Find a way to embed the time limits deep in the recesses of the contracts so he's basically unaware of how long the agreement lasts—in perpetuity is a good term. Forever is a long time. Solve this problem, Allen. And make sure, if anything happens to Orson everything goes to MAC-ROWORLD. What if he turns up sick, disabled or worse? You're the legal wizard here. Cover all the bases and do it today."

"But, Peyton—"

"Just do it!"

I slammed the phone down and swallowed the last of the whiskey. Whirling my chair around to face the view from my window, I waited for the feeling of power to return. It did, but with a dark shadow cooling the passion.

"Andrea?" I punched the intercom button several times before I was sure she heard me. "I'm going home early. Call the car."

Minutes later, I sat safely hidden in the rear of the limousine, behind the nearly black tinted glass. I drank one more whiskey on the way, and as soon as I closed the front door behind me, I poured another to consume in the Jacuzzi. I had to unwind. I had to release the tension and uncertainty Orson had forced upon me. That ratty little weasel with his brilliant mind had outsmarted me. No one gets away with the manipulation of Peyton Staley. The flow of warm water from the jets in the tub massaged my legs and back. The whiskey massaged my consciousness, and I began to drift in and out of a light dream state. I was aware that time was passing, since the water had grown cool. I watched the bright after-noon sun fade to dusk, as I awakened from the last nap.

I liked living alone. I liked my solitude. But there was something different in the apartment. I felt a presence. The luxury of the gray marble bathroom, the mirrored alcove, where I dressed each morning, and the two-sided fireplace on the wall across from the Jacuzzi reflected my unrest. I heard sounds, creaking and shudders that I had never noticed before. I turned on the hot water to warm the tub. The noise of the water couldn't drown these intruding sensations. My imagination was working overtime. Nothing intimidated me. I poured out the half-finished whiskey and pulled a pitcher of ice water from the miniature refrigerator under the sink to pour myself a glass of arctic sobriety.

Why had Orson been able to force my hand so effort-lessly? I focused on the water rushing around my body. How could he say I have no scruples? I had kept him working when no one else would have him, hadn't I? A quiet thud interrupted me, like a door closing. Would Allen be able to make changes in the contracts and patent ownership fast enough? The bureaucracy usually ground to a halt when you needed it to move quickly. Turning off the water jets and listening, imagining movement in the rooms beyond the bathroom door, I held my breath to hear only ambient sound. Silence. I returned to my worries. What was to keep Orson from bolting anyway? Maybe Allen was right. Maybe I shouldn't cave in so fast. Turning the water jets back on and moving the towels closer, I drank more ice water.

Unidentified sounds kept swirling in and out of each other like the water in the tub. For the first time, indecision immobilized me. Doubt numbed my reactions. Demons tempted me to pour another whiskey. My slower reflexes prevented me from responding to the first instinctive feelings of an intruder moving in my living room. Curiosity took the helm of my dim awareness. Again, I turned off the water jets, pulled the plug and started to get out of the tub.

A whisper of motion caught my peripheral vision. Just a hint of movement through the two-sided fireplace screen stopped me from drying myself. A chill gripped my spinal column. I wrapped the towel around my waist, the corner tucked in tight to hold it in place. Every muscle in my body tightened. Creasing my forehead to open my eyes wide enough to take in every detail in the dim light, I entered the bedroom.

"Hello, Peyton." I recognized the lilt in the soft female voice that greeted me.

"Rebecca?" My whole body released tension as my former fiancée's silhouette came into view from the doorway.

"Did I surprise you?" She smiled coyly, taking a cou-ple of steps toward me.

"Surprise isn't the word. How did you get in?"

"I still have my key, remember? You didn't want it back." She stepped toward me again.

"I hoped you'd—" Her touch on my lips silenced me.

"So, I decided to bring it back now. I won't be needing it any more." She took my hand in hers, turning it palm up and placing the key in the hollow of my hand. She folded my fingers to close my fist over the cold brass. "I'm leaving town. It's unlikely I'll be back."

"Oh?" I noticed a peculiar glint in her eye. Her demeanor was like a child with a secret she was not quite ready to tell, but you knew she would soon.

"Yes, I have other commitments to keep in San Francisco." Her voice was playful, twisting the words slowly, as if daring me to ask her for more detail. I decided not to play along.

"Thanks for the key. It was thoughtful of you to bring it back, even if unannounced and uninvited." I kept my tone businesslike and unassuming. "Why don't you go into the living room for a moment. I'll dress in a flash and we can go out for a bite to eat. You can tell me all about your plans at a sort of good-bye and good luck dinner between two former lovers."

"No, I don't want to. Let's go in the kitchen. I've planned something for you." Her voice grew agitated at the mention of going out.

"Just a minute. I'm going to put on some shorts, at least." I took her by the arm and led her toward the door to the living room. I knew that tone. It sounded wrong for the simplicity of the moment. She had a way of changing moods very quickly, especially if she skipped her pills. Her bipolar personality—actually active manic depression—had destroyed our future together. She flew from exquisite highs of joy and almost compulsive optimism into the caverns of suicidal sadness and irrationality.

"I'll only be a moment." Closing the bedroom door gave me a momentary sense of relief.

Two years ago, she attempted suicide twice and spent some months in treatment afterward. We hoped the problem would pass, but instead she broke our engagement. Now here she was in my apartment uninvited. It felt wrong. The effects of the whiskey were gone. Every nerve in my body was alert.

I wanted her out of the apartment. Pulling on a pair of flannel boxers and a tee shirt, I closed the closet door and picked up the phone to call the office, hoping Andrea would still be there. The in-use light on the kitchen phone gave me away to Rebecca, who very slowly picked up the receiver. I didn't notice the change in the background sounds. The office phone rang four times.

"Shit!" I was certain Andrea had left.

"Mr. Staley's office." Andrea's voice sounded more beautiful than a live symphony.

"Andrea? It's Peyton. Call the police. Have them come to my apartment. Rebecca is here. Something is all wrong about it."

"Are you all right?" Andrea said.

"Yes. Just call them, and tell my doorman to let them in without any buzzers. I want surprise on my side."

"Yes, Sir."

I laid the cordless receiver in its cradle as Rebecca placed the kitchen phone on its holder. I slipped on a pair of loafers. She slipped the knife from its holder. I opened the bedroom door and faced toward the kitchen. She chose her spot between the cooking island in the middle of the kitchen and the swinging door, where I would have to enter the room. I knew I had more time to kill than I wanted in this situation. Rebecca was capable of violent, irrational actions.

What brought her here tonight? It was not that she was leaving town. I paused to think at the front door. Why not just leave? She'd be in the apartment when the police came—they'd find her—no, I was just being paranoid. She was probably going to prepare one of those delicious twenty-minute meals like she used to. I had wanted her to be cured of her illness—I had loved her beyond reason. I had been willing to give up everything for her. She was the one who called off the wedding. Maybe she had gotten a great job out there. That's all it was.

I was trying to talk myself out of the gut wrenching feeling that Rebecca had come here to do harm as I entered the dining room. All my instincts screamed at me to get out of the apartment. I pushed the swinging door and stepped into the kitchen. From behind the door, a flash of light arched in an upward direction. I didn't see the knife come down. I only felt it slice deep into the space between my left shoulder blade and my ribs. Rebecca let go of the knife as I whirled around, staggering from the pain.

"I had to finish you off," she said. "You've been dead in my mind for so long, I had to finish you off." Her eyes were wild with rage. Her voice growled at me. She went for the knife holder, trying to grab another weapon.

I lunged at her, knocking her off balance. It took all my reserve to push her against the counter as hard as possible. I had to keep her from inflicting another wound. This one was taking its toll quickly. My left arm was numb. I couldn't move it. I pinned her into the corner, leaning on her with two hundred and thirty pounds of survival instinct. She was a petite woman, hardly one hundred pounds and barely five feet tall.

"You asshole!" she screamed at me. "Die! Goddamn it! Die!" She struggled against me.

"Not today." I snarled at her. I was panting from the loss of blood, which I was sure was considerable from the exertion of holding her at bay and keeping her confined at the same time.

"What could you possibly have to gain from my death?" I held her left arm with my good right hand, pushing it up behind her and pressing my weight against her torso.

"My freedom. I have everything in place. With you dead, I can simply get on with living. Besides, you never canceled the life insurance policy you provided me."

"You can't collect from death by a murder you commit." Breathing hurt.

"I'm the last person anyone would accuse, if you were murdered. I've been declared cured of my manic depression. I'm free—except for you."

Her wriggling and writhing was wearing me out. The blade felt like it was holding back the flow of lava from a volcano about to erupt in the back of my chest cavity. My left lung was filling with fluid. The urge to cough was overpowering. A coughing spasm forced me away from her, splattering blood on her, on the counters and on the floor, as I hacked and wheezed uncontrollably. I fell to the floor. She pulled the knife from my back and raised it over me.

"One more for the road—" she said just before she screamed. A burly policeman grabbed the hand holding the knife and wrenched it from her. Another policeman grabbed her from behind and subdued her by cuffing her. That was the last image I remembered. My consciousness flowed away from me like the blood draining from my wound.

"Hey, boss. You're going to be all right." The cheerful tone of Orson's voice made me want to laugh it was so comically out of character.

"Uh huh," I groaned. The tubes, the bandaging of my chest and the effects of anesthesia permitted only the slightest response.

"They say you'll be back on your feet in no time." Orson continued his happy-go-lucky performance, trying to keep me from falling back asleep.

"You signed the contracts?" I struggled to whisper.

"Contracts? Oh, sure. Allen took care of everything. We're ready to go. Just need you to get over this and back to the helm at MACROWORLD."

His pretense bothered me. I didn't want him in my hospital room.

"Orson, I need to sleep. Come back in a couple of days. Okay?"

"Sure, boss. Sure." He was backing away from me.

"Orson?" I struggled to speak. "What about Re-becca?"

"Oh, they've booked her on attempted murder charges. Open and shut case. She'll probably get off for insanity and spend the next zillion years in a mental institution." His flippant chatter was so ridiculous.

"Orson?"

"Yes, boss,"

"Cool it, will you?"

"Sure."

Several weeks of rest and treatments returned me to my original strength. Luckily, the knife had not inflicted the damage Rebecca had hoped for. The surgeons stitched me back together, and within two weeks I was spending my days working from my office at home. Orson's cheerfulness was justified. We started the production and promotion of his BMCs and biochips. MACROWORLD stock soared. Our competitors were scrambling. We enjoyed the havoc we were causing in the worldwide microchip markets.

MACROWORLD's BMCs and biochips did for us overnight what XP and ME 2000 did for Microsoft, and what Viagra did for Pfizer Pharmaceutical. The inability among computer builders, IBM, Apple, Dell, Hewlett-Packard and all the rest to compete in the biomolecular arena had effectively allowed us advance our dominance unchecked in this emerging marketplace for more than a year. We had effectively created a completely new market, free from competition and we were still growing.

But threatening storm clouds were gathering on MACRO-WORLD's sunny horizon. Allegations of monopoly began to filter into the media from both government and corporate arenas. Hurriedly convened congressional investiga-tions into MACRO-WORLD's trade practices, coupled with the efforts of incompetent yet vocal competitor companies to flood the market with their inferior versions of the biochip, and our vigorous attempts to stop them, created monolithic obstacles to our continued expansion. It was only a matter of time before MACROWORLD would be drawn-and-quartered and sold to the highest bidder.

When I was also indicted for insider trading, which I found humorous since I had no doubt that my manipulation of the merger would play out in the courts as the antitrust case of the century, I decided to take evasive action. I thought charges of insider trading were the least of my worries, and I knew it was certain I would not be so lucky as to get off with a short sentence in some country club prison and a small portion of the fortune I had amassed as majority stockholder in MACROWORLD. No, it was more likely that I'd spend the maximum sentence of thirty years in prison on the insider trading charge alone. The two million dollar maximum fine that went along with the thirty years seemed mild by comparison. The fact that I could take no one else down with me—my broker, my lawyer and my collaborators were firmly under my control and made no material misstatements or omissions that I hadn't directed them to make— sealed my fate as the principal perpetrator of the crime and so the man who would go to jail.

The SEC had made new rules of particular interest to me, namely New Rule 10b5-1 that would allow those who could "demonstrate that their transaction occurred pursuant to a binding plan of trading that had been established before they learned the material non-public information." In my case, there simply was no access to material non-public information for anyone but me, since I had created the fictional deflation of the MACROWORLD stocks and then quietly bought up the chaff that remained from the rapid panic sell-off of the company's holdings. On the other hand, the second part of New Rule 10b5-1 required that "the entity," in this case MACROWORLD, have "policies in place that were designed to ensure that the individual making trading decisions would not violate the insider trading laws." MACROWORLD had no such policies, and if they had, I certainly had not followed them, neither in the spirit nor the letter of the law.

No, the financial barracudas held me in their jaws, and only had to finish their meal to eliminate me from the scene. In retaliation, I decided to save them the trouble and deny them the pleasure.

"Allen, could you come in here for a moment?"

"What's up, Peyton?" Allen already knew what I would say next.

"Draw up my resignation papers. I'm taking myself away for an extended vacation."

"Peyton, even if you resign, you won't escape prosecution." Allen looked ashamed to tell me the obvious.

"I know that. I just want to buy a few weeks of seclusion, that's all."

"You can't leave the country as it is—"

"Stop reasoning with me. I want out, and I want it now." I stood up from my leather chair for emphasis. "You have an hour. I'll sign the resignation and I'll be gone. Simple as that."

"All right, but I must say as your attorney this isn't…"

"Allen?" I raised my voice. "Just do it. My plane leaves in less than two hours."

He left the room. I sat in my chair for the last time, swinging it around to the windows. No sense of power washed over me. Instead, I heard a strange voice.

"So, Peyton, you have lived your Sidetrack. It is time for your Final Decision Symposium." I recognized Javier, and he was speaking to me.

"I want to leave Orson a message—I can't just disappear."

"No, he is not actually a living being, remember? All this has been a Sidetrack. You have no choice."

My office, the panoramic view, my life at the top all evaporated. The next thing I knew, I was standing in the cave with Hannah.

23

"Are you all right?" Peyton looked a lot worse for wear than the last time I had seen him.

"I guess so. And you?" We were both dressed like we were about to set out on safari in khaki shirts and pants, complete with hiking boots.

"Yes. But I have a bad feeling about this Final Decision Symposium thing they're going to put us through. If your sidetrack was any part as difficult as mine was, then we're in for a very rough time. I nearly died! I mean it. They nearly killed me."

"My ex-fiancée stabbed her way out of my life. Not a fun time, I must say." Peyton winced at the thought.

"So, have you got a plan for our escape?"

"I was just thinking about how as a kid I tried spe-lunking in some of the random tunnels and washouts in the hills around my Kentucky hometown. Shall we try to find a way out of here before they come for us?"

Peyton was silent as he turned in a full circle, slowly surveying the perimeter of the cavern. I stepped out of his way and squinted into the shadows beyond the light that spilled into the center of the natural cathedral from the sizable fissure in the overhead rocks.

"Why not try to get up there?" Peyton pointed to a spot where the fissure began near the highest point of the wall. "It looks like the striations in the rock would provide good footholds and grip points to make climbing at least possible."

"And when we get up there, you plan to fly out the narrow gap in the ceiling?"

"No—not fly—slither is more like it."

"Slither—upward with no hand holds—the rocks are smooth."

"But, there are vines hanging within reach—see them?" Peyton again pointed to the tangle of vegetation snarled at the base of the opening. "I'll bet they're strong enough to hold one of us at a time."

"At least they have green leaves—growing vines are usually anchored better than dead, dry ones."

Taking my hand, Peyton simply walked me over to the wall, like he was taking a small child across the street. He put his arms around me and pulled me close.

"If we ever get out of here, if we are together—even if we're not—I want you to know I care about you. I—hope this works out."

I returned his hug and turned my face toward his unaware of the passion my kisses would ignite in his soul. He gently slid his hands down my back. I caressed his legs and ran my fingers up his arms to his neck. He was kissing the most sensitive part of my neck, just below the ear and under her jaw. We were sinking to the floor of the cavern, which is soft along the base of the walls.

I responded to him like I had known him all my life.

The first tremor was very subtle.

"Did you feel that?" I said, wishing to make love to him but knowing the moment had passed.

"You are phenomenal, Hannah."

"No, I mean, did you feel that?"

"Feel what?"

The next tremor was more convincing. We were up and dusting ourselves off instantaneously as the tremors continued in shorter and shorter succession.

"Give me a boost—"

Instantly, we were scaling the wall like spiders. I had never done anything like this. The rocks formed gently curved, concave walls, like a giant bowl, pockmarked with holes that gave us easy access upward. Peyton kept saying how simple our escape could have been without the tremors. Every placement of hand and foot brought us closer to the fissure. What had seemed a narrow crack from below proved to be a wide opening, certainly large enough for us to climb through, if the vines held.

"Let me get ahead of you," Peyton said from just below my left foot. "Just stop there."

He worked his way around me, as I clung to the wall for a moment's rest. We continued upwards. The tremors subsided just as the walls became more vertical near the top of the cavern. Hand and footholds were not as conveniently placed. I had to stretch farther than my arms and legs could easily reach. Peyton made his way much more easily than I did, owing to his longer arms, legs and torso.

"Hey!" I shouted upward. "I can't reach any hand hold. I'm stuck," A momentary chill of panic seized me.

"Stay there. I'll come down to you."

Peyton retraced his route downward. He found a placement even with me and began to move sideways in my direction.

"Follow me, use the same holes I do."

We slowly made our way upward. As he moved a foot, I put a hand in the spot. This method slowed our progress. The fissure loomed above us, and the leading tendrils of the vines dangled just out of reach above Peyton's head.

"We're almost there," he said, trying to reassure me. "I can almost each the vines." The powerful vibrations of the renewed tremors compromised our contact with the wall. I flattened myself into the rock, praying the shock waves would not shake a foot loose or cause me to lose my grip.

"Take this," Peyton commanded. He was holding a vine toward me a few feet up from where I had last seen him. With my left hand, I grabbed the woody tendrils and wrapped them around my arm with a twisting motion that sent the end flying in ellipses.

"What about you?" I said, since he had given me the closest vine.

"I'll get the next one," Peyton said as casually as if talking about a taxi he was surrendering to a pretty woman. He moved up and away from me to capture the vine he intended to use.

The next tremor doubled the duration and intensity of the first ones. I clung with all my strength to the vine, terrified to look up or down, holding my breath and feeling my foothold on the stone let go.

Peyton and I swung away from the wall on our vines, not by choice, but in helpless submission to the earthquake. Rocks shook loose and fell past us, crashing in dust clouds to the cavern floor below. A paralysis of fear held us dangling like ornaments on some giant's necklace.

"Climb!" Peyton shouted at me. "Climb for your life!"

Peyton's words freed me. I pulled myself up, hand over hand, winding the vine around my legs the way I had learned to climb the rope in a high school gymnastics class. My strength was going as I struggled to reach the fissure. Peyton was already half way into the opening. The light from above made his hair glow like an illumination in a fourteenth century Italian painting.

"Hurry, Hannah! We have to get out. Pull yourself up! Hurry!"

"Save yourself!" I shouted back. "I'll catch up with you!" The thunder from the dissolving cavern drowned my voice. I could hardly breathe. The dust was suffocating. I climbed toward the light, every move sapping my energy. I could hear Peyton calling to me, and I followed the sound of his voice, arriving at the top of the opening as the tremors subsided again. Peyton's hand appeared above me in the light.

"Hannah!" he shouted. "Take my hand."

I reached for him as he grabbed my arm and pulled me clear of the fissure and onto the flat rock beyond the cavern. We both collapsed and rolled onto our backs.

"Oh, my God! Oh, my God. Oh, God." I was trembling from the exertion as much as from fear.

"Hey, Hannah. Open your eyes. Look at me." Peyton rolled onto his stomach and inched himself toward me. He shook me gently.

I wiped the dust from my eyes with the back of my hands before I dared open them.

"Hannah. We're alive. How about that?" Peyton's laughter brought me to my senses.

"We are?"

I laughed uncontrollably. Peyton put his arms around me and rocked me, closing his eyes as much to control his own emotions as to calm mine.

I let him engulf me with his strength to feel safe for a moment. Then, almost by reflex, I looked beyond his shoul-der to see where we had come to.

"Peyton?" I felt very small as I spoke.

"Yes?" He stopped rocking me.

Look where we are."

My voice was shaking. His silence suited the moment perfect-ly. We were surrounded by an amphitheater filled with hundreds of

Agents. The flooring of the arena was highly polished white marble, and the fissure we had just escaped was gone. The simple design of the architecture suggested extreme austerity, so clean, so perfect that it exuded a cold beauty unknown in earthly structures. The walls behind the seating areas were translucent and glowed as if illuminated from the base by intensely focused colored lights. The wavelike shimmers from the wall reminded me of the aurora borealis, which I had seen only once as a small child.

All the Agents were dressed in form-fitting silver body suits that minimized any individual characteristics and maximized the homogenizing effect of conformity. Males were only distinguishable from females by the baldness of their heads. The women wore blond or brunette hair pulled back severely. Their expressionless faces made them seem like mannequins carefully placed for theatrical effect. We both searched the arena for a familiar face.

"I don't see anyone I know," Peyton whispered.

"I don't either." I was trying not to move my lips. "Let's just stay where we are and see what happens."

"Hannah Sebastian, please stand." The Voice boomed from beyond. No one in the arena spoke or even blinked as I stood.

"Peyton Staley, please stand." The reverberation of the Voice made non-compliance impossible. We stood close together, weak-kneed and uncertain how to act.

"The Final Decision Symposium is about to begin," said the Voice. "You will approach the Tribunal."

We looked at each other. Neither of us understood the reference, since there was no structure in the space that suggested a Tribunal.

"Behind you," the Voice said in a tone irritated by impatience.

We turned to see a judge's bench rise from the floor. Seated at the bench were three judges. One man sat in the center, flanked by two women. The woman judge on the right spoke first.

"You have learned the source of your early confu-sions in life. You have experienced your Sidetracks. You have survived The Cavern by choosing to escape and doing so successfully. You have worked together as a team. These are good things."

The woman judge on the left spoke next. "Those in the earthly realm who are trying to help you return are very close to discovering the source of your arrival here. The violence that was done to you in your earthly lives will not kill either of you. You have proven your resilience here. These are good things."

"However," said the male judge in the center, his tone revealing that his would be less positive news, "Whether you will return and go on with your lives on their original roads, or on different roads is what we determine in this Final Decision Symposium. You may select one of us as an advocate, or you may defend yourselves, alone or together. The Agents will recommend your fate to the Processor, who, of course, will make the Final Decision."

When the male judge stopped speaking, the silence was excruciating.

"Could Hannah and I have a moment to decide what to do?" The simplicity of Peyton's question drew only a nod from the judges. We stepped away to confer.

"I think we should try to do this on our own. I don't want to trust them with my future—our future."

"I'm afraid we'll be at a disadvantage, not knowing the way things are done here. What if we make some kind of stupid mistake in our arguments?'

"Self-determination is the primary core of any reasonable code of ethics. Even God's Will is actually Self-will. 'God helps those who help themselves'—remember? We were given the ability to choose our course of action. I'm not about to give it up here."

"Okay. We'll do this on our own—together, right?"

"Okay." Turning back toward the judges, Peyton drew a deep breath, exhaled, and paused, fixing his gaze on the male judge in the center. "We'll speak for ourselves," he said in a firm, clear tone. His demeanor radiated self-confidence.

"Fine." The judges stood together and stepped down from the bench, taking seats in the front row of the Agents. The bench lowered into the floor, leaving us standing in the center of the arena. The shimmering lights faded. The atmosphere of the amphitheater took on a somber cast, similar to the lighting in a movie theater just before the film begins. We could see silhouettes of the Agents, but their faces were lost in the shadows. The back walls glowed soft blue, accentuating the blackness of the figures in the seating areas. A circle in the floor around us glowed brightly, washing us in white light.

The Voice spoke.

"What direction do you think you deserve, to return to life as it was or to begin a new path?"

"To return to life as it was," we both said simultane-ously.

"Explain your motives for returning to life as it was."

"To move forward in life together," Peyton said.

"You were unknown to each other."

"We knew each other briefly, I delivered her flowers. If that doesn't count for something, then we will find each other," he said.

"Only if it is intended," boomed the Voice.

"It is intended, or we would not have met here." Peyton stayed calm.

"That was a mistake."

"A mistake?" he asked.

"The transport sent Peyton Staley into Hannah Sebastian's compartment by mistake."

"It was not our mistake. It was the Processor's mistake." Peyton enjoyed the observation.

"Not the Processor's mistake! The Processor makes no mistakes!" the Voice shouted.

"Whose, then?" Peyton said.

"The transport's error. Some malfunction. It happens some-times. That's why there are deformities, multiple births, mental vari-ances, genetic errors, miscarriages and the like. They're all just trans-port errors."

"Useful information," Peyton whispered to me. "I'll bet mis-takes are common."

"Silence. You may not confer at this time," the Voice said.

"Objection," Peyton said. "We must confer to defend ourselves. Fair is fair."

"Over-ruled. Nothing is fair. Fair is not a consideration."

"Objection," Peyton said. "We insist on time to confer." The strength of conviction was powerful. A moment passed in silence.

"Granted," the Voice said. "Explain how you will change in the earthly realm."

"Change what?" Peyton asked.

"Change behavior. Change relationships. Change goals for life."

"One or all three?" Peyton countered.

"All three!" the Voice boomed.

"Together or individually?" Peyton was gaining confidence from this exchange.

"Individually! You must reveal what you have learned," the Voice roared.

"Let me go first." Hannah whispered to Peyton.

Turning to the audience of Agents, she cleared her throat to buy a moment to think. She spoke from the heart.

"Thank you for this moment. Please bear with me if my words fall short. I learned from the Formation Environ-ment that as a child, I understandably believed I could trust the people around me—my family in particular. The most profound mistake of my life proved to be my unwillingness to let go of that belief. Trust in everyone but myself caused me to lose my self-worth, my children, my hope." She glanced at Peyton for encouragement. His eyes gave her all the support she needed.

"In my Sidetrack," I continued, "I lived the horrific events my misguided trust could have inflicted upon me if my choices had been only slightly different. The Sidetrack speaks to me as an allegory for my adult life where the effects of my misguided trust were no less dramatic. I gave up my right to choose through my fear of confrontation. I clung to the vain hope that others would do right by me. I handed over my soul's power to any person who tried to take it. I allowed my personal strength to flow away from me like a river swollen from heavy rain. I allowed others to rape me, emotionally, financially, and professionally without protest."

The expressions in sea of faces were softening. I felt their sympathy as I tapped into the well of pent-up anguish.

"My mother first took my power. Later, my brother. Eventually, my first husband. After my second husband's death, I let go, completely retreating into my pain. I allowed others to flatter me and steal away my creative energies." Tears ran down my cheeks. Sobs broke my train of thought. Trying to regain control, I breathed deeply.

"I never fought a hard battle, only easy battles. I didn't look at long-range consequences, only for relief from the immediate discomfort. Confrontation of any kind made me run away. I couldn't ask any hard questions. I couldn't stand firm." I straightened my back, squaring my shoulders to strengthen my resolve.

"In the earthly realm, when I return, I will retrieve my personal power. I will not drink and drive. I will not drink at all. I will confront the people who have taken advantage of me. I will end the abuse to regain control of my life and reclaim my personal dignity."

The applause was deafening. I knew the words had come from my soul and not from my head. Peyton was staring at me.

"Tough act to follow," Peyton said. I smiled at him, overcome by emotion. I let my tears flow.

"Opinion considered," the Voice said. "Peyton Staley must speak."

I stepped sideways separating myself from Hannah. I let my eyes wander over the motionless faces as I gathered my thoughts.

"I also thank you for this opportunity to speak. I learned in the Formation Environment that during my childhood, poverty, abuse, and the lack of parental guidance were presented as the normal way of life. I let myself accept my father's beatings, my employer's manipulation and the profound unawareness that I could achieve better." I felt the strain take over my face. I took a deep breath.

"As I grew older, after losing a few battles at work and in my personal life, I stayed as detached from emotion as I could, the way real men are supposed to react under pressure—tough, unflinching, cool. I knew if I allowed myself to feel, I would be overwhelmed by regret. So, I just ignored the consequences of my actions and the feelings that went along with them. My Sidetrack proved to me what I already knew—that power corrupted by greed eventually isolates and destroys its controller. It showed me how fear of success pushed me to build the walls thick enough and high enough around myself so I would not have to accept responsibility for my failures. I wouldn't have to look at my personal reality if I kept my vision blurred. I knew there was a part of me that could be ruthless, and I feared that. Over time, it became easier to back away from a fight than risk the transformation into a corrupted, self-serving winner. "

I was shaking. The tremors of admission reached my fingers and knees at the same time. I looked at Hannah for support. She smiled and nodded.

"In the earthly realm, when I return, I will rebuild my life to my own specifications. I will give myself a chance to succeed."

My speech had reached the Agents.

"I don't know where that came from," I said to Hannah through the thundering applause.

"Your heart."

"Opinion considered," the Voice said. "The Agents will now evaluate your opinions and the Processor will decide your futures. Wait in there."

The Agents turned their heads in unison toward a black door to the right. We walked toward the opening, drawn by an irresistible force. We could not have done otherwise.

24

*L*ynn arrived in front of the Dayton-Holland Indus-tries Building on the north shore of the Chicago River only ten minutes after leaving Detective O'Riley at Barnaby's Pub. Her briefcase carried the court filed documents suing Lenny Miller for Breach of Trust on behalf of his only living sister, Hannah Sebastian. Lynn's less than conventional decision to personally deliver the papers allowed her the chance to meet Lenny face to face and evaluate him first hand.

Lynn paid the cab fare and wedged herself into the flow of shoppers and workers rushing in opposite directions to their secret destinations. She carefully chose her way through the commotion of bodies in the noon rush to enter the silence of the red marble entrance with a feeling of exhilaration and relief. The stark coldness of the highly polished rotunda, the sophisticated chime of the elevator signals, the genteel hush and swish of the elevator doors increased her anticipation of the battle with Lenny Miller who lay in wait like a predator stalking its prey just ahead.

Arriving almost instantly at the forty-fifth floor, Lynn observed the austere character of the reception room of Dayton-Holland Industries before stepping from the elevator. Black marble walls, chrome-edged windows and picture frames, sculpted gray carpeting, and black leather armchairs placed in simple groups of two and three around square glass tables choreographed a ballet of power to intimidate all those who passed through the doors. Only a freeform glass vase holding a spray of white calla lilies accented by the arching stark, chartreuse stems arranged like arrows dropped into a too large quiver softened the hard lines of the room.

"May I help you?" The receptionist, dressed in a white gabardine suit, posed the question with a rich, throaty voice that matched the elegance of the single strand of pearls encircling her neck.

"Yes." Lynn responded with her most professional voice, trying not to betray how effectively the décor had made her feel shabby in dress, in demeanor and in her intent to confront. "My name is Lynn Hargrove. I am the chief attorney with Hargrove and Associates. I have papers for a Mr. Lenny Miller in regards to a suit filed on behalf of his sister, Hannah Sebastian."

"Do you have an appointment?" The receptionist's voice rose to pose the question and effectively gave its own answer. Lynn avoided the negative implied and informed rather than answered the receptionist.

"The court requires that Mr. Miller be served these papers personally. Please tell him I am here." Lynn's statement had turned the game to her own advantage, leaving no room for refusal.

"Just a moment. Please take a seat over there. I will make Mr. Miller aware you are here."

The receptionist typed for a brief moment at the computer keyboard. She watched the screen, as if waiting for a reply. Lynn looked for a door or a hallway leading into the offices behind the reception area. Not finding any, she decided security concerns are better served by architecture cleverly designed to mask any obvious appearance of an opening.

"You may go inside." A door slid sideways to open a portal in the marble.

"Like a submarine—Or a vault."

Seated at an expansive desk with the back of the black leather executive chair facing the door, Lenny Miller spoke indistinctly, as if holding something between his teeth.

"Ms. Hargrove?" The chair swiveled, bringing Lenny Miller, powerbroker industrialist and his Cuban cigar face to face with Lynn Hargrove, self-employed attorney. "Welcome to my home away from home. It is a pleasure to meet you, at last." He reached across the desk, but did not stand, to shake her hand. Lynn ignored the gesture.

"Mr. Miller."

"Lenny."

"Mr. Miller, these papers are self-explanatory. They bring suit against you on Hannah Sebastian's behalf to reclaim her inheritance."

"Why don't you sit down? You look uncomfortable standing there like that." Lenny Miller looked her up and down, the way a construction worker looked at a pretty woman walking past his work site.

"No, Mr. Miller. What I have for you won't take that long." Lynn placed the envelope containing the court documents on the desk. "Your willful mishandling of the money in the Miller Family Trust for your own personal benefit is, in a word, unseemly. It is also illegal. Hannah's also due half of the money that would have stayed with Donna, had she lived." Lynn waited for Lenny to respond.

"Donna died of natural causes in a hospice."

"Did she? Why didn't you notify Hannah?"

"She wouldn't have cared. Besides, there was nothing to notify her about. Donna died, was cremated and dispersed. That's all there is to it."

"No, you received all of Donna's money, not that we're talking huge amounts here. I wonder why a rich man like you has been manipulating the trust as you have."

"I haven't."

"I believe you have. And I believe you are responsible for Hannah's injuries."

"That's a mighty big leap of logic."

"No, Mr. Miller, it isn't. Antonio Cordoba, Hannah's attacker, is dead. The police found him in the river with one bullet in his gut and one in his brain. His fingerprints are on the cell phone the police found in Hannah's foyer the day she was attacked. A Dayton-Holland identification label was on the phone. He apparently dropped it as he escaped the crime scene, leaving Hannah and Mr. Staley for dead."

"Assumptions on your part."

"No, Mr. Miller. Not assumptions—hard DNA evidence such as his blood on the dog's snout where she had locked onto his arm, and dripping down the steps to the house. So, the question is: Why would a small time street boss be using a Dayton-Holland Industries cell phone? Why would he take it with him to the home of an unsuspecting middle-aged woman? Why did he shoot her and the deliveryman in her bathroom and leave them for dead? What did he take from her office, which was ransacked? Why did he turn up dead himself a day or so later?"

"I'm sure I don't know." Lenny was squirming almost visibly in his chair. As he listened miniature beads of perspi-ration appeared on Lenny's forehead the way dew appears on grass at dawn.

"I believe you do. I believe there is a connection between you and Cordoba." Lynn paused for a response. Getting nothing, she continued. "Perhaps you wanted Hannah dead so you could get the rest of the money from the trust or something even more valuable from the ransacked files."

"Get out! Get out! I won't hear any more of this insanity! Get out and take your fucking law suit with you!" Lenny rose from his chair, snatched the envelope and threw it at Lynn.

"I see I've touched a nerve." Her calm intensified his unrest.

"You bitch! Get out of my sight!"

"No, Mr. Miller." Lynn showed no emotion, picking up the envelope and gently placing it on the desk. "The suit stands. You will answer the demands of the court, and provide a full and complete accounting of the trust and anything else that is turned up by the court date. Hannah's interests will be served. Her inheritance will come to her in time to pay her medical bills. As for the other issues, the police will be in touch with you shortly. You will be brought to justice, Mr. Miller."

Lynn stared hard and long at Lenny to watch his reaction. He leaned forward on the desk to stare her down, unblinking.

"Justice means different things to different people, Ms. Hargrove. Nothing the courts could demand of me could weigh as much as the emotional rejection Hannah inflicted on our mother. That pain cannot be undone. The courts cannot punish me enough to repay the agony Donna caused our mother by disappearing for years and years. That agony cannot be undone."

Lenny paused, standing away from the desk and squaring his shoulders, as if gathering strength to go on.

"I'm not worried about being brought to justice by you or anyone else. I live with my hatred. I was a better son to Mother than either of them ever were daughters. They don't deserve a cent of Mother's money. They deserve what they got. Anything I may have done to reclaim Mother's dignity could never be enough." By the time he paused again, Lenny was sweating droplets that ran down his face and splashed on his tie and the lapels of his suit.

"Mr. Miller, I will have to tell the police what you have just told me."

"Go ahead. You can't hurt me. The courts can't hurt me. Bring on your goddamned lawsuit. Bring on the cops. Nothing can hurt me. Now, get out!" He was screaming uncontrollably. He took a glass art nouveau paperweight and hurled it at the door.

Lynn read the rage and the insanity in Lenny's eyes that made her feel genuinely unsafe in his presence. As the door to the reception area opened, she walked quickly to the elevators. Waiting only a few seconds for the doors to open and close, she pushed the ground floor button. Her stomach floated upward as the high-speed elevator plummeted downward. Her thoughts were racing. As the elevator slowed to a stop, Lynn took a deep breath and hurried to the revolving doors of the lobby and into the street.

"What a psycho! Thank God for crowds." She worked her way along the city side streets toward Michigan Avenue. Thoughts run at lightning speed.

You can't let him get away with any of this. Think. You can't go back to the office. Think—before you meet O'Riley tonight—what was taken from her office? What is missing in this puzzle?

The rumble of the traffic shook the bridge under her feet as she walked across the river away from the high rent, exclusive shopping district of the Magnificent Mile toward the business district south of Wacker Drive. At the intersection of the Michigan Avenue Bridge and Wacker Drive, the stairway leading down to the Chicago River's edge beckoned to her. The last of the tourist boats floated forlorn and nearly empty of passengers as the wind of the approaching winter choked the last of the summer warmth from the air. For no reason at all, in an impulsive response to her confusion, Lynn hurried down the stone steps to the waiting boat.

"When does this one go out?" she asked the young attendant, who stood slouched against the railing to relax while chewing a large wad of gum.

"In about five minutes. You got to pay over there, lady." He pointed toward the ticket window. She read the sign advertising the different cruises, trying to decide which one to take.

"How much for the hour and a half cruise. Please?"

"Thirteen dollars."

Lynn handed the attendant some money.

"Thank you. Enjoy your cruise," The young woman returned the change with the ticket.

"Yes. I hope so."

She boarded the boat, stepping over the gap between solid land and floating vessel, as if escaping from a self-made prison. There were only five other passengers in her section. An elderly woman in a wheelchair with an oxygen tank and her companion nurse sat near the right, front exit. A young couple sat kissing and giggling in the last center seats nearest the rear. A middle-aged man boarded last and moved to the side railing about halfway to the rear. He remained standing, leaning over the railing to stare into the choppy, gray water.

Lynn took a seat on the left, just behind the bulkhead where the lifejackets were stowed. Lynn read the emergency instructions to pass the time and to distract her mind from the frenzy of the encounter with Lenny Miller.

Let your subconscious sort this out. You know the solution to will appear in the void. Keep your thoughts focused on the wind whipping the water, the rocking of the boat, the silhouette of the Chicago skyline against the gray, churning clouds. Let it come to you.

The attendants scurried from side to side, releasing the ropes, pulling up the gangplank, and counting the people on the boat. The microphone crackled as an athletic young woman flicked the switch to talk to everyone.

"Welcome to the Star Ship Line. We offer the most informative cruises in the city—" The voice droned into the background when the engines revved to move the boat away from the dock. Lynn's gaze drifted between the architecture and the water while the boat moved slowly along the river toward the Sears Tower. She noticed the No Wake sign as the boat came about and retraced its route toward the lake.

In which part of the river did they dump Antonio Cordoba's body? Look at those pylons lining the water's edge—clusters of pylons, lashed together with rusty chains and scattered in odd parts of the river's bend leading toward the industrial estuaries. Hmmm, no one would look there right away. Strange that he turned up so fast.

"I'll have to ask O'Riley about that," she said aloud, feeling slightly embarrassed when the elderly woman's companion glanced over at her. She watched the bridges pass overhead until the boat approached the locks that allowed the altered river to flow away from the lake. Within minutes, the boat ran free of the river and onto the lake. The cold wind whipped the waves over the bow, sending rivulets of icy water down the aisles between the seats. The gray clouds hung low, obscuring the eastern horizon. Black and powerful in near silhouette, Chicago rose to the west along the shore. The tops of the tallest buildings pierced the clouds as if to cause the rain to fall as the heavy mist that soaked the translucent blue awnings of the cruise boat. Relief. Let your thoughts blur, just absorb the panorama of the skyline.

"Not a good day, huh?" The middle-aged man's voice broke across her mind like the waves across the bow of the boat.

"Uh—well, I guess not."

"What brings a pretty young woman like you onto the lake on a day like this? Shouldn't you be working?"

"I am working. I'd like to keep on working, without interruption, thank you."

"You don't have to be rude."

"Apparently, I do." She turned her face into the wind and away from him.

"I have a message for you—" he said over her shoulder.

Lynn turned to look at the man. Her eyes showed the question.

"—from Lenny Miller."

The man handed her a thick manila envelope and moved away to give her privacy. Lynn removed the rubber band that held it closed. Lifting the flap, she saw three packets of money bound in the middle by paper strips. A piece of torn yellow paper peeked out from the neat edges of the money. Lynn pulled it out. Scrawled diagonally across the rough rectangle she saw the message:

"Take this. Disappear."

She thumbed through the money. Three packets of one hundred bills each in thousand dollar denominations flipped back at her.

Three hundred thousand dollars!

She folded the flap down and put the rubber band around the envelope.

"Sir?"

"Yes, ma'am." He moved back to her side.

"Take this back."

"I can't."

"You will." She put the envelope in the space between his arm and his side. "I cannot be influenced. Tell him that."

"He'll kill me."

"That's your problem. Now leave me alone."

"Listen, lady. It's not like you think."

"This is a bribe."

"He told me you'd refuse it—that I should explain."

"There's nothing to explain. Now, leave—me—alone." Lynn worked her way forward and sat on one of the benches near the front bulkhead. The man followed her.

"I can't get off this boat with this money. It's some kind of in-heritance money. You have to take it. My life depends on it."

"You should keep better company. And, no, I don't have to take it. You have to deal with it. Just throw it overboard if you must. I am not taking it."

"Lady, be reasonable—"

"I am being reasonable. Take the money yourself and leave the country. You can do pretty well with that kind of money in small, underdeveloped countries."

Look, Lenny Miller is not the kind of guy you double cross." He paused a moment to think. "He wants you to give up the lawsuit and just take this money for your friend. Use it for her."

"I guess I've not been clear enough. Hear me, who-ever you are. Tell this to Lenny Miller. I am not giving up the lawsuit, I am not taking this money, and you can do whatever you want with it. Give it back, keep it and evaporate, throw it overboard. I don't care in the least. Now, get away from me before I tell someone you're harassing me."

"You'll never win. He's too rich, too powerful." The man put the envelope back in his coat. He then walked to the rear of the boat.

Lynn kept an eye on him for the next hour until the boat docked. He jumped the gangplank to run up the stairs and across Michigan Avenue Bridge before anyone else could get off the boat.

I have just enough time to grab something to eat before meeting O'Riley at Barnaby's.

The rain had stopped, and most of the workers were gone. The streets were less populated than usual.

Something is wrong. Get a grip. Just sit down in that corner res-taurant over there.

She crossed the street in a daze, took a seat at the counter, picked up the sticky plastic-covered menu, looking at it without reading.

Why the incident on the boat? Lenny Miller couldn't have had enough time to think out the bribe plan and carry it out by the time I went to the boat. That was such a spontaneous act on my part; he couldn't have known where I was going. I didn't know myself. That man had to have been following me from the time I left Dayton-Holland. The money has to be part of Lenny's master plan. He was already prepared to buy me off even before I arrived at his office.

"What can I get for you?" The waitress' voice brought Lynn back to the moment.

"I'll—uh, I'll take a cup of black coffee."

"Dinner?"

"No, thank you. But—a blueberry muffin, if you have any."

The waitress reached into the nearly empty plastic covered carousel at the end of the counter and retrieved a muffin. She put it on a small plate and dropped two pats of butter next to it. She slid it in front of Lynn.

"Here you go."

"Thanks."

The hot coffee chased away the chill from the boat ride as she picked at the day old muffin. *I still have enough time to walk to Barnaby's. I'll just take the route past Dayton-Holland for the hell of it.*

Lynn dropped a five-dollar bill on the counter and left, wrapping her coat around her she returned to the corner where she had seen the man turn off Michigan Avenue. She followed her gut instincts that led her along the deserted street. As she walked, clouds deepened the dusk until the streetlights began to emit the warm orange light so character-istic of Chicago at night.

Lynn had a habit of looking at the ground as she walked, especially when she was alone. She rarely looked for anything in particular as she made her way. But this time she noticed an odd swirl of droplets, like someone had dribbled brick red paint from an over loaded brush. The swirl started at the curb and continued in an un-even zigzag back and forth across the sidewalk like a boat tacking into the wind on a choppy lake. The haphazard movement of the droplets fascinated her. The way they increased in size and number as she con-tinued walking seemed odd and sensible at the same time.

She followed the swaggering design, stopping to see if the drop-lets were still wet. Sliding her shoe across one part of a swirl, the fluid smeared. Every nerve energized. Adrenaline flushed through her veins.

It's not paint. This is fresh blood. Whose? How did it get here?

Lynn searched the immediate surroundings, her eyes working the growing gloom like a periscope peering through fog.

Details. Look for out of place details. Nothing seems dis-turbed.

She crossed the next alley, following the trail as it con-tinued an erratic course along the walkway. Suddenly it made a strong right turn around the corner.

"Oh, my God! Oh, my God," she gasped. The swirls stopped in the stream of blood that flowed from the body into the gutter along the sidewalk. The man from the boat lay face down, sprawled where he fell. A sinister sensation lingered in the air. Lynn's instincts told her to run. She reached into her purse for her cell phone as she stepped into the shadows along the wall. She dialed 9-1-1.

"9-1-1," the dispatcher answered.

"Send an ambulance immediately to the corner of Kinzie and Orleans." Lynn spoke in a hushed voice. "There's been a murder. A man is dead on the street."

"Kinzie and Orleans? North side of the river?"

"Yes, and hurry. This just happened. I don't know why he is here." Yes, I do.

"I'll send the paramedics right away."

"Thank you. I'll wait, but—hurry." The connection crackled into silence.

Lynn backed up against the building, standing frozen as a statue, hoping no one would drive past or walk by until the paramedics arrived. Minutes seemed like hours. Her nerves tingled from anticipation. Every sound was sharpened by fear. She felt someone watching her. The sensation was almost overwhelming. The scuffle of heavy footsteps walking along the sidewalk reached her from the same direction she had come. They were uneven in pacing, progressing in fits and starts, as if the person was stopping to look at something and then moved on. They slowed as they came closer, stopping just before reaching the corner. Lynn stared at the edge of the building. Her breath came in shallow gasps. In the distance, she could hear the Sirens of the ambulance reverberating against the canyon-like walls of the city streets.

Hurry! Hurry! I need help! Her mind focused on the Sirens, calling them to her rescue. She saw the toe of a man's shoe step beyond the invisible barrier she had mentally placed at the edge of the building. The male form was large, yet blurred by the darkness. He held something in his hand, raising it in her direction. The Sirens approached, louder by the second. A blinding light caught her in the face.

"Ms. Hargrove! What are you doing here?" Detective O'Riley lowered the flashlight toward the body. "Are you all right?"

"Oh!" Lynn exhaled. "O'Riley! Oh my, God. Yes, I'm all right. How do I explain this?" Lynn took several deep breaths to try to regain control. "Why are you here?"

"I heard the 9-1-1 call, and not being too far—on my way to Barnaby's to meet you—I decided to respond. But you're the last person I thought I'd find standing over the body."

"Me too." The sirens of the arriving ambulance and police cars drowned out her voice.

Within minutes, the crime scene investigators set up the

perimeter, and the police photographers took the neces-sary photos of the body. Lynn and Detective O'Riley stood by, watching the process.

"So? Why are you here?"

"I didn't go shopping when I left you. I went to Dayton-Holland Industries to serve the papers for the lawsuit to get Hannah's inheritance from Lenny Miller. He and I had a very interesting exchange, to say the least. I was so frus-trated when I left his office, I decided to take a boat ride on the lake, just to sort things through."

O'Riley nodded every few seconds as he listened.

"On the cruise, there was this man, who offered me three hundred thousand dollars—from Lenny Miller—to drop the suit. He told me if I didn't take the money—which I didn't, by the way, Lenny Miller would kill him. I still refused the money."

"Three hundred thousand dollars—to drop the suit against Lenny Miller. A bribe?"

"I thought so. But the man said it was supposed to replace the inheritance and that I should use it for Hannah. Then he warned me that I couldn't win—that Lenny Miller was too rich and powerful. When the boat docked, he jumped the gangplank and ran in this direction before I could get off the boat."

"So, you followed him here."

"Well, not immediately. I stopped for some coffee to pull myself together. Then I realized that the man and the money must have been part of Lenny's plan all along. So, I figured I'd walk to Barnaby's via Dayton-Holland Industries—just to see what I could see. This is what I found."

"We're ready to move the body, Sir," a young paramedic said to Detective O'Riley. "He's been shot several times."

Detective O'Riley spoke with the head crime scene analyst. "So, they let you out of the office today I see, huh, Henry? Can you tell us how he died?"

"It looks like the killer wanted him to try to run. Judging from the blood trail, it was a drive-by shooting. It seems likely they shot him in the leg, then in the arm, then in the side—maybe not in that order—and finally in the head and neck. The increasing volume of blood on the ground indicates a progressive series of injuries, one after the other, until he fell dead right here."

"Did you find anything on him?" Lynn asked.

"You mean other than his clothing?"

"Did he have a manila envelope in his coat pockets?"

"No, nothing, except this cell phone." He held up a plastic bag containing a cell phone identical to the one found at Hannah's house.

"May I see that?" The investigator handed her the phone. She turned it over to look at the back.

"Property of Dayton-Holland Industries," Lynn read aloud.

"We'd better compare what ballistics finds on these bullets with the ones we found in Antonio Cordoba," O'Riley told the analyst. "See to it for me, would you, Henry?"

"Sure, Jim. Just as soon as they have the results, you'll have the results."

"Thanks. Come on, Ms. Hargrove. We still have to talk with the bartender at Barnaby's."

$\approx\!\!\approx$

25

$\approx\!\!\approx$

A few minutes past nine, Lynn and O'Riley arrived at Barnaby's Pub. Entertainment was in full swing. The bar was crowded with a mixture of young single men and older businessmen. At the far end, four nearly naked women danced on the round stage, which was bathed in intense color by the rotating overhead lighting. The suggestion of their dancing left little to the imagination. Rock music blared from the speakers placed on either side of the stage, and the cheap mirrored globe scattered points of light around the room in a mediocre parody of a bad seventies movie.

"There's Angel," Lynn pointed at the first woman on the stage. "Is this what they mean by exotic dancing?"

"Are you really that inexperienced?" O'Riley laughed.

"I guess so. But I am surprised that Angel is a dancer."

"I'm not. I had her pegged the first time I saw her. The way she didn't slouch and the way she walked, toes touching the ground first, plus the decorated nails and heavy makeup gave it away."

The music stopped. The dancers left the stage. Fending off the pats and pinches of her more drunken customers, Angel made her way through the crowd.

"Hello, Detective O'Riley." She completely ignored Lynn. "What brings you here? Oh yes, you want to talk with Jack."

"Good memory, for one so young. Is he here?"

"Yes, he's in back getting ready for a long night. The natives are rowdy tonight. Must be the bad weather—cooped up in little cubicles all day, they just have to come out at night and let off the steam. Rain makes it worse."

"We'd like to have a word with him before he gets caught up in the ruckus."

"Follow me. I can't guarantee anything. It all depends on his mood."

Angel led them through the crowd to the back dressing room that also served as the office for the club. A closet, a small bathroom and a changing area defined by curtains hanging from a wire across the corner of the back two walls took up most of the room. A computer, a phone, and a calculator crowded onto a small desk that squeezed into the corner under a wall mounted bookshelf. At the desk, the phone clamped between his ear and his shoulder sat Jack.

"Jack? These people are here to talk with you. This is Detective O'Riley and Ms. Hargrove. Can you take a minute?"

Jack mumbled something into the phone and hung up. "Yeah? I got about two minutes. What do you want?" His thick West Chicago accent fit his out of shape gut, squat stature and balding head perfectly.

"We're trying to find out the series of events that led to the shooting of one of your customers—Peyton Staley."

"Yeah? So, what makes you think I know anything?"

"He was in here a little over a week ago. According to Angel, you were the last person to see him, because you threw him out after closing."

"Yeah? I throw a lot of guys out of here. What makes him so special?"

"He was shot the next morning, just after he delivered flowers to a woman on the Gold Coast."

The phone rang. Jack picked up the receiver. "Uh, excuse me a minute. I got to put this through to one of our guys out there." He pushed the hold button and left the room.

"I've got to go back to the stage and work, too," Angel said. "I'll tell him to come back in here."

"Thanks," O'Riley said. "Guess we can cool our heels a bit. Have a seat." He waved Lynn toward the stool in front of the makeshift dressing table as he sat at the desk. Jack's chair was still warm.

Lynn noticed Angel's purse. She glanced at O'Riley, who was sitting with his back to her, reading one of Jack's Playboy Magazines. What was in the purse? She unsnapped the clasp to peek inside.

"O'Riley - look at this. Isn't this a .22 caliber pistol?"

"Yes, it is."

"Weren't the bullets in Peyton's chest and Hannah's leg .22 caliber bullets?"

"Yes, they were."

"So, could there be a connection?" She raised her eyebrows to suggest something illicit.

"Possibly. Probably not."

Lynn closed the purse. "I think we need to find out if there was anything going on between Peyton and Angel."

"What makes you say that?"

"Call it women's intuition—I just have a feeling. Jack will know, I bet."

The door opened. Jack's voice and cigar filled the room. "All right. Make it quick, I got to take care of business out there."

"I was wondering, Jack, if Angel ever dates any of the customers," O'Riley said.

"Not usually. I don't notice things like that. If she dances sexy and sells the booze, I don't care what else she does."

"Did she have anything going with Peyton Staley?"

"Who? Oh, you mean that guy that got shot a week ago—the morning after getting wasted in here the night before?"

"Yes, that's who I mean."

"What difference does it make?"

"I'm not sure if it does, but it's possibly a piece of the puzzle we're trying to figure out."

"Well, they've been getting the rocks off, so to speak, for a couple of months. I noticed Angel softened up as soon as she started seeing him. He must do something right, because she's a savvy woman. Not much she hasn't seen or done."

"Anything more than a casual relationship?"

"Maybe for Angel. That night he was in here I know she was going to ask him if they could move in together—you know, make it a permanent shack instead of the now and again thing it actually was. He must have said no, or some equivalent, because within a very short time from the beginning of their conversation, Angel stormed into the back and wouldn't come out until it was her time to dance."

"What happened then?"

"He starting slamming 'em down, one right after the other. He's an Irish whiskey drinker—so, I noticed. He must have had seven or eight drinks by the time the bar closed."

"Did he talk with anyone else that night?"

"I saw him talking with a couple of young street punks who came in an hour or so later. They pestered him a while, but left him alone when Angel finally came out and started dancing. The other girls were off, so Angel had to work alone that night."

"What time was that, approximately?"

"I don't know. It was late, maybe around two, two-thirty. We close at three."

"Bar time?"

"Yeah, so it was really only about between one forty-five and two-fifteen. Angel finished dancing and went in back to change into street clothes. I started cleaning up a little early, since he was the only guy left in the place and snoring himself hoarse. When I rousted him and threw him out, Angel came out of the back, and she watched him from the window."

"What was her mood then?"

"She was just watching. No emotion at all—which, now that I think about it, was strange all by itself."

"Did you hear anything unusual from outside?"

"No, just the usual street noise—cars without muf-flers gunning their engines, backfiring, hot-rodding up and down the street. The creeps and punks come out at that time of night to race each other—showing off for the girls, you know, gang stuff."

"How long did Angel watch?"

"Only a couple of minutes. Then she said good night and went in back for her coat and purse."

"So, all in all, a normal night, right?"

"Right."

"If you had to describe Angel, what would you say?"

"Me? Oh, I'd say she is tough, proud—and—well," his voice cracked with emotion, "—an incredibly sexy woman when she wants to be."

"Anything negative?"

"Yeah. She's a jealous bitch." Jack took a deep breath. A hostile edge came into his voice. He folded his arms and hunched his shoulders. "She knows about taking revenge, that one. And—she hates not getting her way. Personally, I'd never want her mad at me. She can be nasty."

"Does she have it in her to shoot someone?"

Jack looked at O'Riley, sizing up the need to answer the question. "Yeah, I think so, but only to protect herself."

"Could she hire someone to shoot someone else?"

"Put out a contract? I don't think so."

"Did you know she carries a piece in her purse."

"Yeah, you would too, if you looked like her and worked nights in a neighborhood like this. Now, I got to get to work. We got a real rowdy bunch out there tonight."

"Thanks, Jack. You've been helpful."

Jack left the room.

"I think I'll have to ask her to come in for question-ing," O'Riley said.

"Why is that? She didn't do anything but get angry." Lynn frowned her disapproval.

"Probably, but two things don't sit right—the fact that Angel's got a thing for Peyton, and said nothing about it, and that Jack said they had an argument, and she said nothing about that."

"So, you think one of them is lying."

He shook his head. "Maybe both of them are coloring the truth to their advantage."

"I think Jack is covering for Angel. There was something in his description of her that makes me think he's in love with her." Lynn smiled, broadly, showing her teeth in a gesture of humorous victory.

"Woman's intuition again?"

"More than that. Did you notice the difference in the tone of his voice, and the way he crossed his arms when he told us she could be a bitch?"

"Sort of."

"The emotion in his voice when he described her as tough and proud and sexy, that gave it all away for me. His body language showed a classic gesture of self-protection, like she'd hurt him. It matched with his comment that he didn't want to be on the receiving end of her anger. I'll bet he has been, and more than once, too."

"You got all that from his voice and arms?"

"You have to read people, not just hear their words."

O'Riley gallantly opened the door. "Ready?"

"You want me to come with you?" Lynn said.

"I think it would be helpful. She'll relate to you better than to me, I bet. At least you can read her for me."

"Like I read you." They both laughed.

They walked into the noisy, smoke filled club, taking a place to the side of the stage. Angel saw them, nodding in acknowledgment. O'Riley motioned to her to come over to them. She kept dancing until the music stopped. She walked to the steps leading from the stage, and made her way over to them. The music picked up again, and the other girls started a new routine without Angel.

"Detective O'Riley—Ms. Hargrove, did Jack fill you in?"

"Yes, ma'am, he did," O'Riley said. "I need you to come with us to the station. He gave us some information only you can help us follow up on. How fast can you change?"

"I can't go now, I'm working. This is a crazy night—Jack needs my help." Angel's reluctance spoke volumes to Lynn.

"I think Jack will manage just fine. I'll clear it with him. Now, please, go change so we can leave." O'Riley's professional manner left her no room to object. "Ms. Hargrove will go with you."

"What? You think I'll try to run?" Angel trembled, her nerves rising to meet the challenge. "I've got nothing to hide or to run from." She pushed her hair out of her face. "Are you saying I've done something wrong?"

"Not that you've done something wrong, but that we need your help and more information. This just isn't the place to talk." Lynn tried to set Angel more at ease. "Come on. I have a couple of things I want to ask you without Detective O'Riley around—you know, girl stuff."

Angel looked at Lynn, sizing up her comments. "All right. It'll only take me a minute to change. You'll clear it with Jack, right, Officer?"

"That's right."

The two women left the commotion of the club behind. The relative quiet of the dressing room helped Lynn retrieve her thoughts.

"I'll bet you can tell, I'm a rather middle-class working girl. I went to school, got my law degree and went to work. The road was all laid out for me by the time I was sixteen. But, you're the first woman I've ever met I feel I can ask about how a woman gets into this kind of business. And how do you stay in shape? I'd be embarrassed out there."

Angel laughed. "You get into this business because there's nothing else you can do. I flunked out of high school. My body has always been my best asset. Dancing is a great way to stay in shape. I've been doing this so long, I wouldn't know what else to do." She slathered lotion on her face to help remove the make-up.

"This question may be way out of line, and if it is, you just tell me."

"Okay, try me." Angel was wiping away layers of foundation and eye shadow with several Kleenex tissues. A softer, gentler face was emerging from behind the mask.

"Have you ever taken money for love?"

"Oh, you mean, sex—not love, and you mean am I a prostitute?"

Lynn nodded hoping the directness of her question would get Angel to open up.

"Well, a few years ago, I augmented my lifestyle by accepting the gifts and money men would feel they wanted to give me. But, I never worked for a house or a pimp. The gifts never hurt, and the money definitely helped." She wiped the edges of her face clear of make-up. "If that is prostitution, then, yes, I have been a prostitute."

She stepped behind the curtain, taking her street clothes with her. "But if you think about it, it's not all that much different than what wives do for their husbands in exchange for a lifestyle they want to live and not pay for." The skimpy, cobalt blue sequin-spangled costume flipped over the curtain wire and hung limp like a shiny, wet noodle.

"I just can't understand the women who take a lot of abuse, get no money and end up with a bunch of snotty-nosed kids to support when their husbands leave them for some young bimbette. They're the ones who get the raw end of the sex-for-money deal."

"I suppose they are. You seem pretty cynical about it, though. Haven't you ever been in love?"

"In love?" Angel stepped out from behind the curtain, wearing a long black skirt and a soft, cream-colored sweater. "You must be kidding. That's just a notion some men cooked up to get women into bed for free."

"Oh, and not a notion some women cooked up to get men to support them?"

"Look, you may want to give yourself away to become some man's recyclable sex object, but not me. If I give it, I'm going to get it, if you know what I mean."

"Yes, I think I do. Shall we go make Detective O'Riley a happy man and answer his questions?" Lynn had set the stage for the harder questions Angel was going to hear at the station. She liked this woman, even though she sensed an unhappy rage boiling beneath the carefully constructed surface appearances.

"Sure." They went into the club together and joined Detective O'Riley at the bar.

"Ready? Jack agreed to let you out of the cage for tonight." Angel glanced at Jack, who nodded with the intent of communicating more than his agreement to let her leave. Angel read him. He was hoping she'd keep things straight.

"See you tomorrow, Jack." She winked at him. They left through the side door.

"The police station is only a few blocks away. What do you say we walk?" Detective O'Riley said, as they stepped onto the sidewalk.

"Sure," the two women said simultaneously. They walked for nearly two blocks in silence. None of them had any desire to make small talk.

Lynn's mind was racing. *We're leading a lamb to slaughter. She doesn't have an attorney—she may not have anyone other than Jack to call if she is booked. She needs representation, and she needs someone other than O'Riley during the questioning.*

O'Riley welcomed the silence. His thoughts were forming a web for Angel to catch herself in.

You've got to squeeze Angel enough to get her to tell the truth about what really happened that night. Maybe you should get a little rough with her—and you've got to get her gun from her. Maybe you should accuse her of hiring someone to shoot Peyton. Yeah, that's it. Tell her you think she's guilty of conspiring to commit murder and see what happens.

Angel looked sideways at the others, more uncom-fortable with every step. She slowed her forward motion. Uneasiness set into her mind.

Something isn't right. I shouldn't have agreed to this. What's with this silence—they're up to something. I have to keep my mouth shut. What did Jack say to them? That he threw Peyton out—that's easy. But did he let on that you were making it with Peyton? Man! I can't let them know about that. They'll crucify me.

"Detective O'Riley, I don't think I can go through with this. I don't know why you want to talk with me. I don't really know anything that can help you."

"Let me be the judge of that." O'Riley's response was crisp and short.

O'Riley's going to be rough on her. Lynn acted fast.

"Angel, do you have an attorney?"

"You must be kidding. Why do I need an attorney?"

"Well," Lynn continued, ignoring Detective O'Riley's facial contortions. "I think everyone who goes to a police station to answer questions should have an attorney present."

"I can't pay any attorney. I'll just have to go it alone."

"No, you don't have to go it alone. I'll represent you if you want me to," Lynn said, glaring at Detective O'Riley. "I won't charge you a penny."

"I don't think any of this is necessary. You're not in any trouble, I just want talk about that night in detail," O'Riley said, seething inside.

"Ms. Hargrove, do you really think I need your help?"

"Yes, Angel, I think it's a good idea, in spite of Detec-tive O'Riley's words to the contrary. I just want to be there to make sure the conversation is appropriate." Lynn stared at him and then smiled. "Better safe than sorry."

By the time Angel agreed to accept Lynn's help, they were crossing the street in front of the police station. Detective O'Riley walked several strides ahead of the women.

Damn! Just like a woman. I thought that Lynn and I were a team, now we're not. She could keep me from getting everything I can from Angel.

"Follow me," O'Riley said, leading them through the station, past a few tired cops questioning a few tired teenagers, to the small, unadorned interrogation room. The old, damaged conference table consumed most of the space, leaving a narrow perimeter where a few uncomfortable chairs waited for someone to sit in them. He indicated that they sit on the far side, across from the two-way mirror. He stood at the end of the room nearest the door. A filthy, frosted glass window glowed from the streetlights just outside. The overhead lamp emitted a harsh light from unprotected bulbs dangling from the tin-shaded fixture. The dingy green walls begged for a fresh coat of paint that clearly had been denied for decades.

O'Riley cleared his throat. "Angel, would you just tell me what happened the night before Peyton Staley was shot?"

"Honestly, Sir, I've already told you what I know. Peyton came into the bar, he drank a lot of Irish whiskey, and Jack threw him out at closing."

"You know I spoke with Jack earlier tonight, right?"

"Yes."

"He said you and Peyton had a conversation, and that you were furious at Peyton for some reason, and that you stormed into the back of the pub, unwilling to come out until it was time to dance. Is that true?"

Angel's face turned pale. "Yes, that's true."

"Tell me what that conversation was about." O'Riley maintained his hard-nosed cop posture.

"It was personal in nature. It had no bearing on the events that night or the next morning."

"And what if in that conversation, Peyton Staley told you he was not interested in the relationship you thought was becoming long term?" He was trying to get a rise from her.

"Did Jack say that? He's guessing. The real fact of that conversation has nothing to do with anything."

"Then you won't mind telling me what it was about." O'Riley was firm.

Angel looked to Lynn for guidance. She nodded.

"Well, I'm sure Jack told you that Peyton and I were lovers.

Nothing serious, just an arrangement for recreational sex." Angel took a deep breath to calm her nerves. "That night, I told him that I was pregnant, just a few weeks. I told him I missed a period and waited only long enough to get a read from the home pregnancy test before telling him. And then, I told him I was scheduled for an abortion the next morning. I asked him to come with me. He was furious. He didn't want me to have an abortion. I didn't want to have a baby. He told me he wouldn't come witness the death of his child. He said that if I wanted to kill a baby, I'd have to do it alone." Angel began to cry.

Thinking better of his intention to accuse her of attempted murder O'Riley chose a more open-ended ap-proach. "What happened then?"

"I was hurt and angry." She took a Kleenex from her purse and wiped her nose. "I blew up at him. I escaped to the dressing room to try to get control of myself."

"Did you get the abortion?" Angel ignored O'Riley's question, just glaring at him for having asked it. He tried a different direction. "Do you know who the two young men were who talked to Peyton?"

"I saw them as I passed by on my way to dance. No, I don't know who they were. They came over to the stage and sat in the front. The other patrons were very subdued, everyone was too drunk to get all worked up, even for my dance. These two guys just leered at me like they had never seen an exotic dancer before."

"Did they stay long?"

"They watched most of my dance. Then they left."

"And then—"

"When I finished dancing, I went in the back to change my clothes. By that time, Peyton was passed out, and Jack was cleaning up."

"Did you notice anything else? Anything out of the ordinary?"

"I'm not sure this is what you mean, but when I went into the dressing room, the window was open. I shut it, figuring Jack had left it open to air the place out. Once I got dressed, I went back out front to tell Jack I was leaving. He was just pushing Peyton out the door."

Angel shifted her weight in the chair. "I went to the window and watched Peyton as he stumbled and fell and then dragged himself over to the park bench. He pulled himself onto the bench and passed out again. I figured he'd wake up and get a cab or a bus or something."

She put her head in her hands, trying to remember what happened next. "I stopped to talk with Jack for a just a couple of minutes about the next day's schedule. I told him I had a doctor's appointment in the morning and asked him if I could come in late."

Angel's eyes filled with fear. "Then, I went back into the dressing room to get my purse. Here's what's strange. The window was open again, only just a crack this time. I know Jack was cleaning up the whole time I was in front. Neither of us went in back. Why was the window open again?"

"You didn't close it tight the first time," Lynn said.

"No, I'm sure I slammed it shut. The lock is broken, though, so I couldn't lock it."

There was a momentary silence. Everyone was trying to put it together.

"Could you identify the two men Peyton was talking with if you saw their pictures?" O'Riley asked.

"Maybe."

"And—could we have your gun for testing?" Lynn said.

"My gun? How did you know I have a gun?" Angel opened her purse.

"I looked in your purse when we were waiting for Jack. It could be that someone used the window to get in to steal your gun. But, when you came into the room to change, they had to get out. You closed the window, left the room after getting dressed, and they came in again. Maybe they swapped your gun with a different one and skipped out the window a second time. They only had to know you have a gun. Then someone used yours to shoot Hannah and Peyton the next morning."

"It's a fair assumption because of what I do and where I do it," Angel said. "It's not impossible for someone to get in. But why would they? Street punks have their own guns. They wouldn't need mine."

"Maybe someone was paying them to take Hannah out, and they took your gun because they could get it and it wouldn't be traced to them—only to you." O'Riley said.

"Why didn't they just throw the gun away?"

"Maybe they did, and the one that's in your purse isn't yours. " Lynn could see the possibilities.

"Could we take your gun to check the registration?"

"Sure," Angel said, taking the gun from her purse and handing it to Office O'Riley. "It looks like my gun. Same feel."

"Let's see if we can find these two guys in the files. That might point us in the direction of whoever it is that wants trouble for Peyton Staley." O'Riley opened the door. "Hey, Joe, get me the mug shots— just the last year or so, okay? And bring a baggy for this gun. I want you to check the registration and then take it to ballistics."

"Sure, Jim. And here are the results from the bullets in the dead guy. They match the bullets we found in Cordoba. The same gun killed them both," Joe said, "a .22 caliber pistol."

Angel looked through five volumes of mug shots. It was nearly two in the morning when she turned the tenth page in the sixth volume.

"Here's one. Here's one of them." She pointed at the mug book. "This guy kept staring at me as I danced that night."

O'Riley took the ID number from the photo and punched it into the computer.

"His name is Jose Mendosa, twenty-three years old. He's been arrested for petty theft, willful damage to property—smashing car windows, and defacing public property—painting graffiti on the subway platforms. Never convicted on the theft charges, and spent a couple of nights in jail for the others. Not much of a rap sheet." O'Riley kept reading. "Here it is. He's one of Antonio Cordoba's boys. Keep looking, Angel let's find the other guy."

"He looked younger than this guy. As I remember, he wasn't Hispanic either."

Another hour passed before Angel found the second face she was looking for. "This is him," she said, pointing at the photo of a sandy-haired, blue-eyed young man. "I remember he looked embarrassed by my dancing. He kept trying to get the other guy to leave. I thought they were a strange pair. Miss-matched, you know, like they really didn't belong together."

O'Riley ran his ID. "Even shorter rap sheet. His name is John Linneman. He's only fifteen years old. He was brought in a couple of different times for disorderly conduct and released to his parents. They reported him missing about three months ago. I remember we listed him as a runaway, and Antonio Cordoba probably got his hands on him, if he was with Mendosa."

"So, now what?"

"We'll bring them in and question them. Linneman's parents will be glad if we do find him. The job of locating a couple of street punks can be a trick—even for our best undercover cops."

"It's after three in the morning. Can I leave now?" Angel asked. "No wonder I'm getting tired."

"Sure, but leave your home number with the sergeant at the front desk, so I can reach you if I need to." O'Riley let Angel leave the room.

"What do you think?"

Lynn leaned against the wall to consider the question. "I think Lenny Miller is behind all this. First Cordoba—with a Dayton-Holland cell phone—then the guy from the boat—with a Dayton-Holland cell phone—both turn up dead, shot by the same gun. Then these two kids—connected to Cordoba—turn up at Barnaby's the night before Hannah and Peyton Staley are shot."

"Yeah, and Peyton's ex-wife said Miller was out to ruin him."

"She also said Miller was dangerous. I'll agree to that. I felt very unsafe in his office when he became angry." Taking a legal pad and a pen from her briefcase, Lynn sat down at the table. O'Riley joined her.

"But we don't have motive. What could he possibly gain from all this?" he asked.

"Let's look at the possibilities," she said, scrawling a line down the middle of the page and labeling one side Hannah and the other side Peyton.

"On Hannah's side of the chart: he told me he'd do anything to restore his mother's dignity. So, he lets Donna die—or she is a victim of euthanasia—in a remote and secluded hospice. Then he orders a hit on Hannah to elimi-nate her. He gets their money. He avenges their mother's supposed humiliation. Because Cordoba messed up and didn't kill Hannah, Miller kills him as retribution. And we have the guy who tried to bribe me, dead on the street."

"Why would he kill Cordoba and the boat guy himself?" O'Riley said. "We don't know that he did." He answered his own question. "All we know is the same gun shot both him and the guy from the boat."

"Then, on Peyton's side of the chart," Lynn said writ-ing simul-taneously, "we have him being fired from Dayton-Holland Industries because he was so good at his job that Lenny Miller felt threatened, according to Peyton's ex-wife. If she is to be believed, Miller has it out for Peyton. We have the two punks possibly involved in getting a gun to shoot Hannah, and Peyton just happens to be in the way."

"And, don't forget one pregnant exotic dancer."

"This all adds up to three dead people and one critically injured on Hannah's side, and one fired and shot, one pregnant woman and no one dead on Peyton's side. Kind of lopsided, isn't it?" Lynn mused, frowning at O'Riley.

There was a knock at the door. "Excuse me, Detec-tive O'Riley." Joe was acting embarrassed to interrupt their conversation. "The coroner's office just brought in a body found in a drainage ditch near Calumet Harbor."

"Got any idea who it is?"

"Yes, a Jose Mendosa. Shot in the back of the head. It looks like a professional hit," Joe said. "I thought you'd be interested."

"Anything on a John Linneman," O'Riley asked.

"No, not yet."

"Thanks, Joe. Get me a read on the bullet that killed Mendoza—see if it matches the bullets that killed Cordoba and the guy from tonight. Anything back from ballistics on the .22 caliber weapon I gave you earlier?"

"Not yet. I'll let you know right away." He left the room, closing the door softly behind him.

"Chalk up one dead on Peyton's side of the chart. Now all we have to do is locate John Linneman, if he's still alive, and find out if he knows who's behind all this."

"I'll put my money on Lenny Miller." Lynn stood to leave. "I've got to get some sleep, though. I'll call you in the morning. I'm going over to the hospital to visit Hannah in the early afternoon. I'll stop in to see Peyton, too. See you."

"Yeah, see you."

It was approaching four in the morning when Lynn walked

slowly out of the police station and took a cab to her apartment. The Lexus could wait for her. O'Riley decided to take care of some paperwork, not having a reason to go back to his apartment. Neither of them could imagine the events unfolding at Dayton-Holland Industries.

26

Like the approach of a violent thunderstorm, Lenny's mental and emotional stability swirled more out of control with every passing minute. Nothing could save him from the depression that was drawing him further away from reality and sucking him deeper into the quagmire of total mental disorientation.

Lenny was sitting transfixed, staring out the window of his office waiting for dawn, which was coming far too slowly. "I've done all I can, Mother. Your agony is ended. Mine will end soon."

He stood and walked slowly around the room, turning off the lights, putting any out of place knick-knack back in the exact spot he wanted it to be found. With a single motion, Lenny swept up one bookend and threw it at the huge painting over the leather couch, tearing a six-inch hole in the canvas. He tipped the torchière on its side and kicked out the halogen bulb. He opened the wall safe, rifled through the papers and scattered a few on the floor for effect. He picked up the lock box in the safe and placed it carefully next to the leather-bound calendar pad on the center of his enormous desk. He used the letter opener to split a couple of the couch cushions. He tipped over the chairs, adjusting them carefully askew in front of his desk.

When the room looked the way he wanted it, Lenny stepped back to his desk. He stood motionless for a moment, and then put the lock box on top of the calendar pad, opening it to see that the certificates were safely accounted for. He picked up the fragile papers, leafing through them as if counting them. Then he carefully aligned them and held them up to his lips. He kissed them.

"Mother, your wishes have been fulfilled. I have done everything I could to regain your dignity and avenge your humiliation. Your irresponsible daughters have been punished. Everything I have done, I did for you. You needed me to take care of you, and I did. These stocks will repay me for the effort when my private banker retrieves them in the morning, cashes them out, and sends the funds to my off-shore account."

Then, carrying the lock box to the safe and placing it inside, Lenny closed the safe door engaging the latch, but not spinning the tumblers in the locking mechanism, effectively leaving it unlocked while securing the contents. He turned toward the window and walked to the space between his chair and the window, facing the enormous tinted pane of glass. His reflection, transparent as a ghost, followed his every move. He opened the side drawer in his desk, picked up the airline ticket, the fake passport in another name, and the gun he had put in the drawer only that morning. He put the gun in the inside pocket of his suit coat, as his mind raced through the next part of his plan. He checked the departure of his flight, and the visa stamped in the passport one last time. All he had to do was get to the airport, fly to Polynesia and disappear forever. He picked up the phone and called a cab.

As he turned to leave, the reflection in the window caught his attention. His reflection, still transparent and wavy in the glass, distorted into his dead sister Donna's form. He stumbled around the end of his desk disoriented by the hallucination. Fearfully he looked back to the window at the phantom.

"You will not escape me," he thought he heard the apparition say. Dropping the airline ticket and the passport in his frantic attempt to pick up a paperweight from his desk, Lenny heaved the heavy brass eagle at the window with all his strength. The paperweight bounced off the tempered glass and fell to the floor, rolling impotently under his desk. Lenny came around the desk, placing himself directly in front of the image. "I'm not afraid of you!" he shouted, raising his left fist and shaking it at the reflection. The apparition again transformed, taking on his mother's elderly silhouette.

"No! Get away! You are nothing to me! I am free. You cannot manipulate me any longer!" He shouted at this second apparition in a tear-filled voice. "I have done all I can do!" The ghost's face smiled at him, an all-knowing expression of the dead in the grimace of a demon. Terrified by the vision, Lenny fumbled in his suit jacket, struggling to get the gun from the pocket in the lining.

"I'm not afraid of you!" he screamed. And then, as if gaining control of the supernatural world itself, Lenny very quietly and calmly said, "Good-bye, Mother." He took careful aim and fired.

The window disintegrated outward as the sudden change in air pressure forced open the office doors across the room. The rush of wind from behind pushed Lenny toward the protruding shards that clung to the frame. He whirled around, facing inward, grasping for any hand-hold he could find. His left hand clawed at the shattered pane as the force of the air pushed him backward through the opening in the window. He caught one saw-toothed section with his palm. It gashed his hand wide open. As his feet lost their footing, he fired the gun again, pathetically into the air. Screaming with unknowable terror, Lenny Miller tumbled toward the earth, almost gracefully, as if floating toward the plaza below. The gun smashed on the pavement not far from his body. Dawn was finally breaking over Lake Michigan.

Lynn turned on her kitchen television as she set the natural cone filter into the automatic drip coffee pot and began to shovel the aromatic gourmet blend she kept as her only culinary luxury. The rugged features of a man filled the screen as his equally rugged voice spoke.

"I couldn't believe my eyes. The pavement was crumbled all around him, like he had fallen from the sky."

"Can you tell us what time it was when you found the body?" the television reporter asked.

"Not more than a few minutes after five a.m. I was on my way to work – I'm a newspaper vendor in the lobby of the Dayton - Holland Building."

"And there you have it. Multimillionaire Dayton - Holland Industry CEO Lenny Miller fell to his death sometime in the wee hours of the morning. Police have very few details as yet and will only acknowledge that his forty-fifth floor office was ransacked and damaged by the force of the change in atmospheric pressure when the window blew out. The ransacked condition of his office leads the police to speculate that he put up a terrific fight with his attacker, who smashed the window and threw Mr. Miller to his death. They also are asking that anyone who may have seen the event to come forward. This is Rosaline Merriweather, reporting for Channel Seven News, Chicago. Stay tuned for further news updates throughout the day. Now back to the newsroom for the traffic report and Evelyn Smith."

"Can you believe it?" Lynn muttered to herself as she punched the coffee pot on button, turned off the television in the kitchen and headed for the shower. The phone rang. It was Detective O'Riley.

SIDETRACKS

"Lynn? Can you meet me at Lenny Miller's office? We've found something in the safe you've got to take a look at. And, they've got a make on the gun found next to Miller's body. It's registered to Angel and it's the same weapon that killed Cordoba, the punk kid, the man from the boat, and matches the bullets from Peyton's chest and Hannah's leg."

"How is that possible?"

"Every bullet matches the barrel markings—and, get this, the only fingerprints on the gun are his. I'd say this lets Angel off the hook. The gun in her purse was not registered at all, and the serial numbers were gone. Can you get here in, say, half an hour?"

"I'm there already."

Detective O'Riley and Lynn Hargove entered the disheveled office of Lenny Miller, as if they were entering a tomb.

"Jesus Christ, can you believe this mess?" Lynn said, stopping to survey the ruins. "I worked in a high-rise once, and they told us never to even think about breaking a window, not even if there was a fire, because of the way these places are built, the air pressure inside is controlled. A break in the windows, and everything is sucked out—like on an airplane." She looked around the office, remembering the sleek decor on the day she had confronted Lenny. "I guess they were right."

"Detective O'Riley?" One of the crime scene specialists interrupted their conversation. "We have been going over the space since Mr. Miller's body was found this morning, and other than the fact that most of the contents of the office have been destroyed or accounted for, we'd like you to look at what we found in the safe." He held a lock box and a writing tablet out for them to take. "It's full of old stock certificates."

SIDETRACKS

Detective O'Riley opened the box and picked up the certificates. "Huh. Five hundred shares of Coca Cola stock dated June 1927. That's nearly seventy-years old. Could they be worth anything?"

"Let me call my friend, Jack Hastings. He's a stock-broker. He could tell me in a heartbeat if they're valuable or not," Lynn said, flipping open her cell phone and dialing a number. "Rats! Voicemail," she whispered to Detective O'Riley. "Hey Jack! Lynn Hargrove. Here's a puzzle for you. How much would five hundred shares of Coca Cola stock from 1927 be worth today? Call back A-S-A-P and tell me, okay? Thanks." She flipped the phone closed.

27

"Peyton?" I kept my voice soft in keeping with the gentle rocking of the compartment.

"Yes?"

"If we ever meet again, do you think we'll remember any of this?"

"I have no idea." He barely moved a muscle to speak. "No, probably not."

"I'm so very sure that we are meant to know each other—not just here, but back there, if we ever do go back there. I've felt this way all my life—separate from my body—but in no way uncertain of the being I am supposed to become."

I waited for his response.

"I can't say I have. I never gave anything like this a thought. I went to Sunday school just to see if I could get into Betsy Nelson's pants. She was the minister's daughter, and hotter than—uh—well, let's just say, all the young boys fell for her, hard and heavy."

"You have never considered the philosophical underpinnings of the human condition?"

"Say that again?"

"You know—read Aristotle, Nietzsche, Camus, Dostoevsky,

and all the rest of them—essentially the basis of the liberal arts tradition in higher education?"

"Can't say that I have—but I have read Ayn Rand, Carl Sagan and Isaac Asimov—along with a healthy dose of Tom Clancy." Peyton's laughter made me angry.

"Peyton, one of these days, your irreverence is going to catch up with you."

"Irreverence? More people claim Atlas Shrugged influenced their lives than the Bible had. The little Russian immigrant woman writing in her second language has more power than the Prophets."

"And you think the marketing of the self-centered Objectivist philosophy she spouts validates her viewpoint as more powerful than the Word of God?"

"God? What's God? There is no God. There is no before or after. There is only the here and now."

"Look where you are, Peyton. Look around you. Explain this place, these people, this moment. What here and now are we living?"

"This is not what I mean."

"This is exactly what I mean—and so do the others. There is much more than what appears to our bodies. There is much more."

"I just want to get back—to go on with my life. I'll say and do anything to get there."

"So, you didn't mean what you said out there."

"Yes, I meant it. But I can't answer all the questions you have. So, stop asking me."

The austerity of the moment depressed me into silence, though my thoughts were flowing like a river over a cliff, tumbling and streaming together. I could see the continuity in my life, the why and wherefore of the events that brought me to the day of my attack. I understood the purposes of each segment of my own history. I could feel there was something more left for me to do before the end of my life, but the particulars are not clear. How could I tell Peyton of these things? He wanted to stay closed off from the possibility of some other dimension to existence. I wanted him to see the strength he holds in his heart.

"Hannah Sebastian, come forward." The resonance of the Voice vibrated through me.

"Wish me luck." Peyton nodded as I moved toward the black door.

"Good luck—see you on the other side."

I found it curious for Peyton to say that as I passed through the opening and returned to the great hall. The Gallery of Others was still packed with Agents, though the Tribunal was again in place and the Judges sat high above the audience.

"Stand in the center." I moved into the light.

"Hannah Sebastian, the Processor has made the Final Decision."

I trembled, my nerves wrangling with my muscles for control.

"You will return to your life. Significant changes have occurred during your absence in the circumstances surround-ing your earthly existence." The Voice paused. "However, you will have some residual physical effects from your injuries that will make your recovery longer than you might like."

"May I know them now?" I was trying to get ready for the worst.

"No!" The Voice boomed at me. "You will know them upon your return."

Then I saw Peyton coming through the black open-ing. He glanced my way as he moved toward the center of the room.

"Stand in the center." I did as they told me and moved into the light. Hannah looked beautiful to me.

"Peyton Staley, the Processor has made the Final Decision."

I felt an unusual sense of calm.

"You will return to your life. Significant changes have occurred during your absence in the circumstances surround-ing your earthly existence and you will return with only a short recovery time to pay." The Voice paused. "However, neither of you will remember anything about the day you were brought here nor anyone you saw that day. You will have to move on in your lives without that knowledge."

Annica came down from the Gallery of Others, approaching us. She held the same book as at the beginning of this adventure.

"Come, it is time for you to leave here. Follow me, please."

"Annica, will we know each other again?"

"That is not for me to say."

"What is going to happen to us?"

"That is not for you to know."

She led us to the corridor. We followed the purple carpet to the farthest end of the hallway. The door disap-peared and we were suddenly alone. The call of a train whistle echoed in the distance as we slipped away.

28

A soft beeping, like a pulse monitor in a hospital, greeted me as I opened my eyes. The lights in the room were dimmed, but still too bright. I squinted, trying to focus on where I had come to. No one else was in the room. I tried to move my arms and legs. Nothing happened. There was a bandage encircling my head. "Okay, let's try the fingers and toes." I could move the fingers on my right hand, not on my left, and the toes on both feet. The rest of my limbs felt so heavy I couldn't muster the energy to lift any other part of my body. I then realized I was strapped to the bed.

"That explains it—I'm not necessarily paralyzed." I turned my head to watch the door, hoping someone would come in. Time passed. I drifted in and out of sleep. I heard voices in the hallway and opened my eyes.

"She's in here. We moved her to the extended care wing just this morning. She's doing pretty well, considering. We've strapped her to the bed to contain the spastic flailing that occurs now and then. She can move, but she has no control of the movements—we hope that's due to being unconscious."

Lynn entered the room along with a doctor.

"Hi. Been away a while, have I?" My words startled both Lynn and the doctor.

"Hannah!" Lynn was clearly surprised to see me awake. "How are you?" she said, taking my hand as she tried not to cry. "I have arranged for the kids to come visit in a few weeks—I thought you'd like to see them again." I nodded, chocked up by the tears that trickled from the sides of my eyes as she told me the news. "How are you feeling?"

"Actually, I'm feeling rested. What's with these straps, doctor?"

"Just preventive measures—to keep you from hurting yourself. Shall we try it without the straps?"

"Fine. Let's go for it." I felt energized—like lying in a hospital bed was the most inappropriate thing for me to be doing. The doctor removed the restraints and pulled back the sheets.

"Lift your right arm."

"It's tingling—like it has been asleep." It floated upward as I wriggled my fingers. The tingling in my muscles intensified and then faded. We continued with the other limbs to discover my left arm didn't function normally.

"I can feel you touching my hand," I told the doctor, "but I can't make it move."

"That you can feel is a good sign. With time and therapy, you should regain at least some function. The way you hit your head when you fell could have killed you. The faucet hit only millimeters from crushing your spinal cord. It's too soon yet to know how much or how long it will take to regain your mobility." I smiled at him.

"That's all right. I'm just glad to be here."

"Can we spend a few minutes alone, Doctor?" Lynn asked.

"Of course. I'll come back in a little while."

"Listen, Hannah. So much happened in the time you've been gone. I don't know where to begin. I—"

"Wait. Let's just sit for a while and enjoy the moment."

She wanted to tell me what had gone on. And someday I would want to hear the details of how I had gotten hurt and who had caused it all. But, not now. She could understand that. Lynn sat down, smiling. I smiled at my friend that goofy smile that happens when words fail the feeling of joy. A few minutes later, Lynn moved toward the door to leave.

"I have to visit one other person while I'm here. Do you think I could do that now? It'll only take a couple of minutes."

"Sure, Lynn. Is it anyone I know?"

"I don't think so. He's just a guy I've gotten to know in the last few days. He came in with you. I'll explain it to you when we go through all the events that have happened since your fall. He's in the next room."

She started for the door. "Hey, Lynn," I said. "Could you turn on the television? Maybe I could catch a few minutes of Oprah."

"Sure," Lynn said, picking up the remote and clicking it to the right channel. "Be right back."

I watched and listened to the sights and sounds com-ing from the television, but I couldn't focus on what they were saying. I was trying to hold on to my new reality, trying to understand my circumstances, but unable to grasp sense of where I was and why.

Lynn was gone only a few minutes.

"How is your friend?"

"He's happily sitting up in bed, eating ravenously." She smiled at me. "Are you hungry?"

"Sure. How's about pheasant under glass?" We both laughed at the idea. I couldn't stop laughing. One of those giggle spells hit me, and my laughter filled the room and spilled into the hallway.

Lynn opened the blinds to let in the morning sun. "It looks like a beautiful day, Hannah. Want to go for a wheelchair ride? You could eat outside in the courtyard. The doctor suggested it might be good for you."

"Sure, but only if you come with me."

Lynn helped me get into the chair and like a couple of old ladies we waddled down the hall toward the courtyard. My meal tray didn't offer high cuisine, but I was hungry and it only took me a few minutes to clean the tray of any edible substance. We talked for a while, and she rolled me around the courtyard, which was large and inviting. But within a short half hour, I was fatigued.

"I'm afraid all this activity is wearing me out. I think I should probably get a little nap in before dinner, okay?"

"Sure." Lynn rolled me toward the corridor to return me to my room to rest. I understood that at my age I would spend more time than I wanted getting over my injuries and trying to figure out what to do with my life once I was healthy.

A week later, Detective O'Riley walked into Lynn Hargrove's office, a bouquet of grocery store flowers in his hand.

"Hello, may I help you?" Marjorie asked, somewhat flustered by Detective O'Riley's appearance before her.

"Yes, I'm here to see Lynn Hargrove, please. I'm De-tective O'Riley."

"Oh! Detective O'Riley! At last, we meet. I've heard so much about you." Marjorie smiled more broadly than would be normal, as she looked at the flowers and back again to his face. "Just a moment," she said, scurrying into Lynn's inner office. "Lynn? Detective O'Riley is here to see you. He has flowers!"

"Thanks, Marjorie. Give me just a moment, and I'll come out." Lynn ran her fingers through her hair, puffed into her hand to check her breath, and straightened her suit. Certain it would not actually matter how she looked, she then stepped into the reception room. "Hello, Detective O'Riley. How goes it today?"

"Call me Jim. I'm here to thank you for all you have done."

The sudden entrance of the mailman, who tossed the day's mail on Marjorie's desk, tipped his hat and disappeared, interrupted Detective O'Riley mid-sentence. Lynn picked up the rubber-banded stack of mail, slipped the elastic off, and began to sort it, dropping the junk mail into the wicker wastebasket next to Marjorie's desk.

"You were saying?"

"Well, I came by to thank you, and, well, uh, to ask you to go to dinner this evening, uh, just to celebrate the end of the case, such as it is."

Still sorting and tossing, Lynn abruptly looked up. "Dinner? Sure. That'd be great."

An awkward silence clung to the air the way a wet shirt clings to the back. Finally, O'Riley broke it with a cough.

"I have a bit more news about the motives that drove Lenny to his death," Detective O'Riley said. "We found an airline ticket to some remote island in Polynesia and a falsified passport on the floor behind his desk."

"So he was going to cash in and disappear?"

"Apparently," O'Riley said. "Did you know that Dayton-Holland Industries was bankrupt? The contents of the lock box in the safe belonged to Margaret Miller. According to Hannah, her mother apparently bought these stock certificates in 1927 on the advice of her employer, who advised her not to purchase a fur coat, but instead to purchase Coca Cola stock. Years before Mrs. Miller died she had given them to Hannah. Neither of them was aware of the value of the certificates."

"Yes, I knew that. And, Jack Hastings, my stockbroker friend, told me those certificates were worth roughly 113 million dollars, with all the stock splits since Margaret Miller purchased them in 1927. So, I guess Hannah will have enough money to pay her medical bills." Lynn smiled at O'Riley as she handed the sorted stack of mail to Marjorie.

"And then some," Detective O'Riley said. "We found John Linneman, who—without much coaxing, I might add—filled in the blanks on the entire scam before we turned him over to the Juvenile Department. Lenny hired Antonio Cordoba to eliminate Donna so she would not be able to benefit from the certificates. Then he contracted Cordoba to kill Hannah and retrieve the certificates from her possession."

"And the gun?"

"Linneman told us that Lenny paid him and Mendosa to steal the gun from Angel."

"Why her?"

"Because he knew Peyton frequented her pub and was involved with her. He also paid the boys to burglarize Hannah's house to get the lock box, but he killed Jose Mendoza, when they failed. Linneman managed to escape and disappear, till he turned up a couple of days ago in a halfway house for teens."

Lynn picked up on the logical stream of events. "So, Lenny gave the gun to Cordoba to use and then ordered him to return to Hannah's to get the lock box and to kill her. When Cordoba failed to kill Hannah, Lenny took things into his own hands and used the gun to kill him and had his body dumped in the river."

"That's right. Lenny kept the lock box, hired the courier to carry the bribery money to you, and when he failed to bribe you, Lenny killed him, too."

"And all this was accomplished with the same gun?" "Yup."

"Motive, opportunity and means. He had them all."

SIDETRACKS

Another awkward silence punctuated the end of the adventure that had consumed so much of their time.

"Seven o'clock then? I'll pick you up here, if that's all right," O'Riley said as casually as he could.

"Seven it is."

EPILOGUE
Several months later

I had a lunch date with Lynn, at a great little Thai restaurant on Oak Street in the rich Gold Coast quarter of Chicago's Magnificent Mile. It was late in the spring, and I was feeling pretty much myself, finally having regained my independence from the rehab center. It was my first solo outing in months—the first time no one had to drive me somewhere, to go with me to the corner grocery, or to bring me my mail. I loved the smell of the first flowers, and the warmth of the sun cutting through the coolness of the lake side air. She was waiting at the 'Please Wait To Be Seated' sign at the entrance to the restaurant.

"So, have you been waiting long?" I asked, knowing she had just arrived.

"No, no. Only a couple of minutes. How are you doing?"

"Fine. Just fine," I said, knowing my smile betrayed my liberated psyche. "I like being a cultured lady of leisure. I just wish I had more time to work on the 'cultured' part. Want to go to the Art Institute this afternoon?"

"Tempting, dear girlfriend, but I am a working lawyer, and I must attend to business after this respite."

"This way please," indicated the lanky young hostess, dressed in a form-fitting black and white uniform, and wearing those awful four inch heels that I gave up eons ago. We followed her to a table under one of those huge square restaurant umbrellas that don't always block the sun. The removable fencing, hung with flower boxes that artfully spilled trailing geraniums and variegated vinca over their sides, separated us from the bustle of the street, while the white table linens, better than ordinary table settings, and cut glass goblets filled with lemon-laced water promised that the cuisine would be delectable, no matter what we ordered.

"I have invited someone else, too," Lynn said, trying to sound like I wouldn't be curious about it.

"Oh? Any one I know?"

"I think so. Maybe not very well, but I think you'll remember him."

"Him?"

She glanced a couple of times toward the entrance to the interior of the restaurant to hint that I should look in that direction. There was the delivery driver I had met a few times when he brought other men's flowers to my house.

"Peyton, the delivery guy?"

"So, you do remember him."

"Yes, of course, but why did you invite him here?"

She raised her hand and waved at Peyton, who saw us then, and smiling that wonderful, broad, engaging grin of his, made his way through the other tables to ours.

"Hello, ladies. Is this where I'm supposed to be?" he asked, shaking hands with Lynn and sitting down next to me.

"Yes, it certainly is," Lynn replied. "Peyton, this is Hannah Sebastian, my good friend. Hannah, this is Peyton Staley, your good Samaritan."

I smiled at him, but I'm sure my eyes were just ques-tion marks. "Good Samaritan?"

"Yes, I, uh—I pulled you from your tub the day you hit your

head. I was delivering a huge bouquet of roses to your place, and, well, you know what happened."

I was dumbfounded. "Lynn? You didn't tell me about that part." I blushed, and couldn't find the right words.

"No, I didn't. But, I just knew you'd want to thank Peyton for saving your life at the right time."

I was still at a loss for words, but taking her cue man-aged to say, "Yes, I do want to thank you for saving my life." I felt oddly foolish, because there was something about this man—a feeling that I knew him better than I could possibly know him, having just been introduced. He was looking at me with a questioning expression, like he was trying to place me among all the other women he'd ever met.

"So, Peyton," Lynn interrupted our silent staring contest, "What ever happened to Angel?"

He broke his gaze, and turned to Lynn. "Oh, she eventually married Jack. The baby is due next month, and they finally worked out the fact that they wanted to actually be parents to their child. It turns out she never meant to make me a father before my time. And Detective O'Riley? Do you ever see him?"

"Just for business. That man is a workaholic par excellence. Never quits. Has no life outside his work. But, that's what makes him so good at what he does, and also interesting to have as a friend."

At just that moment, our waiter approached our table. Tall, lanky in stature he reminded me of a basketball player ill at ease with his height. His brown hair fell in unruly curls to his shoulders and he walked with a slouch as if accustomed to ducking under doorways and the umbrellas shading the café tables.

At the moment I saw the waiter's face, it was like a floodgate had opened, and my mind instantly sorted through the puzzle of memories I thought were only dreams. I looked at Peyton. His mouth was slightly open, his eyes wide with surprise. He looked at me, and the recognition of how we knew each other beyond the limits of my front hallway came rushing toward us both.

"Good afternoon! My name is Javier, and I'll be your waiter today."

Not a word was spoken, but we understood it all, as we smiled and nodded in that subtly accepting way people nod as they pass through a door on their way to the next moment in their lives.

ABOUT THE AUTHOR

Valerie Connelly lives with her husband, Michael, in the northern Midwest. She divides her time between writing, publishing, speaking, painting landscapes and waterscapes, composing and traveling to visit grown children.

An educator and international traveller since her days as a Peace Corps volunteer in Togo, West Africa in 1969, she made her living teaching French literature, language, and culture in the United States and in France, as well as teaching English as a Second Language (ESL) in West Africa, Iran and the United States.

Ms. Connelly founded Nightengale Press in 2003, and by 2008 had published eighty titles for authors in the USA, Australia, Canada, Dubai, Cyprus, and with her husband formed Nightengale Media LLC, which launched WEB4W.com and YourBookTube.com early in 2009 to meet the internet needs of authors.

She has hosted a weekly internet radio program, *Calling All Authors* on Global Talk Radio since 2005. Listen to the archives at www.globaltalkradio.com/shows/callingallauthors

Her mystery thrillers, SACRED NIGHT and SIDETRACKS, CALLING ALL AUTHORS, How to Publish with Your Eyes Wide Open, an information-packed guide for authors, and ARTHUR, THE CHRISTMAS ELF, a holiday adventure tale with a craft section for children of all ages are all available at:
www.nightengalepress.com
all online bookstores,
and upon request in bricks and mortar stores.